Prel

by

Morgan W. Silver

This is a work of fiction. Similarities to real people, places, or events are entirely coincidental.

PRELUDE TO POISON

First edition. January 1, 2020.

ISBN: 978-9083038827

Written by Morgan W. Silver.

Also by Morgan W. Silver

Maggie's Murder Mysteries
Prelude to Poison
Poised to Quill
Booked For Murder

Maid for Murder
The Missing Maid

Monday Moody
The Chrono Unit
Unparalleled Affairs

Standalone
The Exciting Life of a Minor Character

Watch for more at www.authormw.com.

I dedicate this book to all the oddballs out there.

You know who you are. Always be proud of your inner Pandora.

Chapter 1

The lifeless body of Marlene Green was draped across the carpet as if she were sleeping. Only the pool of blood that surrounded her head like a halo and the lifeless expression in her open eyes indicated otherwise. She was known for her looks, but now that she was nothing but an empty shell, the mere residue of a person, her beauty seemed to be a cruel joke, like a broken piece of jewellery.

Detective Black stared at the body, wondering what she'd been like when she still had a pulse, when she was breathing, her heart beating in her small-framed chest. Had she been a morning person? Had she loved animals or been afraid of the dark?

I STOPPED WRITING AND stared at the page before hitting the delete button for the seventh time. In the last two hours I had rewritten the opening paragraph of my latest novel six times, and at this rate I'd be working on it until the sun imploded. Which would be a welcome distraction.

"Why are you doubting yourself, dear Maggie?" Detective Black asked from behind me. He moved past my table in the local pub and sat across from me. It wasn't busy at eleven o'clock in the morning, and I sat all the way in the back. On the rare occasions that my writing drove me mad in my own office, I sought refuge in The Rose where I could be driven mad in public.

I bit my lip and stared at Detective Black, unsure of how to answer him. "I'm n—" I started, but just then Callum popped out from behind the bar with a fresh pot of tea. He was dressed way too stylishly for his job as a bartender, in his blazer and bow tie. But he was only doing this kind of work so that he could pay for acting classes.

"Talking to yourself, Mags?" he asked as he poured me a hot cup of tea before putting the pot down. There was barely any room for it since I had littered the table with my laptop, several notebooks, and too many pens and Post-its.

"Just my characters," I said, and glanced at the seat across from me, which was empty now.

"Seeing as how you barely started, will you please put me in your novel?" Callum asked with a hint of excitement in his voice.

"Why would you want that? All new characters are either suspects or murder victims." He wasn't the only one who had asked me this, but I always held my ground because otherwise I'd soon be writing about my entire village.

"I'm trying to impress my new beau," he said. "He reads a lot. He wears glasses and even has a bookcase."

"Amazing," I managed to say without rolling my eyes. Callum didn't read anything other than menus and his text messages. It was wise not to remind him of the fact that most people owned bookcases, and even wiser not to mention the four that I had.

"Right? And look, I can make an excellent corpse." He flopped down to the floor and remained motionless, staring at the ceiling.

"Okay, yes, very good." He really was good at not blinking, I had to hand him that.

He remained motionless and showed no signs of getting up.

I laughed. "You can get up now. You look too nice to lie on the floor."

"So will you put me in your novel?" he asked as he bounced to his feet again.

"No. And what happened to your previous boyfriend who owned the tattoo parlour?"

He made a face. "He owned a tattoo parlour."

"Right." Despite his whimsical interests, I couldn't help but admire how easily he found these boyfriends, especially since he always joked he was the only gay in the village. Whatever dark forces he was using, I wanted in. I mean, I was completely willing to ritually sacrifice a pen or two. "Now that you have a boyfriend who is into reading, can I tempt you to enter my bookshop and actually purchase a book?" I wiggled my eyebrows.

He laughed. "How cute you are." Then he turned and walked away.

I grumbled something and attempted to write one more hour before returning to The Wicked Bookworm to put my stuff away. I wanted to visit Beth and didn't want to be too late. Especially since I had something else planned for later today.

When I arrived at my shop, it was busy. No, Saturdays were busy. This was mayhem.

I checked out the queues and heaps of cackling women in my store. Not that I didn't love the women in this village, but they did have a tendency to gossip about trivial things and frown upon every woman in her late twenties, such as myself, who hadn't reproduced yet. Thursdays normally didn't bring such chaos, but the new novel *True Love* had been released today. I had expected some buzz, but not this much. It appeared to be a flimsy book and even just the cover was sweet enough to give me diabetes.

Instead of running upstairs to my flat, I slipped behind the counter and went through the curtain and into the small room I shared with my aunt Nancy. It functioned as a tiny break room, with a sink and small fridge, as well as some cleaning supplies. Her occult store was on the other side of her curtain. I put down my bag and hurried back out. My best friend Eddie had red cheeks and shot terrified glances at the chatting women in the queue. He was wearing a T-shirt and jeans. He never wore anything else. Even in winter.

My other employee, a woman a few years younger than me, Susan, was also at the counter, but she showed no signs of stress whatsoever.

As soon as I opened another cash register, it attracted the flock of women who had been standing in line for Eddie. Most of the women I knew by name, and others I recognised from around. The majority of them were part of the Castlefield Book Club. They sometimes held their meetings at my bookshop and though I hadn't ever attended, Nancy had. She said the meetings consisted mostly of gossip and cakes.

It also meant that I had dirt on most of these women, since Nancy relayed any noteworthy information to me.

Poppy Kilkenny, for instance, went through a phase where she put on cat fashion shows for herself. She dressed up the cats in knitted clothing that she'd made for them. Apparently she had a playlist, special lamps, everything. She was a widow in her eighties and I didn't blame her for finding ways to keep busy. She was now third in the queue and every time I saw her, I'd ask about her cats. It was a bit mean since she had no idea those fashion shows were now common knowledge and she always responded in earnest, but I couldn't resist.

Jessica Parsley collected hamster wheels. To this day she still didn't have a hamster. Phoebe Rivers made her own dollhouses, which I found cool, but she was adamant that nobody ever see them. She had three alarm systems in her house.

My favourite bit of info was about Lily Cromwell, who was still a bit sore about the fact that I had exposed her cousin as a garden gnome thief. She considered herself an inventor, which was no secret, and liked to tinker with things. One of the things she had invented was a coffee mug that also served as an iron. As well as a teapot with two spouts.

Normally these women would all have a little chat with me when I was at the counter, but this time they were too excited about the new novel. I could hardly judge them for it, since I knew the power of good books all too well. Books had been my sanctuary as a kid when home wasn't.

The women continued talking to each other while I rang up their books and it wasn't until an hour later that it finally quieted down enough to breathe. Eddie sighed next to me.

"You okay?" I asked while I handed my final customer a plastic bag with my bookshop's logo on it; an open book with a bookworm.

Eddie moved his hand through his red, curly hair. "I'm fairly sure that even my sweat is sweating." He chuckled his boyish chuckle.

"You survived and that's all that matters. I'm proud of you." It wasn't just the sudden rush, but I knew he disliked the women mainly because of the way they had gossiped about his parents when they split up, as if it had been pure entertainment for them, which it probably had been. This Cornish village didn't elicit much excitement, except for when the gnomes were stolen and my books got published. The first time my Detective Black novel came out, the Castlefield Book Club threw a huge party during which I mostly cried with pure joy.

From the corner of my eye I spotted the vicar's wife lingering near a stack of *True Love*. "One moment," I said to Eddie and strode over.

She looked up and soft lines appeared around her warm brown eyes. "Hi, Maggie." She squeezed my arm.

"Eleanor," I said, though it made my toes tingle every time I said it. She had made me address her by her first name since I was sixteen, but I respected her too much to utter the name without my body protesting a little. "There is one steamy scene in it, the rest is pretty sappy," I said as I picked up one of the books.

She chuckled. "Don't you remember that I bought a certain romance book about bondage?"

My eyes widened. "No. I am sure I would have remembered that. In fact, I'm sure the memory would have engraved itself in my brain." I was uncertain how I felt about this little piece of info, but decided I rather liked it.

"Then why the hesitation?" I asked.

She sighed. "I just feel like I've read them all, you know? I feel like reading something different."

"Then why don't you? I don't think any person reads just one genre. I think you should read what the mood dictates. What do you feel like reading?"

She tilted her head as she contemplated an answer. A streak of greyish black hair fell over her shoulder. "Violence," she said.

I burst out laughing.

"What?"

"Nothing. I just like these surprises you keep throwing at me. Follow me, I have some cool thrillers about women who kick ass."

"Oh, I'd very much like that," she said as she followed me to the right bookshelves. After a few moments we returned to the register and I rang up her books. "Enjoy the violence," I said with a smile.

She laughed. "Not too loud or I'll be hearing about this at the next Castlefield Book Club meeting."

"You know they'll all be distracted by the new romance novel, right? They'll talk about bare chests and dramatic hair sweeping gestures that make them swoon."

She made a face. "I better start preparing myself mentally, then." With a wave of her thin hand, she headed out.

I turned to Eddie. "I'm sorry, I have to go visit Beth. I'll see you later." I grabbed two books from under the counter that I had reserved just for her. "Will you be okay?"

"Of course. Though I can't guarantee that I won't fake my death at least several times today."

I laughed. "That will probably only attract more customers." I left and as I passed my aunt Nancy's store, I was forced to stop. A man darted out in front of me clutching his head while Nancy hit him repeatedly with a broom.

"How dare you? Get out and don't come back." She hit him once more before he ran off across the cobbled street. Several people stared and by dinnertime the whole village would know about this. Luckily for Nancy it meant that customers would come in to hear her version and also buy something.

My aunt had raised me and I was always glad to see her, even when she had her volatile outbursts. Which could be quite frequent and would always make me laugh on the inside. When I was ten, I witnessed her shove a pie in a man's face at the church's bake sale after he'd touched her bum. As I recall, she even won the bake sale, but that was probably because people were afraid of her. It didn't help that every time someone asked her about her glass eye, she came up with a new gruesome story of how it had happened.

And yet people flocked to her for ointments, spells, and advice. She was even asked to put a spell on Pandora the psycho chicken that terrorises Castlefield. She has a tendency to peck everyone in sight. People cross the street just to avoid her. Much to the dismay of every one of us, she had declined and said that Pandora was working through some issues and who were we to interfere? She made it up by never turning down any humans. Except for now. Hitting someone with a broom, sure. But hitting a customer with a broom? No.

"What the sweet muffin was that about?" I asked.

She huffed. "He wanted some herbs to put his wife to sleep so he could go out all night and spend time with his mistress."

"What? Really?" I wanted to go after him with a broom myself.

"Well, he said he wanted them so his wife would sleep and he could stay out all night. But it was all there in his lewd eyes and lustful aura. I can read between the lines, you know?"

She had never been wrong as long as I remembered, and I had places to be. I was already late. "I believe you," I said, holding up my hand. "I'll talk to you later, I'm going to visit Beth now."

"Is she doing any better?" Nancy's voice was calmer as we moved on to the topic of Beth. She was one of the oldest women in the village and though she had her moments, she was getting confused about reality. She remembered things that weren't memories, but bits from books or films she'd seen and most of the time they were harmless. Although she did once tackle Dawn the postwoman because she thought the package that was being delivered was a bomb. She broke her hip doing so.

She'd always been like a granny to me and she had no family around, so I took it upon myself to visit her a few times a week and spend time with her. I usually brought her romance books, because they contained no dangerous situations or threats that she could perceive as real.

"Last week she wanted me to chase off a dinosaur in her garden because she'd seen a documentary about them. That's when I unplugged the TV and gave her a few books to read. I'm bringing over a new batch now."

"You know Patricia Woodsbury has been making her a charity case. She and her gang visit her every Sunday to play bridge with her and afterwards she boasts about how kind she's being." Nancy made a face. "And then she bathes in the blood of innocents."

I laughed. "I don't like her either, but it's good that she's entertaining Beth, no matter her motivation."

Nancy grumbled.

She'd never liked the woman, not since she stole her boyfriend in secondary school, just because she could.

"Okay, I'm off. See you."

"See you later, love."

BETH'S COTTAGE WAS near the vicarage where Eleanor and Harold, the vicar, lived. It was a cute cottage with a rose garden in the front that was regularly tended to by Eleanor. Olivia, the baker's wife, also occasionally brought her baked goods, so she was in good hands. It was also the main reason I loved this village so much. Despite the gossip and the rare rotten apples, people genuinely cared about each other. No matter where you were from or what you looked like, or who you dated.

I picked up the key from under the flower pot and entered. "Hi, Beth. It's me," I shouted and went through the reception area, which was empty, and straight to the kitchen.

Beth shrieked when she saw me and held a rolling pin above her head. She had a wild look in her eyes and was trembling.

"What's wrong?" I asked. "It's me, Maggie."

"Maggie?" She slowly lowered the rolling pin and then her expression changed. She broke out in a smile. "Hello, dear. How are you doing? So nice to see you."

"And nice to see you." I gave her a kiss on her cheek and took the rolling pin from her, hoping that whatever had frightened her was now forgotten. "I brought you two new books." I put them on the counter. "Why don't you sit down in your chair and I'll make us some tea."

"No!" she dashed forward and yanked me back from the teapot. "No, don't do that. It's poisoned."

Chapter 2

As soon as I had put Beth in her favourite armchair with one of the books I had brought, she calmed down. In fact, she quickly forgot the whole thing, unlike me. Instead of making her tea, I inspected all of her teacups, tea bags, loose herbal tea, and even her teaspoons while Detective Black looked over my shoulder and listed signs of poison. Not that there were any to be found. There was nothing suspicious, and all appeared normal. It was safe.

"But what about untraceable poison?" Detective Black whispered in my ear.

A moment later I put down a steaming mug of black sludge on the coffee table. "I made you coffee," I said.

"How nice," Beth muttered as she continued reading. As long as she had a book in front of her, she would be fine. It was when she got up to pee or to eat that she usually forgot that she had a book unless she returned to her armchair. Which is why I had trained her to put her book on the chair each time she got out of it. That way she had to pick it up if she sat down and usually she went straight back to reading. But this was only if she had one of her unclear moments. The moments that she was her real self were fine.

After that I took out the trash, which included all of the tea, hoovered, and then ran to the grocery store to buy her all kinds of new teas. I couldn't help myself and swallowed the big ball of flaming fear that accompanied my paranoia, as I remembered how my mother could be.

At some point Beth looked up while I was sitting on the sofa, flipping through the other book I had brought, getting over the poison scare. It was a warm spring day and there were fresh roses in a vase on the table next to me. The entire room smelt nice.

"Do you know Alistair Ashworth, Maggie?" she asked in a very clear, crisp voice.

I automatically sat up straight and if I had been a cat, my ears would have perked up. "Yes," I said, trying to sound normal.

"Oh, boy," Detective Black said. "Don't go all cuckoo over a man. Have some pride."

I glared at him and returned my attention to Beth who touched the rollers in her white hair and squinted at me. "He's a detective that moved to London. Broke his poor mother's heart, you know? She was a good hairdresser, she was. She always did my hair really well. Anyway, Alistair turned out to be a fine young man."

My heart was racing by now, and I wanted to yell at her to hurry up, though I managed to contain myself. "What about him?" I asked quietly while a storm of feelings raged inside of me. Why hadn't I gotten a haircut recently? I was hyper-aware of the fact that my once coloured bob had now morphed into something more like a dark blond blob.

"Oh, right. He's moved back to the village," she said and rattled on, but her voice was drowned out by the sound of trumpets and fireworks.

Detective Black rolled his eyes.

She managed to inform me that he actually lived across from her in the cottage where Mr Simms used to live. He had raised sheepdogs until he moved to the Caribbean to marry a former stripper. To each their own. Point is, as soon as I would step outside of this cottage, I could see Alistair's home. I could potentially see him as well. *Should I ring the doorbell? No, I'll go home to change. And I should bring something. Flowers? No. Chocolate? No. Alcohol. Yes.*

"What are you getting worked up over?" Detective Black asked. "It's been years since you last saw him. He won't even remember you and he'll probably be married with five kids."

I made a face, but realised part of that could be true. "Is he married?" I blurted out and Beth stopped talking. Then she shrugged. "Don't know, actually. I have only caught a glimpse of him and only just yesterday evening. But Dawn delivered some post and told me it was him and that he had moved back. He's got a lovely black Volkswagen Beetle. I love those cars."

"Right, right." I stayed with Beth a little while longer as I complained about my writer's block and then left. The cobbled street was quiet and I stared at Alistair's cottage for a moment. Finally I decided that if I was going to see him, I would have to be prepared. As I made my way home, I saw the familiar figure that belonged to Victor Woodsbury. He had stopped to look at something, maybe his phone? Unlike his wife, Patricia, I had liked Victor ever since he ran into me as I was wandering the streets, blubbering because I found out my boyfriend at the time had cheated on me. He had taken me to his place, made me a cup of tea and showed me photo albums just to get my mind off it. Luckily enough, Patricia hadn't been there.

I sneaked up to him and saw that he was looking at a beautiful jewellery box with a heart-shaped necklace in it. "Boo," I said.

He jumped up and then snapped the box shut before whirling around. The muscles in his face relaxed as he realised it was me and he managed a smile. He put the box in his jacket. "Maggie, our favourite author," he said, apparently speaking on behalf of the village.

"How are you, Victor? Haven't seen you around in a while." He was dressed in an expensive suit with a purple silk tie that matched the blazer he was wearing.

"Work's been busy." He glanced around, and his expression turned more serious. "Actually, I could use some advice."

"Oh?" Finally someone was coming to me for advice instead of to my aunt. Perhaps people were catching on that as a writer I could be very insightful. Dare I say wise?

"Could you ask your aunt to stop by sometime tomorrow?"

My face fell. "Sure."

"And perhaps you should come along as well. After all, you did solve that case of the missing garden gnomes."

"I did. I also found out at uni who stole girls' underwear. Anyway, I'd be happy to help."

He nodded, then gripped my upper arms firmly. "It's important you don't tell anyone. I mean it. And that goes for your aunt as well. This is important."

I swallowed. "Okay, I got it. You can stop squeezing my arms now. Any longer and you'll cut off my blood supply."

He immediately let go. "Sorry, I guess I just—well, just be sure to see me first thing tomorrow. I've taken the morning off and I'm staying at the Pembroke Hotel. I'll have a room and you can come up."

"What? You—really? The Pembroke Hotel?" It had recently been renovated by a Mr and Mrs Field and before that it had a horrible history even though it was a gorgeous Victorian estate. Just the name alone gave me the heebie-jeebies and the fact that we were meeting there made this whole thing feel more serious than I had thought.

"Perhaps it is a mystery," Detective Black said. "One that will lead to danger and death."

I hoped not.

Victor glanced around again, and then strode off whistling as if nothing was the matter. This whole thing was very strange, but I couldn't think about it too long. I hurried back home. Instead of going through the bookshop, I took the back entrance and walked up the stairs to my flat.

I was running slightly late and though Detective Black was eager to get back to his novel and make me bleed ink, I had something else planned. I swapped my black shirt for a red one since it was supposed to be a seductive colour. What I really needed to do was go shopping and buy myself a new wardrobe. Shirts and jeans were alright when I was nineteen, but my style had changed. Even if right now it had changed in my head only. It was time I bought some more feminine and colourful clothes.

After putting on some extra mascara, I squeezed myself into a corset. It took five minutes and afterwards I could barely breathe. This was my first date since my ex, and I couldn't help but feel extra self-conscious. I was desperate to hide my tummy and look as sexy as possible. The only reason I didn't wear high heels was because I knew I'd fall over in them. I was already prone to accidents when I wore flats. Add heels and I was a hazard to people's safety.

My date's name was Danny, and we met on one of those online dating apps that I decided to give a go last week. So far I had encountered rude guys, shy guys, weird guys, and Danny. Danny loved books and he made me laugh, which was all I wanted. He was also easy on the eyes.

I couldn't take my aunt's Land Rover because it meant explaining where I was going, and I didn't want that. I also didn't want the entire village to find out about it and ask me how it went. This was a first date and it could go either way. Which is also why I tried not to get excited, but as I made my way to the bus stop, my nerves fluttered like birds.

The entire ride I went over the icebreakers that I'd Googled yesterday and felt semi-confident when the bus stopped outside the pub The Black Dog. It was located in the village next to ours; I didn't want to run into anyone I knew. With great difficulty I pushed myself out of my seat, but at least I had a flat stomach and right now that was a priority.

I was glad I was doing this. I needed this in order to avoid becoming a hermit.

And so I entered the dark pub and scanned the thin crowd for Danny. When I was certain he wasn't here yet—it was now ten minutes past our meeting time—I sat down where I had a view of the door.

The owner, a middle-aged man with a red face, took my order and later brought me my lemonade.

The door opened a few times, but each time it was someone else. I checked my phone for messages, but there was nothing. I was beginning to get worried.

"Don't be. He might have decided not to come," Detective Black said.

"Why would he do that? He's the one who asked me out." I glanced around to make sure nobody was looking at me like I was crazy. Then I played a game on my phone to pass the time and so I wouldn't fret.

Thirty minutes later the owner showed up at my table with a look of sympathy. "Sorry, luv. But if he ain't here now, he ain't coming." He put his hand on my shoulder. "Go home and don't call him." He grabbed my empty glass and went back to the bar.

Tears filled my eyes, and I blinked them away. He was right. Even if Danny was running late, he would have let me know. I got up and left. On my way back to Castlefield, I picked a quiet spot on the bus where I could cry silent tears. By the time I arrived at the bookshop, I was fine. Enough.

Susan was closing up while Eddie stood behind the counter, his cheeks no longer flushed.

"I see you survived the day," I said. Eddie was my best friend and I could tell him anything, but that didn't mean I wanted to. My disastrous non-date would not be mentioned. Ever.

"I came close to death a few times. Particularly when Mrs Dowry asked where the sex books were." He pretended to gag.

"Hey, age is nothing but a number."

He shook his head vehemently, and I laughed.

"Can I go now?" Susan asked, startling us both.

I blinked. "Sure. We'll finish up."

She nodded and disappeared behind the curtain to grab her jacket and her bag. Then she took the back entrance, which was through the door marked *Private.* She'd pass the bottom of the stairs that led to my flat.

"You know, just for fun I feel like pretending to confess my undying love to her, just to see how she'll react," Eddie said as he watched her leave.

I smiled. "She'll probably nod and then continue working."

"Or she'll malfunction and her hard drive will explode."

"Eddie! She's not a robot."

He leaned forward, a playful grin on his face. "Are you sure?"

I laughed and threw a pen at him. "Come on, let's balance the cash register so we can get you home."

"Ah, yes. The joys of warming up a microwave meal for one."

"I recognise your subtle hint of wanting to be invited for dinner, and since I was going to eat at The Rose anyway, I guess you can tag along. We can discuss how I'm failing horribly as a writer." Plus, I needed a distraction from Danny.

"Is it that bad, huh? I'm sure a good meal with your friend Eddie will make you feel better. Are you buying?"

"No."

"It was worth a shot."

I glared at him.

"What? Free food just tastes better." He grinned at me.

"Let's just go before I change my mind."

Chapter 3

An hour later Eddie and I sat in the local pub, munching on our fish and chips. It could be quite packed around dinner time, but this evening we were two of the few customers. We had picked a quiet corner close to the kitchen to avoid the four middle-aged men who were laughing loudly at the bar. One of them was the baker from across my bookshop, Stanley. His wife would not be happy tonight. He was supposed to be on a diet with a strict zero tolerance for alcohol. He was also the one who was laughing the loudest. I liked him. He sometimes gave me an extra scone for free. Which was bad for my waistline, but good for my mood.

The pub was cosy and charming, with dark tones and soft lighting. The food was also very good, and it had been a while since I had an evening meal here. Which is probably also why I finished my plate so quickly. Though I always ate my meals faster than Eddie. It was probably a sign that I should eat more regularly, but when I was writing, or trying to, I could sometimes forget basic human needs.

"I visited Beth today."

Eddie looked up, stuffing his face with the last piece of his cod.

"She told me that Alistair moved back." My voice was a bit higher.

"Alistair? Alistair Ashworth? The one you had a major crush on all throughout secondary school?"

"Yeah, that Alistair." My face warmed. In fact, my whole body started radiating heat. Soon I'd be attracting cats.

"I thought he joined the Met."

"Yeah, he did. I was extremely jealous of the fact that he got to be a real-life detective. Although, in hindsight, I'm glad I don't have to deal with gruesome deaths. Except for in my novels, of course."

"Right. Well, have you seen him yet? Where does he live?"

"Opposite Beth, actually. And no I haven't seen him. I'm thinking of stopping by, though I'm not sure what I should say to him."

"What? You don't still like him, do you? Then again, you have been single for a few months. You might as well get out there and try. It's been long enough since Co—"

I held up my finger to his lips as I leaned over the table. "Don't even say his name." I removed my finger and leaned back.

"Fine. He-Who-Shall-Not-Be-Named does not deserve to be thought about anymore. So go say hi, but just keep in mind that Alistair might not be the person you remember him to be. Everybody changes." He toyed with the extra packets of ketchup and mayonnaise and finally tucked them into his trousers.

I glanced around. "Why do you always do that?"

"Free stuff is free stuff. We can't all be loaded authors like you."

"I am not loaded and right now I have a serious lack of inspiration so who knows, I might end up being nothing more than an eccentric bookshop owner."

He waved his hand. "Don't worry about that. You went to London and you've done all the boring parts of being an author lately. You should relax and read a few books and let your creative well fill up."

I chuckled.

"What?"

"Nothing. You just don't usually use metaphors."

"I can be writery if I want to be. You must be rubbing off on me." He smirked.

I slurped my lemonade and looked up when a couple in their late forties sat down. They didn't look like they were from around here. They had that twinkle in their eyes and that new-people vibe about them, untainted by the views and style of the Castlefield villagers.

Eddie leaned in. "Those are the people that bought the Pembroke estate and fixed it up."

So that was them. The Pembroke estate was gorgeous, but had an association with tragedy as a serial killer had originally built the estate, creating secret tunnels and rooms to trap victims. She used it as a hotel to kill mostly maids and guests. After that a family ran the hotel, but married men disappeared and were said to be cheaters who died because of the curse.

It had been empty for a long time before Mr and Mrs Field bought it and renovated it. They knew their audience, since they hired my aunt to cleanse the hotel, which even featured in the local newspaper. When they opened, they got

Eleanor and the vicar involved and there were loads of baked goods, as well as a balloon artist and a bouncy castle for the kids. At Eddie's request, they even allowed him and his friend Brian to use their ghost-busting equipment to check if there really weren't any vengeful spirits anymore. When Eddie shared that info, I considered putting on a sheet with two holes to mess with them, but the bouncy castle had been too much fun.

I was contemplating whether or not I should introduce myself when Mrs Field leaned towards me. "Excuse me," she said. "I don't mean to bother you, but aren't you that mystery author? Maggie Matthews?" She had a gorgeous smile with dimples.

"Yes, I am." I beamed. There weren't a lot of newcomers in this village, so being recognised didn't happen that often and always made me feel special. It helped that in the past few years I'd done a few book tours in neighbouring areas here in Cornwall, as well as one in London.

"I just loved your latest novel."

Now I was beaming even more. Any more compliments and I'd be blinding astronauts looking down at Earth. "Thank you so much. I'm glad to hear it." I had rehearsed plenty of standard phrases that made me sound professional. The first time I had gotten recognised, I was so excited that I had asked for *her* autograph. The woman didn't mind. In fact, I think I have a fan club that consists only of her. She still sends me Christmas cards.

"I'm glad you got the Pembroke Hotel up and running again. I'll definitely visit sometime soon," I added.

"That would be lovely. I look forward to it," she said.

I nodded at her and her husband, who gave me a tight smile. "Enjoy your evening," I murmured and we went back to our business. "They seem nice," I said to Eddie.

"They are."

I leaned back and sighed. "I didn't realise I've been working so hard until experiencing the outside world in all its glory again." Even such a small thing as having dinner at the pub with Eddie was enough to lift my spirits, pun not intended. I also made a promise to myself to go out more and not just to the pub.

"Yeah, you needed this. But that's what friends are for."

"That and to tell each other they look horrible in certain outfits."

Eddie pretended to be shocked. "Are you trying to tell me something?"

I chuckled.

"So, shall we go?" Eddie glanced at his watch.

"We shall," I said. "I just need to nip to the bathroom, be right back."

"Sure."

The bathrooms were located past the bar, near the entrance. When I pushed open the door, the scent of lavender struck me. Ever since they had a new female bartender working two nights a week, this was what the women's bathroom smelt like. I was forever grateful. Not that it smelt bad before, but this was definitely nicer.

After I'd gone to the toilet, I washed my hands with the lavender soap and checked myself in the mirror. My complexion was pale with dark circles around my eyes. My short hair was cut in an uneven bob and had almost grown long enough to reach my shoulders. I rubbed my cheeks to get some colour in them. It was spring. I really had to stop locking myself in my office.

A woman strutted into the bathroom as I was about to leave. She moved so quickly that I was unable to dash out of the way. We collided. I grabbed hold of her, but lost my balance, and we tumbled to the floor. I fell on top of her. "I'm so s—oh, that's a nice perfume," I said.

"Get off," she said and waved her hands as if to fan me away from her.

I rose to my feet and helped her up. "Are you alright? That sort of stuff never happens to me." It did. It totally did. I once managed to sprain my ankle while putting on a dress.

She narrowed her eyes at me, still looking attractive with her short pixie cut and leather jacket. She definitely looked new as well. How many new people had we attracted to Castlefield? It meant Eleanor would have some baking to do, together with Olivia. They usually welcomed newcomers that way.

She opened her mouth, no doubt to say something nasty, but instead her face scrunched up like an accordion, and she burst into tears.

"Uh-oh." I patted her on the shoulder. "Are you okay?"

She mumbled incoherently and I caught snippets: "...moved here... boyfriend... London... different...lonely."

Luckily I was fluent in sobbing. "Well, it's a good sign that you were willing to follow your boyfriend here from London. It means you really love him. And of course it will be a big change from a busy city, but take time to get used to it. Also, remember that London is a train ride away, and if you really don't like it here, you should have an honest conversation with him and see what's what."

She patted her red cheeks dry and blinked at me.

"Not everybody is lucky enough to find that special someone. At least, not yet. So if he's worth fighting for, do it. Besides, when I first came here, I felt completely lost and alone. These people were amazing. They made me feel like I was part of their family, it's the warmest feeling." I smiled at her. "So don't write it off just yet."

Her cheeks were blotchy, but she had stopped crying and managed to return my smile. "Thanks. I'm Christina." She held out her hand.

I took it. "Maggie. If you do ever find yourself bored, stop by the local bookshop. It's called The Wicked Bookworm and I own it. Ask for me and I'll give you a discount."

"Great. Thank you so much." Then she rushed to the mirror to adjust the make-up that was now smeared across her cheeks.

I left feeling the warmth that accompanied a good deed and headed outside where Eddie was waiting for me. I glanced back to see a man with his back to me. He was on his phone. The lamp above him was broken, and I could hardly make him out. Still, there was something familiar about him.

Eddie and I split up to get home. We hugged goodbye, and he headed to the cottages where he lived with his dad. Instead of returning to my own flat, I used the key I had for Nancy's flat and went up.

She was on the sofa watching *Coronation Street* with a glass of white wine and her Border Terrier Bailey at her feet.

His little tail wagged as he saw me, but he was too lazy to get up and properly greet me.

"Hey, love," she said. "Oh, do you know who's moved back to the village?" She wore a red headscarf that stood out against her platinum blonde hair.

"Alistair Ashworth. Yeah, I heard." I plopped down next to her.

She turned down the volume. "Have you seen him?"

"No. You?"

"Nope. Didn't you used to have a crush on him?"

I did all but stalk him. "Did I? Can't remember."

"Hm. Olivia said he's hot. Do you want me to give you a love potion?"

"Nancy, no! And I know I'm single, but I'm not that single."

"Are you sure about that?" She chuckled.

"Anyway," I said loudly as I glared at her. "Victor wants us to visit him. He was being very secretive and dramatic. He said he needed advice, and he wanted us both to come and meet him first thing tomorrow morning at the Pembroke Hotel. He'll have a hotel room."

Nancy's eyebrows shot up. "The pervert."

"Nance, come on. It's not like that."

"I should hope so or I'll throw him out the window."

"He looked quite spooked."

"He's a serial cheater, is what he is. The only thing he should be worried about is an STD." She downed the rest of her drink. "But sure, we'll go. No harm in visiting a cursed hotel, is there?"

"Excuse me? You cleansed it. It better not be cursed."

"There are no spirits, but that doesn't mean it's not cursed." She grinned at me. "Don't worry, dear. You've got nothing to fear."

I hoped that was true, because I was about to visit that hotel and though it was pretty on the outside, it had death traps on the inside and possibly even bodies that hadn't been found yet.

I really didn't want to find any bodies.

Chapter 4

That next morning I decided to read instead of write, hoping it would get me back on the literary horse. I was halfway through the third chapter of a mystery novel I'd read before when Nancy rang the bell at the back of the store. I was already dressed and only had to collect a handbag and my courage before making my way downstairs. I opened the door and stepped out. Nancy was dressed entirely in white and tapped her foot impatiently. Her hair resembled that of a beehive, and her lipstick was bright pink. She wasn't one to blend in.

"This advice he needs better be worth giving," she said. "If it's anything like that man requested yesterday, I'll hit him with a chair. Hotel rooms have chairs, right? Should I bring my broom?"

"No, don't bring a broom. I'm sure he needs our help with something entirely innocent."

"Sure, and that's why he's staying home from work and wants us to meet him at a hotel room in the same village. This whole thing is very odd."

"I know it's odd, and that's why we have to go. Whatever it is, it must be important." I grabbed her arm as we made our way to the bridge and in the direction of the hill on which the hotel was situated. We came across Pandora the chicken who stared us down in the middle of the street, but just as I was about to make a run for it, Nancy squeezed my arm and kept on walking. We went straight towards her. Her brownish-red feathers were pretty, but her beady eyes were evil.

Any moment she could charge at us, but she did nothing. She let us pass without so much as a strange clucking sound. If anybody had seen us, they would have thought it was Nancy's magic. And maybe it was.

The hotel was a Victorian estate with bay windows and castle-like features. Pink climbing roses adorned the white archway by the entrance. It was well-kept and looked gorgeous, yet at the same time I couldn't help but feel sad as I looked at it.

Mrs Field was the one attending the reception desk. It was an old mahogany desk with an old-fashioned ledger for guests to sign in, but there was also a computer in the corner. "Miss Matthews," she said as soon as she spotted me. "And Nancy, welcome back. How delightful to see you both."

Nancy just murmured some general pleasantries.

"Please call me Maggie," I said. "It's nice to see you too. We're here to visit Victor Woodsbury. Do you have his room number?"

"Of course. It's 205. The second floor."

"Thank you."

Mrs Field asked me to stop by at the reception desk before leaving so I could sign her book and after I said I would, we went up the broad staircase with the swirling banister. The carpet absorbed our footfalls as we made our way up. It was very beautiful on the inside and didn't feel like it had once belonged to a serial killer. They really had done their best to renovate it and maintain some of the old features.

We made our way up to the second floor while Nancy was telling me about where she would hit Victor with the chair when we arrived at his hotel room. I knocked on the door and made sure I was positioned between Victor and Nancy when he'd open the door. Just in case.

Silence.

I knocked again, then tried the handle. The door opened. All the doors had old-fashioned keys, so they didn't lock automatically.

"That's never a good sign," Detective Black said.

"Uh-oh," I said. "Stay back."

"No way. You stay back. If this means there's trouble, then I'm going in. I've read your books and I watch crime dramas. I know exactly what to do." She grabbed a tea kettle from her handbag.

"What? Why did you bring a tea kettle?"

"My broom didn't fit in my handbag." She pushed open the door.

"If there is a murderer in there, go for the eyes, the groin, or the throat," Detective Black said.

We tiptoed into the room as I stayed glued to Nancy in case I needed to defend her. She was good with household appliances, but still. There was an empty tea cup on the desk and other than that the room looked like nobody had been in there. Of course, he hadn't spent the night here. For some reason he only rented this room so we would have a place to talk while his wife thought he was at work.

"Victor?" I asked. "Are you there?" My voice trembled. I went over to the bathroom and tried the door. It was locked. "Victor?" I tapped on the door.

Nothing.

I banged this time, though I couldn't imagine why he couldn't hear me. Especially when he was expecting us. A ball of barbed wire settled in my stomach.

"I can think of a reason why he wouldn't answer," Detective Black said.

"Nance, give me your credit card."

"You make your own money, use your own," she said.

"No, I know a trick so I can open the lock. It's one of those hook-and-eye latches. I noticed that when I checked out pictures on their website. Give me a card that you don't mind getting scratched."

She sighed. "Fine. But I'm telling you he's just being an arse, because he is, in fact, an arse." She said that last bit loud enough for him to hear. She handed me a card.

I wiggled it between the door and the doorpost, hoping it would be under the lock. It was difficult because I had to guess. I shimmied the card upwards until I felt resistance. It meant I was in the right place. I kept wiggling until I felt no resistance and there was a sound against the door. I had gotten it out of the hook. I opened the door as I held my breath.

He was in the bath with his back to me, but I could immediately tell that he was dead. He was leaning over the edge of the tub and had clearly been sick. His skin had an unnatural colour. This couldn't be happening. It had to be a nightmare.

I screamed my lungs out.

WE HAD TO WAIT DOWNSTAIRS in the lounge area while the crime scene unit processed the room, and the coroner and detectives were called. Somewhere in the back of my mind I wondered if Alistair would be the detective on the case, but it barely reached my conscious mind. I trembled on the comfortable sofa while Nancy kept rubbing my back and offering me water even though I didn't want any, nor did I see how water could help me unsee what I had seen.

The other guests downstairs were eyeing me with curiosity, but only one had tried to approach me. She had backed off when Nancy growled at her. Still, they already knew someone had died and that that someone was Victor Woodsbury. It wouldn't be long now till the village mentioned the curse. I hated that, because no curse had killed Victor, and I didn't want people to use that as an excuse not to pay attention to their surroundings. Victor had seemed scared. Perhaps other people had noticed something about him. *Of course, it could just be a coincidence.*

"There are no coincidences when it comes to a sudden death," Detective Black said.

Which I agreed with, but I also considered that perhaps my imaginative mind had taken over. Perhaps Victor had simply become a bit dramatic now that he'd reached his fifties.

It seemed to take forever until someone cleared their throat. I looked up at Alistair, recognising him immediately. He was wearing a grey suit and black shoes. His black hair was half-long. His shoulders were broad and he still had that air of coolness about him. He was also very good at maintaining a poker face, since I couldn't tell if he knew who I was.

"I'm DS Ashworth and this is DC Daniels," he said.

It wasn't until then that I noticed the man standing behind him. He looked slender and smiled sheepishly.

"I realise you two have had quite the shock," Alistair continued, "but I'm going to have to ask you some questions. Is that okay?"

I nodded.

"You two found the body?" he asked.

"Victor," I said.

"Excuse me?"

"His name is Victor. Victor Woodsbury." I managed a feeble smile, though in reality it probably looked like a grimace.

"Of course. Victor. And you found him?"

"So what? If it hadn't been for us, it would have been the maid or something," Nancy said. "We were just minding our own business."

Alistair frowned. "In his hotel room?"

"He invited us over," I said. "Yesterday. He said he needed advice and he wanted my aunt to come over, then he added that I should come as well. He said I couldn't tell anyone and that we were to meet him at the hotel. He indicated that he'd pretend to go to work and nobody would know he'd be here. Except us."

Alistair scribbled something in his notebook. "And did he mention what he needed advice about?"

I shook my head.

"And then what happened when you arrived?"

"We asked for his room number and then went up. When we got to his door, it was unlocked. My aunt Nancy took out a tea kettle as a potential weapon since we both thought it ominous that his door was open. Which was silly, I guess, but we watch a lot of crime dramas. Also, it did turn out to be ... you know?"

"A body."

"Yep," I said in a high voice.

"And why did you bring a tea kettle to this meeting?" Alistair asked Nancy.

"Because his intentions could have been impure. He was a cheating bastard," she said.

"He was? How do you know?"

"Everybody knows." She leaned forward. "And in case you don't remember, we gossip a lot."

He flashed her a professional smile. "And then what happened?"

"Everything looked like a normal empty hotel room except for one cup of tea. I tried the bathroom but it was locked."

"Locked? You're sure?" He scribbled something down again. "How did you get into the bathroom then?"

I felt my cheeks get warm.

Alistair stopped writing and observed my expression. He sat down on the edge of the coffee table in front of me, suddenly quite close. Our knees were nearly touching. He smelt woody and I wanted to hug him. "I just want to know the truth. You're not in any trouble, but it's important we get all the facts."

"I used a credit card to open the lock. I simply pushed the card up, and then it opened. I had to do that once for research purposes. As a mystery writer."

He simply smiled. "Then what happened?"

Nancy scoffed. "Then a marching band came out of the bathroom to perform for us. What do you think? We saw the dead body, she screamed her head off, and we ran out of there to get Mrs Field. She rang the police and here we are."

"So nobody stayed with the—Victor?" Alistair asked.

"What did you want? For us to sit there and braid his hair?" Nancy said with a frown on her face.

"Nance," I warned.

"What? It's a stupid question. Are you really the detective on this case?" she said. "Lovely to have you back, though." And just like that the switch had flipped, and she stared at him affectionately. "How is your mother? She must be happy to have you back."

He blinked. "Right. I'm—" his voice trailed off and he cleared his throat. "One more question. Did either of you touch anything?"

"I touched the door handle to the bathroom, other than that we didn't touch anything. Did we?" I asked Nancy.

She shook her head vehemently.

Alistair got up. "I might stop by later to ask some more questions. For now I'll need the tea kettle that you brought." He held out his hand to Nancy.

She gasped dramatically. "Why? What has this tea kettle ever done to you?"

"Miss Knightley, please."

She growled, then took out the tea kettle and pressed it into his hands. "Just be gentle with it. It's a delicate kettle."

"I thought you brought it as a weapon?"

"Reluctantly. My broom didn't fit in my handbag."

After he gave Nancy a look I couldn't decipher, he left. I watched him go, noting that he hadn't shown any signs of recognition. No warmth or kindness. Just a professional attitude that told me I didn't have a shot. Not in a million years.

"Thanks for the ointment you gave my mum," DC Daniels said to Nancy.

"You're very welcome, dear. Say hi to her for me. She's a lovely woman." Her voice was soft as warm milk.

DC Daniels smiled and then trotted off in the direction Alistair had gone.

"You do realise that Alistair thinks you're crazy now?"

"But I am, so why would I mind that? Now, let's get you home."

NANCY BROUGHT ME TO her place where Bailey snuggled up on my lap after she placed me on the sofa with a mug of herbal tea and a blanket. I had thought of getting a pet myself, but I didn't have time to walk a dog every day, nor did I want to. And with a cat I'd have to wear a hazmat suit every time I had to clean the litter box. The only thing that came close to being desirable was a bunny.

Nancy was never sick, nor had she ever hired anyone to cover for her in her shop. This time wasn't any different. After she made sure I was okay, she went downstairs to open up for business and gossip, no doubt.

By that time I had stopped shaking, even if I still couldn't believe what had happened. Despite that time that Victor had comforted me, we hadn't spoken much. Perhaps a few words in the street or the time that he frequented the bookshop. It only lasted a few weeks, and then he stopped. Even if he was a cheater, I had liked him and I was sad to know he'd died. Victor and Patricia were quite popular in this village, and I imagined this would be hot news. Quite a lot of people would be upset. Victor had always been charming.

"Death is always lurking where you least expect it," Detective Black said and pulled up the blanket to my chin. "Get some rest."

I closed my eyes and fell asleep immediately. I didn't wake until noon and went downstairs. I left through the back only to get into my own store, but before I could face anybody in there, I rushed upstairs to put on some make-up. I hadn't bothered with that this morning, and to my horror I looked as bad as I felt. It was a miracle that Alistair hadn't run away.

When I felt a bit more like myself, I went downstairs to see Eddie and Susan. No doubt it would be busy. When there was a piece of news like this, people met up wherever they could. And I knew the book club ladies would be there, because no doubt they'd also heard it was Nancy and I who had found Victor.

"Maggie," Eddie shouted as he spotted me from across the store. He was setting up a new display but abandoned it to rush over and hug me. "Are you okay? Nancy said you were at her place, resting. How are you?"

"I'm much better now, thank you."

"They say Victor was poisoned," Eddie said, looking rather pale himself.

"Poison? Really?" I asked. "I didn't even know that. It's not like I inspected his ... body." Had the poison been in the tea cup? Or had someone injected something? Poison was usually used by women, and it had the benefit of not having to be around to kill someone. Could it have been his wife? But who knew he would be there? Was Mrs Field in on it? My mind was a tornado of thoughts.

The women of the Castlefield Book Club gathered around. Eleanor gave me a kiss on the cheek and was kind enough to bring home-made scones.

"Thank you for coming, ladies."

"It's just so awful," Poppy said.

Several women had burst into tears, even the usually distant Lily. Victor had been even more popular than his wife. I tried to assess if any of them could have been his lover, but I detected nothing suspicious. Poppy clutched my arm and dabbed a lace handkerchief at the corner of her eye, even if she wasn't crying any more.

"Maggie, can't you do something? This is just so awful and you've helped us before." She made a very obvious gesture with her head towards Lily who instantly shot her nose up in the air and looked away. If anybody was to blame, it was her thieving cousin.

"This is not really my area of expertise," I said, flattered they thought it was.

Ava, Dawn's wife, scoffed. "Are you joking?" she said in a Scottish accent. "You write about murders. You get into killers' heads." She tapped her temple and then blew a few strands of her fringe away. "If anybody knows how a psycho killer operates, it's you."

Eleanor cleared her throat and then smiled at me as if to say she didn't mean it like that. She had to do that a lot when Ava spoke.

"Yeah, thanks, Ava. I'll see what I can do."

There was a collective sigh of relief that startled me. Had my concession really been that important to them? And how the hell was I going to live up to their expectations? I could hardly solve a *real* murder, could I? I pictured the sense of pride and accomplishment if I actually managed it. Not just to be able to solve something so complex, but to set something right for Victor and to protect the villagers. Perhaps even impress a certain detective. Also, if a killer could strike once, he could strike again.

"Of course you can do it," Detective Black said from behind me. "I'll help you."

When I glanced back, he was gone again. What the holy muffin had I just said yes to?

Chapter 5

The women stayed in the back of the bookshop where the scones, tea and armchairs were, so that at least Poppy could sit down. I went to the front to greet Susan, who looked pale and rattled. Her hair was not its usual tight ponytail, and strands of her hair dangled in front of her face.

"Are you okay?" I asked her.

"Fine," she said curtly, as if to indicate that there was no room for any more questions.

"Just take it easy today," I said. Apparently, it took a murder to awaken her emotions.

Was it the fact that a murder was committed? Something else entirely? Or had she known Victor better than I thought? There was a time when he frequented the bookshop not too long ago. Was I being paranoid?

"Being paranoid is a good thing for a detective," Detective Black said.

"Not for your personal life," I said.

"What?" Susan came out from behind the curtain where she'd put her bag.

"What? Err, just let me know if you need anything."

"I'm fine," she said again as if I'd insulted her.

"Good, good, good." I moved away and returned to the ladies in the back.

"Do we still have our book club meeting tonight?" Poppy asked after she grabbed her third scone. She had strawberry jam on her chin.

"Of course," Eleanor said. "We need it now more than ever. Ah, Maggie. Is it okay if we have our meeting here tonight? I'd like to go all out. I'll ask Olivia to come and bring a cake or two."

The women all made excited noises, and I guess it didn't matter if I was okay with it or not. Eleanor was right, they needed this. Perhaps even I needed this.

"Does this mean you'll all be discussing the book you're currently reading? *True Love*?" I managed to say it without making a face.

Eleanor inhaled slowly. "Right, yes. I suppose we will discuss that book. No spoilers, though."

The women cheered.

"It's so good. Have you lasses reached chapter four yet? I read it last night and had to fan myself to cool down," Ava said.

"Do you—do you like that sort of thing if a man's involved?" Poppy asked with wide eyes.

"Lass, I may not particularly like pianos, but that doesn't mean I don't enjoy watching someone else play on it." Ava laughed.

Leave it to Ava to call someone thirty years older than her 'lass'.

Poppy nodded, but looked as though she still didn't understand. I stopped myself from chuckling. Poppy's expression was usually made up of confusion and added to her charm. She had been single most of her life, only married briefly, and I wondered how much she had seen of the world.

Soon the women moved on to who Victor's potential lover could be, and I tried to convince them that the curse was baloney. They said they believed me, because how could someone like Victor cheat? But I could see in their faces that that wasn't what they really thought. The curse was part of this village, unfortunately, just as much as Eleanor's scones.

It was what made me decide to close early. I understood the reason for wanting to discuss the murder, but I could only take so much of it. Eddie took a while to be convinced that I was fine and after he went home, I went up to Nancy's flat and made some macaroni and cheese. I put the leftovers in the fridge for Nancy. Bailey stared at my every move the whole time. He was six years old, and when we first got him, I occasionally fed him my vegetables. Hence the love for human food. Oops.

After I finished dinner, I took Bailey for a walk. I needed some fresh air, and it was still nice and warm outside. Bailey wagged his tail as he darted forward. I had to pull him back or I'd end up being dragged around by him. He was strong for a small dog. I walked around for ten minutes without a clear purpose, but ended up in the street where Patricia Woodsbury lived. How was she taking the news of her dead husband and had she known that he had been having an affair? It depended on how long the affair was going on and how good he was at lying. Did the wife always know? Still, even if he was having an affair, why kill him? What was wrong with a good old-fashioned divorce?

The Tudor-style house looked spacious and well kept. It was a detached home, surrounded by high bushes at the sides and a wooden fence at the front, rose bushes placed alongside it. A small fountain was placed in the middle of the front garden and a white bench was below one of the windows.

Bailey pulled on the leash. He was about to pee against the tyre of a car. When I pulled him back, I recognised the car as a Volkswagen Beetle. I swallowed. Beth had said Alistair had a car like that. He was probably talking to Patricia.

"Hmm. I'd love to be a fly on the wall during their conversation," I said to Bailey and pulled him along as he sniffed the ground. He didn't seem to agree with me, though, and pulled me in the other direction. He let out a little bark.

The front door opened and the sudden sound of voices startled me into action. I scooped up Bailey and rushed behind the bushes that separated Patricia's front garden from that of her neighbour's. Hidden behind the hedge, I lost my balance and fell into the prickly twigs of the English laurel. I was afraid to move as I heard Alistair, DC Daniels and Patricia walk the path to the pavement and Alistair's car. Bailey licked my face and I held my breath, afraid any sound would give me away.

"Thank you for your time, Mrs Woodsbury," Alistair said. "If anything comes to mind, please don't hesitate to contact us."

"Yes, I have your number. Please do keep me posted on your investigation. I need to know what happened to my husband," Patricia said.

"Will do, Mrs Woodsbury. Take care," Alistair said. Two car doors slammed and the engine was turned on. After the car drove off, Patricia spoke like she was talking on the phone.

"The police just came." A pause. "Yes, I'll see you in five minutes." Then her footsteps retreated back to the front door and it slammed shut.

I sighed with relief, then struggled as I tried to push myself forward and out of the hedge. Bailey jumped out of my arms before I could put him back on the ground. Then he looked ahead of us. I followed his gaze to Patricia's neighbour who stared at me with an open mouth, holding a shopping bag.

There were some plants planted along the path to the front door, but the rest was grass, so luckily I hadn't trampled on anything. The neighbour was still gaping at me: the weirdo that had been standing still, half fallen into her hedge whilst holding a dog.

"Err, there was a squirrel," I said. "A really big one. You're supposed to stand still and avoid eye contact. That way they don't see you." I took a few steps in the direction of the pavement. "They can be very dangerous. I think it's the tail and the teeth. Very ... yeah. Bye." I waved and scurried past Patricia's house. From my hair I pulled a twig and hoped it didn't show that I had just been hiding in a hedge.

Patricia's phone call bounced around in my head. Was she having an affair too? Also, when I wrote my grieving characters they were much more upset than Patricia seemed to be, but then again I'd never written a character like her before.

I lingered on the corner of the street where I still had a visual of Patricia's house. Bailey had decided to lie down at my feet instead of pulling at the leash. Perhaps he sensed that what I was doing was important, or at least more exciting than typing on my laptop.

One by one I spotted the fancy hats on top of the heads of Patricia's loyal gang of friends. I knew their names. Frances, Dorothy, and Anne. So nothing sinister then, just a couple of girlfriends coming to support her.

My faith in people was restored, for now.

THAT EVENING AT THE bookshop, Nancy and I moved things around to make room. Eleanor had provided plenty of chairs that she set in a circle with Lily and Poppy. Olivia and her husband brought a long table to put all the food on, and Jessica had brought a radio that she'd taken from her daughter's room since her daughter was away at uni. Apparently this book club had wild intentions. I had put enough copies of the book on the chairs for them, so they didn't have to bring their own. My plan had been to help them set up, but instead I decided to stay. It would be a welcome distraction.

Ava and Phoebe were the last to show up. Ava came in laughing and pointed at Phoebe when she found she couldn't speak. Phoebe was wearing a onesie that was meant to resemble a cow. She had her hands stuck in the udders.

"What?" she said. "I'm going to bed after this, and it's very comfortable and warm."

Ava caught her breath long enough to shout, wheezing: "Sh—she's a cow."

Phoebe's cheeks turned red with anger, and she stomped off to the table with the cakes, lemon tarts, and scones. We would all have to be rolled home after tonight.

The other women started to giggle. It wasn't so much because of the situation, but we needed to discharge all the heavy feelings related to the murder, and this was the perfect excuse. The giggle rose to a burst of laughter, and soon we were all laughing, even Phoebe.

Instead of composing ourselves and demurely sitting down in the circle, I put out half the lights and Ava plugged her phone into the radio and started blasting Imagine Dragons. It wasn't the best music to dance to, but we did it anyway. Phoebe moved her arms up and down, looking more like she was flailing and Eleanor danced circles around Poppy. I danced with Ava, and even Lily at some point. Nancy was moving to her own music, which was apparently very slow as she made calm, fluid motions. Then she paused and started headbanging.

At some point I sneaked upstairs to my flat and got a few bottles of whiskey and vodka. I started handing out drinks, and soon Ava was dancing on one of the chairs while Phoebe tried limbo dancing even though there was no bar. Poppy kept meowing like a cat and Jessica was giving Phoebe a makeover with a couple of red markers and a pen. Nancy danced with a mop.

There was a pleasant buzz that had started in my head and spread out through my body. Nothing seemed to matter, nothing but this moment. I didn't have to worry about impressing people or solving things. I could do whatever I wanted, and so I danced.

By the time it finally quieted down, Lily and I sat on the chairs, surveying the damage. Katy Perry was blaring through the radio as Olivia and Eleanor were leaning against a bookcase, both seemingly asleep while Phoebe was lying on the floor, her head on a stack of books. Nancy was stuffing her face with a lemon tart, and Poppy was licking one of the windows.

"Holy hell. What time is it? Two AM? Three?" I asked.

Lily checked her watch. "What time did we start again?" she said with a slur.

"Seven o'clock."

"It's now nine."

I gaped at her. "We are not made for this."

"No, we are not." We clinked our glasses and downed the rest of our drinks.

Chapter 6

That morning I woke up on my own sofa with a vague recollection of how I got there. Slowly, it came back to me. I was fairly sure three women had carried me up the stairs. My hair was a complete mess and someone had drawn on my left leg with a black marker. I couldn't make out what it was, although it had the possibility of being something dirty. I showered for about twenty minutes, had breakfast and then went downstairs to work in the bookshop since I felt like doing something productive.

The shop was busy. People were browsing or buying books while gossiping about the murder. Though the topic of the gossip wasn't fun at all, I still enjoyed the overall cosy vibe that a busy Saturday brought with it.

A few hours later I was working on a new display as Eddie tapped me on the shoulder with repeated vigour.

"What? What? What?" I said without turning around.

"Guess what?"

"You're pregnant?"

"Very funny." He grabbed me by the shoulders and turned me around. His cheeks were flushed.

"Uh-oh, this must be serious."

"It is. You know how everyone thinks it's the curse that killed Victor Woodsbury?"

"How could I forget?" I said.

"Well, it's spread and now there are Welsh ghost hunters coming to the Pembroke Hotel to determine the validity."

"Wow," I said.

"I know."

"No, I mean, I don't think I've ever heard you use the word 'validity' before."

Eddie glared at me. "I'm being serious."

"I know, that's what scares me. The words 'Welsh' and 'ghost hunters' all in one sentence."

He grunted. "I knew I couldn't talk to you about this."

"I'm just messing with you. Sort of." I mumbled that last part. "Are there really people coming here with a bunch of equipment to make sure no ghost has killed Victor Woodsbury?" His death was not some story or show. Certainly not to me.

"Or to make sure a ghost has," Eddie said. "Look, what happened to poor Victor is big news in the ghost community."

"There's a ghost community? Isn't that just the afterlife?"

"And by coming here it will bring lots of publicity to this village, not to mention that we could have a real-life haunted hotel."

"Or not."

He blinked. "I'm choosing to ignore your negativity."

"Or realism."

"I'm going back to work," he said with a frown.

"I don't like this. Victor was a good man. His death should be investigated properly, and it shouldn't become some circus."

Eddie pressed his lips together. "It's not, Maggie. I really think that this will be good. Look, I know you liked him, and I'm sorry. I shouldn't have said this all excited, that was insensitive. However, I do think that it might be possible that ghosts did this, just like a lot of people do. If these ghost hunters prove there are ghosts, it may help us figure out what happened, and if they don't, it will shut people up about the rumour. Either way, win-win."

"Not really. Victor will still be dead."

"Unfortunately dying is part of the being alive deal. He shouldn't have died that way, no. But it happened. There's nothing we can do about it. We don't decide how we go."

"Right. So all we can do is figure out who did it. That's the only way we can make some sort of difference," I said.

"That is not at all what I said."

"Someone's life is the worst thing you could possibly take from them. We can't prevent it from happening, though. The only thing we can do is solve the murder." All I'd be doing was just asking some well-timed questions and paying attention. I already did that anyway. If I was going to do this, I would need a plan.

"I can see that you've zoned out, so I'm going back to work now." He left shaking his head.

"Okay," I murmured, wondering where Detective Black would have started his investigation. I headed over to the counter where there was a man who looked familiar. He turned around and smiled as soon as we made eye contact. It was Danny. He looked exactly like his profile picture. His neatly trimmed hair, his glasses, the wicked smile on his tanned face.

I couldn't believe I was stupid enough to check the news for accidents.

"Maggie." He touched my hand. "Terribly sorry for the delay. I had an important meeting coming up that I couldn't cancel."

"Delay? Our date was yesterday."

He chuckled. "And now I'm here. Why don't you pop on your coat and I'll take you somewhere nice. My treat, of course. It's the least I can do."

Oh, it is. I smiled at him. "Can you give me one moment?" I disappeared behind the curtain and came back out holding a broom.

"What are you—Ouch," he said as I hit him with it. "Are you mad?"

I hit him again and again, chasing him out of my bookshop. "And don't come back, you bastard," I yelled. Across the street Pandora watched him run, and it didn't take long before she started chasing him.

Just then Alistair walked over with his hands in his pockets and in a similar suit to the one he had on yesterday. If he didn't think I was unusual before, he sure did so now.

"I see you're dangerous with a broom as well," he said, and followed me inside where I placed the broom back behind the curtain. I could see why Nancy used it as a weapon. It was strangely therapeutic. I was now completely over the whole Danny-fiasco and even felt smug.

"Is this what you always dress like on weekends?" I said, hoping to change the topic.

He grinned, then his gaze travelled down to take in my outfit. It would surely not impress him, since I wore my standard jeans and shirt. "My boss wants this case solved as soon as possible, and I don't mind working overtime."

"So a bit of a workaholic, huh?" I smiled to soften my words.

He smiled back. "So are you. Don't you have people working for you?"

"I'm experiencing a bit of a writer's block, and I could use the distraction considering what happened. Did you come to ask me more questions?"

"Actually, I'm here to talk to your aunt. I thought this was her shop."

"It used to be, but she split it in half when I wanted to open a bookshop."

"That's very generous of her," he said. His eyes scanned my face, lingering on my lips. Did I have food there? Probably. I ran a finger across my lips just in case.

"She is very generous. Don't let her occasional outbursts fool you. Anyway, you can go through the curtain if you want."

"No, I'll use the normal entrance, thanks. Bye."

Nancy didn't actually have a sign above her shop, but it was too well-known. Everybody knew her shop.

Why bother coming in here?

"Perhaps he wanted to see you, the cheeky bastard," Detective Black said.

"Wait."

Alistair turned back to me. "Yes?"

"I wondered if you perhaps remember me?" He had to, right? We spent that entire afternoon at the fair instead of going to classes.

"Yes. Maggie Matthews, from secondary school."

Right. Just a random person from secondary school. "Great," I said flatly.

"I'm sorry our little reunion couldn't be under better circumstances, and I'm sorry about what you had to go through yesterday. It couldn't have been easy. I hope you understand I was just trying to do my job in questioning you and your aunt." He smiled, turning my limbs into jelly.

"Of course. You can always question me. I mean—" my voice trailed off, and I gave him an innocent smile.

He grinned. "I'll see you around."

"Okidoki." I was sure I'd never said that before, why start? "Take care," I added as I watched him walk away.

Why did I have to be such an awkward idiot?

"You said okidoki, huh?" Eddie asked from behind me.

"You heard all that?" I turned around.

"Yeah. It was riveting."

I narrowed my eyes at him. "He went to talk to Nancy. I wonder why?" I hurried to the back room and stood as close as I could next to the curtain to her store. They must have been standing by the counter, because I could hear them clearly.

"Mr Field said that you cleansed the building before they officially opened," Alistair said. His voice was pleasant, and I wanted to bathe in it.

"That's right. And I did cleanse it. It is spotless," Nancy said.

"I am also to understand that you are known for your ... special abilities."

"Yes, of course. Even your mother visited me for something against hair loss."

A pause. "I see," Alistair said. He sighed as if he didn't want to ask the next question. "And in your opinion, could spirits really cause someone to die?"

"In my opinion, no. I think someone is just using the curse to commit murder."

It was great how we thought alike.

"I'm sorry for having to ask such a question, it's just that the rumour has spread and now everybody believes it's something paranormal. Since you're a respected member of the community, I figured I could refer to your opinion to keep people from blowing this thing up."

"I understand."

"Thank you for your time," Alistair said.

"Are you single?" she asked.

Another pause. "I don't see how that's relevant."

"I do. Maggie's single."

I gasped and pressed my hand to my mouth to keep from making a noise.

"Goodbye, Miss Knightley."

Damn her and her good intentions. Didn't she know she had to keep those on the inside of her mouth? I turned around, bumped into someone, and shrieked. It was Eddie. "You scared me." I pushed him into my shop. "Did you hear all that?"

He made a face. "It reminds me of the time Nancy tried to set me up with this girl in the pub. She'd given her my printed CV."

"If I remember correctly, the girl did go out with you."

"Nancy is eerily good at what she does."

"Don't let her hear that."

He pretended to zip his lips. Then unzipped it. "Want to have a snack in an hour? I didn't have lunch."

"Sure." I glanced around. "Where's Susan?"

"I think she's over at the children's books."

She had been quite upset yesterday. "I'll go check on her."

Susan was at the back of the store putting new children's books on the shelves. Normally she did this with the speed of a Tasmanian Devil on drugs, but today she moved slowly and occasionally stopped to stare ahead.

I observed her for a minute or so before I couldn't take it anymore. "Okay," I said, startling her. "What's going on with you? You may not like talking about it, but it's affecting your job performance. Not that I'm complaining. I'm just worried."

She stared at me and for a brief moment I thought she wouldn't answer me. Then she burst into tears.

I put my arm around her. "Come on," I said and decided to take her upstairs to my flat so that nobody could eavesdrop, and we could have tea in peace. Tea always made everything better.

Susan sat down on my sofa, still sobbing as she wiped her wet cheeks on her sleeves, and I hurried to grab her a box of tissues and made us some tea. I also brought a plate of biscuits in and sat down next to her, awaiting an explanation. It was strange to see her so vulnerable, especially when she was always so composed and cold.

She cleared her throat and took a few shaky breaths. "I had an affair with Victor," she said.

My eyes widened. *Damn.* The thought had crossed my mind, but she was only twenty-six and he was twice her age.

"Teaches you to keep an open mind," Detective Black muttered. "Now, put her at ease and get as many details as you can."

I glared at him. He was right, I had to get as much information out of her now that she was crying and in a talkative mood. I had serious doubts that she had killed him, unless these were tears of guilt, but still, she could know something.

"He visited the bookshop a few times, looking for a gift for his wife," she said and glanced up at me to gauge my reaction. "I know what I did was awful, but he was just so charming. We talked for a while and then he stopped by a few more times after that. At first we just became friends, you know? I didn't want to be someone's mistress. But after I had this horrible date, Victor comforted me, and it just happened. He was so sweet to me."

I remembered the way he had taken care of me when my heart was broken. He had been kind and funny. And yes, he was charming, but I'd never seen him in a romantic light. Not that I was judging her. At least, I tried not to. "And was there anything on his mind? Did he have a problem? He asked me and Nancy to meet him at the hotel and was very secretive and worried."

"I heard that. I don't know why, though. He said he wanted to get a divorce from Patricia, but he'd been saying that for months."

"Months? How long were you together?"

"Four months. But we only met once a week. I would miss him terribly, but when we got together, everything was right again."

"She's got it bad," Detective Black said.

"Is there anything else that might be important? Something you can tell me that might help catch the killer?"

She started crying again. "I can't believe he's been murdered. Who would do such a thing? Please, Maggie. Please find out who did this." She clasped my hand and continued crying.

I left Susan in my flat to calm down and went downstairs to pick up the slack. Eddie was busy himself and barely noticed she wasn't even here. After about twenty minutes she came down, and she looked more like herself. She had redone her ponytail, and something about her demeanour had changed. If I had to venture a guess, it was because she'd got something heavy off her chest. That could do wonders. Perhaps now the ice between us would be melted. Or perhaps that depended entirely on me finding Victor's killer.

I still couldn't believe it was Susan he'd had an affair with. Nancy had called him a cheater, but even then I had still dismissed it, respected him. Now, not so much. Not just because he had cheated on his wife, awful as she was, but also because I couldn't help but feel he'd taken advantage of Susan. There was something lonely about her, and I didn't like that Victor had used that to climb into bed with her. If he had really loved Susan, he would have left Patricia instead of whispering sweet nothings in her ear while going home to have dinner with his wife every night.

I decided I'd tell Alistair about it, but nobody else. I didn't want it coming out, and I just had to hope that Alistair could be discreet when he spoke with her. After all, she knew nothing vital to the investigation, and there was no need for it to come out.

Despite all the gossip that spread like wildfire in Castlefield, I couldn't help but wonder what other things went on that we knew nothing about.

Chapter 7

Around four, Eddie and I left. I felt confident that Susan could manage on her own for about twenty minutes, and she had even regained some of the colour in her cheeks.

Eddie and I went to Stanley's bakery where his wife always helped out. Olivia had done her best to scrub her face, but the markers used for her 'makeover' weren't that easy to remove. The vague outlines were still visible. She had Harry Potter-style glasses drawn on, as well as messy red lips. Her cheeks had perfectly round circles and three horizontal stripes were drawn over her eyebrows in order to resemble cartoon eyelashes. She also kept shushing customers, even though it was relatively quiet, and groaned regularly like a zombie. I'd already heard this from Nancy, who had heard it from Jessica, who had heard it from Dawn.

"Hiyaaaa," I said loudly when we entered. There was only one customer, and she left as we came in.

She growled. "The insolence of youth," she said. "And how dare you not be affected by the booze."

"What booze? What did I miss?" Eddie asked.

"You missed a hell of a party." I chuckled. "I think Poppy was licking windows at some point."

"I didn't think a book club would get so wild," Stanley said and eyed his wife with mock disappointment. The corners of his mouth clearly twitched.

"It was all Maggie's fault. She got the booze. Before that it was perfectly innocent."

"Hardly. I saw Ava twerk."

Eddie laughed. "Man, I can't believe I missed that. Maybe I should join the book club."

"You say that, but we usually talk about how uncomfortable bras are or we Google high heels we are in love with but will never buy because they're so uncomfortable," Olivia said. "Now, what can we get you?"

"Two chicken sandwiches, please. You make the best, Stanley," I said.

"Always love to hear that," he said with a grin as he went to work.

The phone rang and Olivia groaned. She sauntered to the back and picked up the phone.

"So, nasty business about Victor, ain't it?" Stanley said without looking up.

"Very nasty," I said.

"Olivia said the girls asked you to look into it. How is that going?"

"Err, not really a lot of progress yet. It happened yesterday."

"Don't worry about it. If anyone can solve it, it's you. Just don't do anything too dangerous." He winked at me and handed us the paper bag in which he'd put our sandwiches. "On the house."

"Oh, you don't have to—"

"I insist, dearie. You're our local sleuth, and you need your fuel. For the grey cells." He tapped his temple.

"Right." I fought an unsettling feeling without success. "Thank you." After shouting goodbye to Olivia, we left. The bell above the door tinkled.

Eddie took the bag from me as we walked to the small park in front of the store. "You know you don't owe anybody anything, right? I mean, you don't have to solve anything."

"I know. Strange as it may seem, I do want to. I just hope I don't let them down."

"See, that's why I don't like this. You shouldn't put that kind of pressure on yourself. Do you really think you can do what the police do? I mean y—"

"I know. Trust me, I get what you're saying. That's why I didn't want to do it at first. I didn't think I could do it. But I've got nothing to lose if I try." We reached the bench in the park and sat down. Eddie handed me my sandwich.

"It's so nice to be outside and enjoy the warm weather and the gentle breeze." I tilted back my face and enjoyed the rays of sunshine.

"I'm surprised you're not bursting into flames."

I chuckled. "Or that I'm blinded, not to mention that I should really exercise. Right now, the only exercise I get is banging my head on my desk."

"You should go running or hiking. Do something outside."

"I've thought about that. I'm just afraid that if I run, I'll end up in a coma."

He laughed. "If that's how out of shape you are, then you better start running. Speaking of physical activities, there's Alistair. Now is your chance to talk to him, flirt a bit."

When he looked back at me, the seat was empty. "What the—" He glanced around.

I was behind the bench, peering at Alistair in the distance.

"How did you get there so fast?" he asked.

"I have skills," I whispered.

"Why are you whispering when he's at the other side of the park?"

It was a small park, but still, he had a point.

"Okay, forget the flirting. Why don't you just offer to show him around the village or something like that?" He looked at Alistair and then back at me. This time I was back on the bench again. He jumped. "Wow, you move like a ninja."

I grinned, then my face fell. "I don't know. I don't think he wants to talk to me much."

"Why wouldn't he? Even if he was born and raised here, he could use some friends that aren't in their forties."

"I guess I could say hi." But somehow, despite the fact that we had spoken in my bookshop without me being too awkward, I just couldn't approach him. Not without doom scenarios popping up in my head. Not to mention that Nancy had basically already told him I liked him. Or at the very least that she liked to see him with me. Despite that, I got up and started moving his way.

"Good, you're getting up. You're walking. Walking."

I moved forward, then turned left in the direction of The Wicked Bookworm.

"And you're going the wrong way." He ran over to me, grabbed me by the waist and pulled me back.

"No, I don't think he'll want to talk to me."

"Yes, he will."

"I'd like to stay in my comfort zone. Alone."

I had grabbed the bench by now and Eddie was trying to pull me away.

"You won't die if you just talk to him."

He pulled me away from the bench, and I went limp so that he nearly got dragged down by my weight. "Stop fighting me." He tried to pull me up, but we fell down.

I made my way on top of him and pushed him down as I tried to step over him. He grabbed me by the ankle, but I managed to get up from the ground.

"You can't make me do it."

He got up as well and pulled me in, holding my leg to his side as he attempted to move me in the opposite direction. "Yes, I can."

I put my hand on his face and tried to push him away as I was skipping on one leg.

"Maggie?"

We froze and our faces slowly turned in the direction of the voice. It was Alistair. He was standing there in his sharp suit, not a hair out of place as a grin pulled on the corner of his lips.

"Hellooo," Eddie and I both said.

"Everything alright?"

We mumbled something incoherent at the same time.

Alistair nodded. "Well, I'll be on my way then, I was just grabbing some coffee." He turned around and started walking away.

Eddie pushed me forward, and I started following Alistair. I couldn't have him think that Eddie and I were performing some kind of strange mating ritual. "So, Alistair," I started as I walked next to him. "How do you like being back?"

He glanced at me. "The village hasn't changed at all. Neither have the people. Not much anyway."

"Except that you sometimes think you know someone, and they turn out to be cheaters or mistresses, or murderers," I said.

Alistair stopped me with a touch on my arm. His dark eyes assessed me, like he could open up my forehead and see into my mind. If he could, he'd see how messy it was, as well as the heart-shaped posters of him. "Do you know something?"

I fidgeted with my hands. "Maybe," I said in a high voice.

"That's a yes, then." He stood closer. I wasn't sure if he even noticed he did that, but my body certainly did, and it flipped on the heating.

Stupid body. Be cool. I tried a seductive smile, not sure how it came across, and blinked at him.

"Do you have something in your eye?" he asked.

I grumbled something. "My employee Susan was the one who had an affair with him. She admitted that to me a short while ago. I haven't told anyone, and I don't want it to come out. I'm not sure how they'd treat her. The villagers, I mean. Victor and Patricia are popular, I'm sure you remember that. Also, I asked her if she knew anything that could help the investigation, but she didn't. She was very distraught. If you go talk to her, which I'm sure you will, please be discreet about it. There really is no reason for her to get hurt even more."

Alistair stared at me for a moment. "You're very sweet."

I felt my cheeks get warm and giggled. Actually giggled.

"Thank you for telling me. I'll look into it." He put his hands on my arms. "I really appreciate you keeping your eyes and ears open, but please be careful. Everyone is talking about how you're going to solve this, but that means the killer is hearing that as well. Please don't do anything dangerous."

It took me a lot of effort to hear the words instead of getting distracted by the shape of his mouth. "Yep, yep, yep."

He smiled at me.

"Would you like to catch up sometime? Have dinner? I'll cook for you."

He raised his eyebrows and his smile disappeared, so I expected him to say no. "Sure. Monday evening at seven?"

"Really?"

"Here's my card." He fished it from his breast pocket and handed it to me.

I stared at it. It took me all of four seconds to memorise his number. I had a good memory. "Thanks. I'll see you then."

"See you." He turned to leave, and so did I.

Instead of striding away with dignity and grace, I started running back so I could wave the business card in Eddie's face, but I'd only taken three steps before I fell flat on the ground.

Eddie had gotten up from the bench but wasn't moving. *Jerk. Why isn't he helping?* I felt an arm around my waist and Alistair's lips were close to my ear.

"Are you alright?" he asked as he helped me up and turned me to face him. He scanned my body and hands for wounds.

"I like the purple squirrels dancing on your shoulder," I said.

He looked up sharply. "What? Do you really see those?"

"No," I said. "Sorry, I couldn't resist."

He sighed. "I'm glad you're okay. Please be more careful."

"Got it. No pissing off murderers and no tripping."

He managed a smile. "Exactly." Then he gently touched my chin right before he left.

I sighed and watched him go while Eddie's footfalls sounded closer. "Did it go well or poorly? I couldn't tell."

I held up the business card. "I've got a date." *Sort of.*

"Please invite me to the wedding."

"Done."

EVERY SATURDAY NANCY cooked dinner for me and Eddie at her flat. This time she had made her famous lasagna, which was good enough to make me want to marry it. We sat at the dining table, right next to the open-plan kitchen. Our flats were similar, but she had taken down some walls so that only her bedroom and bathroom were separate rooms. It provided her flat with more light and made it seem more spacious. It always smelt of incense and the colour purple was dominant. It was her favourite.

"I taught mindfulness today at the shop. I wasn't sure if there would be many people, but twelve showed up," Nancy said.

"I'm not surprised," I said. "People are upset about what happened. The most exciting thing that's ever happened here is when those garden gnomes went missing, or when we found out that Harry stole those pies from Olivia's windowsill."

Harry was homeless, and once he'd gotten a taste of Olivia's baking, he kept coming back for more. Now she gave him chores once a week in exchange for food. I also hired him whenever I had an event at my bookshop and wanted someone to hand out flyers. In addition to money, I would also pay for a haircut at the barbershop, which Jacob hated because apparently Harry was always rude to him, and many years ago had called him a fanny for cutting hair and shaving beards for a living. Jacob was one to hold a grudge, like most villagers. A few smiles from me would make Jacob do it, though.

"That's not the only thing people are talking about," Eddie said with enthusiasm. "I read on Twitter that those ghost hunters are here. They will start their investigations tonight. They should be at the B&B."

"Oh, no. You're totally going to stalk them, aren't you?" I asked.

"Don't say that like it's a bad thing." Eddie grinned. "Brian and I are going over there to talk to them and see if we can help. Our equipment is pretty good, but these are pros." He turned to Nancy. "Why don't you come with? They could probably use a psychic to come along."

Nancy wrinkled her nose. "I've already been there, and if nobody is going to pay me, I ain't going. Besides, I think those ghost hunters are just a bunch of idiots who scare themselves by turning off the lights and focussing on every little sound."

"Well, we will find out." His eyes held a twinkle.

"Cheers to that." I held up my fork with lasagna.

Nancy chuckled.

"Why am I even friends with you?" Eddie shook his head.

"You're one to talk, Ghostbuster." I stuck out my tongue.

Eddie grabbed a handful of lettuce and threw it at me.

"Hey, no food fighting," Nancy said. "I've been slaving away in the kitchen, you know? It took me several seconds to take that lettuce out of the packaging."

"Fine, I'll be the bigger person." I peeled off a piece of lettuce from my forehead.

Chapter 8

After dinner, Eddie couldn't get his coat on quick enough. "Everybody sure they don't want to come?" he asked as he was struggling to get his arms into his sleeves. He was bent forward with his arms in weird positions, like broken antennas.

"Yes," we said in unison.

Eddie turned to me. "I'm surprised you don't want to go."

"Why?"

"You write mysteries, and this is the biggest and probably only mystery this village has had in our lifetime. Don't you want to check it out?"

"No. They'll be filming stuff in the dark, and they'll focus on spirits. They won't actually check out the room where it happened."

"Ah, I see what's going on," Eddie said as he moved forward, having succeeded in his mission to put on his coat. "You're scared."

"You know what? That is absolutely and completely so not false."

He frowned. "What?"

"You're right." I hit him on the shoulder. "Don't act surprised, we all know what a scaredy-cat I am." Spiders, scary films, heights, people in masks, loud noises, snakes, commitment, confined spaces, and poorly written novels.

"It's true," Nancy nodded.

"Yes," I said.

Eddie shrugged. "It's less fun when you actually admit it."

"I know. You're welcome."

"Fine, don't come, but you'll be missing out on a great adventure and potentially a great source of inspiration for novels to come." He stepped towards the door. "I'm leaving now. Almost at the door."

"YOU ARE SUCH A BRAVE woman. I really admire your strength and perseverance," Eddie said as we stood in front of the B&B. Brian was also there, he wore black-framed glasses and breathed heavily. He had asthma and it was probably an indication that he was getting excited.

I never spent any time with Brian. He was just Eddie's weird friend in my book. Though it was possible that Brian felt that exact same way about me.

"Don't mock me," I said. "I have watched a lot of Jackie Chan films, and I'm not afraid to use that knowledge against you." If I witnessed first-hand what those ghost hunters would find, I'd be even more credible when I told the book club and anybody else that there were no ghosts. It would also mean that Victor's murder would be taken seriously by the villagers, and it could help the police. Besides that, I was also genuinely curious about how something like this would go.

The door opened, and Mrs Suzuki, the owner, stood in the doorway. She was wearing an apron with kittens depicted on it. She had straight long hair that she usually wore in a knot, like today.

"Hey guys, what a nice surprise."

"We heard the ghost hunters were here," Eddie said and bounced up and down as he tried to look past her.

Mrs Suzuki laughed a melodious laugh. "Come in. They are about to leave for the Pembroke Hotel. They're in the front room."

I followed Eddie inside. It had been a while since I'd been here, and I welcomed the cheerful colours and country-like style of the detached house.

In the front room were four people, only one of them a woman. They were packing two bags, one with equipment, and the other one with drinks and snacks.

Eddie didn't waste any time. As soon as he was inside, he began talking. "Hi, guys. I'm Eddie Ellington, nice to meet you. This is my friend Brian and—" He looked up and saw he was pointing at me. He pulled Brian out from behind me. "This is Brian, and that is my friend Maggie."

I waved.

The ghost hunters stood frozen for a second, their eyes on us, probably not sure if this was really happening. Maybe they thought we were ghosts. Ha.

The man closest to us showed the first signs of life and stood up straight. He had blond hair, half-long and curling at the nape of his neck. His eyes were moss green, and he projected a warm smile. He was about our age; they all seemed to be. It surprised me that they all seemed so normal, though

I should know better than anyone to not judge a book by its cover.

"Hi, guys. I'm Nick," he said in a Welsh accent. He stepped forward and shook Eddie's hand first. Then he shook Brian's hand, who began breathing more heavily. When he shook mine, he used both hands. "Nice to meet you."

"Nice to meet you," I said and smiled.

"We're locals, and we know a thing or two about ghost hunting. Not like you do, but still. We were hoping we could help you guys out. We also know about the ghost stories and you know, the recent event," Eddie said.

"Sure, we wouldn't mind some help, but we can't lend out our equipment for insurance reasons," Nick said without discussing it with the other members. He was clearly the leader.

"No problem, we have our own." Eddie smiled proudly.

"Excellent, well, this is Fiona," Nick pointed at the woman with the braid and she gave us a curt nod.

Eddie immediately dashed forward to shake her hand. Subtlety was not his thing.

"Steve." A firm man with a bald head stepped forward to shake Eddie's hand.

"And Eric." A young man with dreadlocks gave Eddie a fist bump.

Nick turned to me. "So you're a ghost hunter, too?"

"No, I'm a writer. I actually write detective stories, and my friend suggested I might come along and help solve a mystery. Gain some inspiration at the same time." I shrugged. "I don't really think there's a curse. Sorry."

Nick smiled. "That's okay. We keep an open mind ourselves. We're after the truth."

"Good, me too." I returned his smile.

He held my gaze for a moment, then turned around. "Alright, guys. Let's get moving. We have a big van. You guys can join us." He winked at me.

Ten minutes later we were in a black van. Luckily, it could hold eight people, so there was no squishing involved. I sat next to the woman, Fiona. She was listening to music and stared out the window, so she wasn't exactly a source of bubbly conversation.

Eddie was in front of me, right between Brian and Steve. He had better luck at striking up a conversation, though their talk of equipment was a little lost on me.

Nick was driving with Eric in the passenger's seat.

I thought about texting Nancy to tell her that parents were right, it's never a good idea to get into a van with strangers, but figured I'd just stick it out. Maybe it wasn't so bad. Nick seemed nice. Still, I felt kind of silly going along with this. Filming stuff in the dark and trying to talk to dead people, all the while being in a place where people died. In bathtubs. Well, let's just say that if I had to do this in a film, I'd get a stunt woman to do it.

When we arrived at the hotel, we parked near the entrance. Mr Field, who seemed even more mousy-looking than when I saw him in the pub, was already waiting for us at the double doors. How did he feel about this? Did he want it to be ghosts or an actual murderer? Which would be better for business?

Mr Field showed us to the reception room which was a large, beautiful room with a fireplace that wasn't burning and antique sofas. Wall lights and a chandelier provided ample light. I hadn't noticed this the last time because of the shock.

"Thank you so much for coming," Mr Field said and indicated we should sit down.

Eddie and I were about to sit down, but everybody else remained upright so just as our behinds were hovering over the seat, we managed to push ourselves up in an awkward way. Nobody noticed.

"I've informed our current guests that you would be here, so I've convinced them that for the next hour they should be out or stay in their rooms. Most of them have gone out to eat, so you should be free to walk around and do what you need to do. The rooms where earlier incidents have occurred are still empty. The doors are open so feel free to walk in. There will be a constable in front of Mr Woodbury's room." His voice was calm and heavy.

"Right," Nick said. "Like I said on the phone, we'll visit each room in the downstairs area and then make our way through the corridor upstairs. We'll review our footage tonight and get back to you tomorrow."

Mr Field nodded. He looked surprisingly calm under these circumstances. His wife was nowhere to be seen.

"Other than the mysterious way in which those cheating men died, is there any sign of a haunting?" Nick asked.

"No, nothing. Just during construction, you know, some misplaced things and accidents. That's why we had the local..." He searched for words.

"Witch?" I said.

"Yes, she came here to do a cleansing."

"Well, let's go find out if she did it right," Nick said and put down his bag with the equipment.

Eddie and I glanced at each other.

They split up in two groups. Nick, Fiona and Eddie were in one, while Steve, Eric and Brian were in the other. They took their equipment and went in opposite directions as they explored the ground floor first.

Nick gave me a walkie-talkie so I could listen in and communicate with them as well. "Are you sure you don't want to come?" Nick asked.

"Nope, I'll just wait here until you guys head upstairs."

He nodded and off they went with their torches and weird equipment.

"I'll be in the back room," Mr Field said. "Thank you for coming."

"Sure," I said. "Bye." I watched him walk away.

"The lights are going to be turned off now," Nick's voice said over the walkie-talkie.

Oh, boy.

As soon as he said this, the lights turned off.

Oh, boy. Oh, boy. Oh, boy.

I turned on my small, pink torch that glowed in the dark and was about the size of my middle finger and let the spot of light glide over the furniture around me. It looked bleak in the light of the torch. A tingling sensation spread throughout my body like I was pricked by hundreds of needles as I stood frozen in the spacious room. What was I trying to prove? I really shouldn't have come here. Fear isn't a sign of weakness, it's a sign that something is wrong.

Chapter 9

I swallowed and moved into the corridor as I shone my torch on the double doors that led to the safety of the outside world. I bit my lip and contemplated running out of here with my tail between my legs. Though if the ghost hunters found me missing, they'd probably think ghosts kidnapped me. I grinned at the thought. I wasn't alone. Eddie was here too. Besides, there was a mystery to solve. I liked mysteries, didn't I? I should be having a blast.

Another reason I'd come along was so I could get a look at the guest register, not that I was sure it would result in anything, but it was worth a shot.

"Perhaps there's some information on the computer," Detective Black said.

I headed over to the reception desk and bumped into it as I hurried to get behind it. "Pardon me," I whispered. The ledger was right there and I didn't waste a second as my nerves started toying with my composure. My fingers trembled as I put the torch in my mouth and flipped through the pages. There were a lot of names, but none that stood out. The rest of the reception desk didn't reveal anything unusual and the computer was password-protected. When the walkie-talkie crackled, I made my way to the bottom of the stairs in time to hear Nick say: "Nothing down here. Shall we go upstairs?"

"We're done here too," Steve's voice said.

A few moments later light shone in my eyes, and I held my hand in front of me.

"Eddie, don't make me hurt you."

"How did you know it was me?" He lowered his torch.

"Like I don't know you well enough?" I grinned.

"Alright, Maggie. Are you ready for some ghost hunting?" Nick asked.

"Sure."

"Good, you can join our group. We'll take the second floor." Then he turned to the others. "You guys will take the first."

A few minutes later we were exploring the second floor. Exploring, in this case, meant that we were sneaking through the corridor while Nick occasionally asked if spirits were present as he held out a small voice recorder. Sandra was filming and Eddie had never been this quiet for so long. His eyes darted around eagerly as if he was afraid to miss a single second. He had probably stopped blinking.

At some point we passed the room where Victor Woodsbury had died. A police constable was guarding it. His eyes forward, his posture straight and unyielding. He didn't seem fazed by the weird people that passed him as they asked if ghosts were present.

I was behind them, glancing at the door and imagining what the last moments of that handsome, older man's life had been like. A shiver crawled up my spine and the sadness swelled up in my chest again. I returned my focus to the corridor. The round light of my torch glided over the dark-red carpet and the off-white walls. My eyes went over every inch, fleeting as it was. Every painting, every lamp, every table with flowers. It all registered in my brain, stored away in the Pembroke Hotel file.

When we were finished exploring the second floor, we joined the others at the third and final floor to walk through together. This floor was practically identical to the second floor, and probably the first, but it had a ceiling hatch at the end of the corridor. An attic.

Detective Black stood below it and pointed upwards.

I glared at him and waved my hand to dismiss him.

He returned the glare and also waved his hand.

Then we returned in the direction of the staircase. It was halfway through the dark corridor that a wailing sound, a cry, travelled through the air. It wasn't that loud, and there was something stifled about it. It stopped abruptly. Brian needed his inhaler when he heard it.

We were close to one of the rooms where someone had died many years ago. Nick waited for the sound to return, but nothing happened. Then he entered the room, followed by everybody but me. I remained in the corridor, my feet glued to the carpet with invisible glue. They returned after about three minutes.

"Anything?" I asked.

"We'll have to find out tomorrow," Nick said businesslike. It was strange how normal this was to him.

Mr Field was waiting downstairs by the time we were done. He sat in an armchair in the corridor with his own torch. He rose to his feet as he saw us coming down.

"And?" he asked.

"We won't know until we listen to the footage, Mr Field," Nick said. "We did hear some strange noises, though. Like crying or a wail, but it was over too fast."

Mr Field swallowed and glanced around as if he was worried a ghost would jump him any second.

"It sounded a lot like the wind, though," I added. "Old buildings and such."

"Ah, I see. Right. Of course." Mr Field lowered his shoulders and exhaled. "Well, I guess I'll see you guys tomorrow. Thanks for coming."

"Not a problem, sir." Nick stepped forward and shook his hand.

"Thank you," Mr Field said again as he held open one of the double doors for us.

THE ROSE WAS PACKED that Saturday night. A small local band was playing. They consisted of three men who worked at a brewery forty minutes away. They might not look like it, but they knew how to play a Beatles' song.

"That was a nice thing you did," Nick said to me when he handed me my coke.

We sat by the window, away from the bar and the loud music, lovely as it was. The others stood by the bar. Eddie was talking animatedly. He was probably sharing that story where he tried to fish for the first time and fell into the water. He loved telling that story because he ended up with a fish on his head.

"What nice thing?"

"Reassuring Mr Field by telling him it might have been the wind."

"Oh, that. Yes, well, he looked so worried. I was afraid he'd have to sleep with a nightlight on otherwise."

Nick chuckled. "You were afraid too, weren't you?" He didn't say it in a mocking way, he was simply asking.

"Not because of ghosts, but because of the crime scene and the thought that Victor died there. I knew him and liked him. Other than that, I don't really like the dark that much. Everything seems scarier then. And though I'm sure that dangerous ghosts exist, I don't think they're here. Whoever hurt Victor is a real person, and that's what we should be afraid of." I hated the fact that someone here could have done that to Victor, but it was very likely. It was too random otherwise.

Nick sighed. "Yes, I'm sorry about that. We didn't come here to step on any toes, just to do some investigating."

"I know. You don't have to apologise. This is what you do, you find evidence of ghosts."

"Yes, well, there's a death tied to this investigation. Could it have been suicide?"

"No, it wasn't suicide." I took a sip from my drink.

"How do you know?" Nick asked.

"He was meeting someone. You don't kill yourself when you're about to meet up."

"True. What do the police think?" he asked.

"I'm pretty sure they don't have much to go on yet. Rumours spread fast and if there was anything new to go on, we would know." I smiled sadly.

Nick shifted in his seat. "So how long have you lived here?"

"Since I was about eleven or twelve."

"You and your parents moved here?"

"No. I did. My parents divorced, and I came to live with my aunt Nancy, who then took care of me." I took another sip, hoping he'd stop the questions there.

"Why didn't you stay with your mum?"

Part of my coke went down the wrong pipe, and I spent about a minute coughing it up.

"Are you okay?" Nick asked. He leaned forward and patted me on the back.

"I'm fine, I'm fine. Sorry." I pressed the back of my hand against my lips and then flashed him a smile. "I'm okay now."

"Good."

"So how are you enjoying this cosy village of Castlefield?" I hurriedly asked, feeling it was too soon to tell this bloke about my mother's mental issues.

"It's nice, but you forgot to tell me why—"

From the corner of my eye I saw the familiar shape that belonged to Alistair. My hand went up in the air and my mouth pushed out his name.

He turned around and I waved. He held up his hand and looked at Nick, then back at me. He scratched his chin before he made his way over.

"Hi," I said.

"Hey, Maggie." His eyes scanned my face, then went over to Nick's.

"I'm Alistair Ashworth." He shook Nick's hand.

"Nick Cavanaugh."

"Are you enjoying your evening?" Alistair asked me.

"Yes, actually. I just visited the Pembroke Hotel."

Alistair's eyes narrowed for a second. "Why?"

"Oh, we just went hunting for ghosts as one does on a Saturday evening." I casually took a sip of my coke. When I looked up, Alistair's mouth was open.

"Yes, me and my gang." Nick pointed at the bar. "We're ghost hunters. We came when we heard about this incident at the hotel."

"Right," Alistair said. "There was a constable at the crime scene, wasn't there?"

"Yes," Nick and I said simultaneously.

"He didn't let yo—"

"No, no, we did our ghost hunting in the corridors and on the ground floor." Nick gave Alistair an innocent smile.

Alistair looked at me and I gave him my most innocent smile as well.

"Fine, well, as long as you're—yes, I'll see you around then. Enjoy your evening."

"You too."

He left and sat down at a table further back. Wooden beams prevented me from spying on him.

"He's a detective, right?"

"Yes, that's right."

"And you're friends?" he asked.

"Well, we went to middle school together, but we never hung out or anything. He lived in London for a while. Apparently he's back."

"He's handsome."

"Yeah, well, he's always had a certain charm. Oh, wait, do you like—"

Nick nearly choked on his drink. "No, no. That's not what I meant."

"I mean, it's okay if you do."

"No, trust me. If I like anyone, it's you, and I'm pretty sure you're a woman." His eyes twinkled as he said this.

A feeling of discomfort rose from my stomach and settled on my cheeks in the form of warmth. "Err, I'm ... I mean, yeah. I am a woman. That I am." I cleared my throat.

Nick laughed. "You're cute when you're nervous."

I muttered something incoherent and held my cool glass against my cheek. If only I didn't have the flirting skills of a lamp post.

TWO HOURS LATER I SAID goodbye to the ghost hunters, as well as to Eddie and Brian, who were still enjoying the riveting stories from their new Welsh friends. Both were hanging onto their every word like kids listening to their favourite fairy tale.

The air was chilly, and I zipped up my red leather jacket. Laughter arose from the pub as I started on my way to the bookshop. I'd only moved a few feet when someone called my name.

It was Alistair.

I waited for him as he made his way towards me, his shoes clicking on the pavement.

"What are you doing?" he asked, his eyes fixed on mine. He sounded angry, though I didn't know why that would be.

"What do you mean?"

"Didn't I tell you to be careful? What are you doing hanging out with these ghost hunters?"

"There's nothing wrong with what they do."

"Except that people might think a curse killed Victor, and they'll dismiss anything they might have seen or heard that could lead to actual clues."

"Or," I said as I folded my arms, "the killer might think he's in the clear and lower his guard. Besides, I only went along to get some inspiration for my novel."

He smiled apologetically and scratched the back of his head. "I'm sorry. You're right. I'm just being—I don't know."

I forgive you so much. "Don't worry about it."

"Let me walk you home."

"Sure."

He matched my casual tempo and occasionally glanced at me. "Do you remember that book fair that Eleanor arranged when I guess you must have been sixteen or something, and you read out that poem?"

"Yeah, I remember."

"I don't recall the words exactly, but it moved me. You wore a red dress and you were so happy reading it out, even though you were nervous. And now you're an author. Funny how life works out. We had no clue back then, did we?"

"You remember that I wore a red dress?"

He smiled. "You were the most beautiful girl there."

My heart warmed.

"Gag," Detective Black said behind me.

"Shut up," I said.

Alistair laughed. "Sorry."

Damn it. "No, I like compliments. Forget I said that." I looked ahead of me and froze.

Alistair followed my gaze. "Where did that chicken come from?"

"Listen, I don't know if your mum ever told you about Pandora, but she's an evil chicken."

"Evil?" He grinned.

"She's a harbinger of death. She's doom and destruction incarnate."

Pandora stood a few feet away from us, assessing us with her black beady eyes.

At this Alistair laughed, startling both me and Pandora. Not a good move.

"She's about to attack us, stop laughing," I said, unable to look away from the demonic poultry.

"It's just a chicken," he said. "Some people literally eat those for breakfast. Granted, not a whole chicken and only in countries where they eat warm meals for breakfast. Probably. Although—"

The chicken made a screeching sound from the back of her throat and came at us. I grabbed Alistair's hand and ran in a random direction. For a chicken she was quite fast and our only hope was to get up high somewhere. She had pecked people's ankles to the point of bleeding and didn't stop. I had nightmares of her sometimes.

"Why are we running?" Alistair asked, forced to keep up with me.

"Because she will kill us and feast on our remains."

He laughed again.

I pulled him along past a narrow street with cottages while Pandora made another screeching sound. She sounded close, but we were still ahead of her. The white fence of the last house on the left came into view, and that would be our salvation. "Do you see that white fence over there?" I said to Alistair, out of breath already. Damn, I was running.

"Yeah," he said, not panting at all. *Bastard.*

"We're going to jump over the fence, and in their garden is like this playhouse with a slide and swings and stuff. We get up on the platform and we'll be safe. You run up the slide, I'll use the stairs at the side. Got it?"

"This is so weird and unnecessary, but okay, I've got it."

We reached the fence as the fluttering of wings and loud cackling sounded closer to us. We'd soon be there. A few more steps. We were still holding hands when we jumped over the fence and both made it without falling. I glanced back in time to see Pandora make it over the fence, though she hit the ground and was slowed down because of it. We let go of each other as Alistair made it up the plastic slide and I dashed up the wooden stairs. There wasn't a lot of room on the platform but we were high off the ground and I hoped Pandora wouldn't be able to get up here. Alistair put his arm around me as we were squished together. I was panting heavily and felt a bit dizzy.

Pandora made it up to the slide and tilted her head. She seemed to be weighing her options but decided it wasn't worth it and sauntered over to the rose bushes where she pecked at the grass.

"Thank goodness," I said.

When Alistair laughed, his breath tickled my ear. "Not that I don't dislike a good workout, but what is so dangerous about that chicken?"

"She pecks people until they bleed, she's a monster. The only person she likes is Nancy." I groaned. "I can't believe I was forced to run. Although, does this mean I've lost a few pounds?"

He frowned. "You don't need to lose any weight, you're perfect."

My stomach did a little flip. "I appreciate that," I said with a smile. We stared at each other and I realised our bodies were touching. Our faces were already close, and I noticed the light-brown spots in his eyes. We both started moving forward so that our lips were almost touching. Just as I thought my heart was going to explode, a door slammed. We both looked up to see that the owner of the cottage had kicked out his Golden Retriever. The dog wagged his tail and sniffed a few plants before spotting Pandora.

Pandora didn't see him yet, but she would and it would mean she'd be distracted.

"This will be our chance," I said and tapped Alistair's arm. "Let's go." I carefully made my way down the slide while the dog approached Pandora with misplaced enthusiasm. She screeched and flapped her wings, making the dog jump back. He wagged his tail and barked excitedly as he moved around her. He wanted to play while she wanted to kill. Probably. Who knew what went on in the mind of a deranged, psychopathic chicken?

I jumped off the slide and Alistair followed. We ran through the garden and jumped the fence again while the dog was still playfully running around Pandora. "Will he be okay, you think?" I asked Alistair.

"Of course. It's just a chicken."

"Milo," a voice called from the back of the house.

"See, that's his owner calling him already," Alistair nudged me along, and we went off in the direction of my bookshop.

In the distance we heard the owner call: "Honey, how attached are we to Milo?"

Alistair walked me to the entrance to my flat. "Goodnight," he said, then seemed to hesitate before he bent down and kissed me on my cheek.

"Goodnight," I said and went up with a smile that was rudely wiped off my face the next morning.

Chapter 10

It was a quiet Sunday morning that I was spending reading in my pyjamas when the doorbell rang. My heart fluttered with the hope that it could be Alistair, though there was no reason for him to be here. Apart from my crazy animal magnetism. I went downstairs and opened the door.

"Eleanor, how nice to see you," I said and eyed the box with baked goods she carried.

She grinned. "These are not for you, sweetheart. I thought that perhaps we could go over to Patricia and express our condolences. I know you were fond of Victor as well."

But not Patricia. "Come on in and let me get changed."

She followed me up the stairs and sat down in the reception area while I changed in my bedroom. Even though she knew I'd always liked Victor, I didn't think she brought me along for that reason. Perhaps part of her was suspicious of Patricia and that's why she wanted me there. Or perhaps she simply didn't want to face her on her own. Either way, this was the perfect opportunity to find out more about her relationship with Victor. She must have suspected he was a cheater. Patricia was a shrewd woman and usually found at the top of the rumour mill.

When I was done, we headed over to Patricia's house. It looked the same as when I walked past it the last time, and I wondered if she was lonely now that he was gone. Even if he was a cheater, she'd lived with him and now there was a void that wasn't easy to fill.

Eleanor rang the doorbell and pasted on a smile before the door even opened. I imagined she had to fake smile a lot around Patricia Woodsbury. Something I wouldn't be doing.

Patricia answered the door after a moment. Her light hair was styled, and her makeup not too heavy. Her outfit matched her shoes, and she looked like she was ready for a photo shoot. It was probably the reason she was so popular. Women looked up to her because she reminded them of a perfectly put-together life. Not that she had one, but because she appeared to have one.

"What a lovely surprise," she said without smiling.

"We just wanted to express our condolences," Eleanor said. "We wanted to give you some time to adjust first. I hope we're not intruding."

"Not at all." She stepped aside to let us in.

The corridor smelt as sweet as her perfume. I managed to keep my expression neutral even if I was vomiting on the inside. We went through to the reception area which held a fireplace and expensive cream-coloured furniture. There wasn't a spot of dirt to be found anywhere. I had to say I was impressed.

"Please, sit. I'll fetch us a spot of tea." Patricia disappeared into the hallway and left us to admire the antique vases displayed in all corners of the room. She had paintings up as well. I didn't recognise them, but they were gorgeous and looked expensive.

We sat down just as Patricia returned with three cups and a plate of biscuits. There were only three of them. The humanity.

"How are you doing?" Eleanor asked with a heavy dose of sympathy.

"It was dreadful, as you can imagine." She narrowed her eyes at me for some reason.

"Yes, of course." Eleanor grabbed a cup of tea and sipped it. "It must have been a huge shock."

I knew Eleanor wouldn't say too much about it, because of the curse and the implication that he was a cheater, which I already knew he was. Eleanor also wouldn't pry because she considered it rude. But that wouldn't stop me, and that's why she'd brought me along, the wily woman. Though married to a vicar, she was still human. She wanted as much information as possible herself, not as gossip material, but simply because she was curious.

"Did you know that he invited us—me and Nancy—to discuss something with him?" I asked.

She lifted her head ever so slightly as if to remind me that she was literally looking down at me. "Not at the time, but afterwards Alistair told me."

Alistair? I clenched my jaw.

"Calm down, girl," Detective Black said. "Keep her talking."

"Do you have any idea what it could have been about?"

"Not at all."

"Had he visited that hotel before?"

"No," she said coldly.

"They have done it up nicely. It's a beautiful place." I grabbed a biscuit. When Patricia didn't reply, I said: "Have you been?"

"No, and I doubt I will." She sipped her tea. "How's your husband?" she asked Eleanor.

The next few minutes consisted of idle chit-chat, but I was willing to play along. She didn't like these questions, probably because she knew I was investigating the murder. But if she knew that and was playing hard to get, didn't that mean she had something to hide? Although she didn't seem like the type to share information about herself anyway.

After an appropriate pause in the conversation, Eleanor excused herself to go to the bathroom and left me alone with the bubbly Patricia.

Crickets might as well have chirped. She refused to make eye contact and continued sipping her tea. But I was not easily deterred.

"I really am sorry about Victor. He seemed like a good man."

She glanced at me. "I appreciate that."

"Do you really have no idea who would want to do something that awful to him?" I asked, my voice soft.

"You mean to me, don't you? He's dead, it doesn't bother him anymore. I'm the one who has to go on without him." There were some cracks of emotion in her self-made mask.

I said nothing.

"But if you must know, I think you should look at the hotel."

"Because of the curse?"

"No," she said, frowning. "Because of those newcomers. I don't trust them. Besides, why—of all places—did he invite you over to that ghastly hotel?"

I had wondered that as well. Perhaps I could find out more about Mr and Mrs Field.

After a few moments Eleanor returned and when the biscuits were all finished—by me—we left. Patricia saw us out and shut the door after a 'toodeloo' which sounded so cavalier that it didn't match the type of conversation we'd had at all. She was definitely a woman who was good at hiding what she thought and felt. Something she actually had in common with Susan.

"Do you think she's the killer?" Eleanor asked.

"I don't know. I'm sure the police have looked into that."

"I heard she had an alibi."

"From whom?" I asked.

"I'm pretty sure from her. Well, not directly. She told Olivia and she told Poppy—"

"I get the picture," I said, holding up my hand. "But we have little to go on when it comes to her. Perhaps Mr and Mrs Field know more about it. I mean, it is weird that he booked a room at the Pembroke just to speak to Nancy and I."

"Maybe he was depressed and wanted to talk about that," Eleanor said.

I narrowed my eyes at her. "What makes you think that?"

"I may have gone upstairs to check out the medicine cabinet."

"Eleanor!"

"Well, I had to do something while you were asking her questions. Anyway, the pills were for him, not her. There was also hemorrhoid cream. That could have been for her." She giggled.

"This is not funny," I said in a stern voice.

"No, quite right." Then she giggled again.

I smiled. "She needs the cream because she has a huge stick up her—"

"Honey," Harold called. He pushed his wheelchair over the cobbled streets with relative ease. He had a lot of practice, after all, having lived here for most of his life. "I need your help at the church. How's Patricia?"

We looked at each other.

"Fine," we said simultaneously.

"Okay," he said with a puzzled look. "And how are you, Maggie? Finding Victor must have been a terrible shock."

"It was, but I'll feel better when I catch his killer."

He nodded slowly. "Just be careful. This is someone who is obviously very perturbed."

"Yes, it is." Which is also why it was important we figured out who it was.

WHEN I ARRIVED AT THE bookshop, I had the intention of going up to read and possibly even write, but instead Eddie came running after he poked his head out from behind the curtain. The closest he usually got to exercise was opening the fridge, not that I was judging him.

"We caught the sounds of a ghost on the equipment," he said, panting with excitement.

"I'm telling you, there are no ghosts, spirits or other curse-related beings in that hotel." We were starting to catch the attention of a few customers, so I moved us to the corner.

"When we played it back and isolated the sound we had heard, it was a clear woman's voice."

"And what did this woman say?"

"Justice."

"Justice?" I muttered. "How lame."

Eddie scoffed. "Don't ridicule the serial killer ghost. She might come after you."

"Better strap a hoover on my back then."

"Okay, don't you dare mock that film." He pointed at me.

"They're the ones mocking themselves." I pointed back at him. "And how do you know it's a ghost?"

"It has to be. It sounded a bit muffled and strange, but powerful."

"And now what? Will the ghost hunters ask the spirit to have some tea with them?" I asked.

"No, they'll just tell Mr Field what they've concluded and leave."

"They'll leave? So basically they'll just tell someone they are haunted and then just leave them with that information?"

Eddie tilted his head as he thought about this, then nodded.

"Well, that's kind of awful. Not that Mr Field has that problem, because it's not a ghost."

Eddie put his hand on his hip. "Really? Have you heard the voice recording? How do you know?"

I grinned. "Actually, I might be able to prove it. I have a plan."

"I'D LIKE TO BOOK A room for one, please," I said to Mr Field that evening.

He raised an eyebrow at me.

"A—are you sure?"

"Yes, I'm sure. I've always wanted to stay in the Pembroke Hotel. It's so beautiful. Besides, I'm experiencing writer's block and a change of scenery will do me good, even if it's only one night."

He forced a smile. "I hope so."

After he made me sign the ledger and handed me the key to my room, 109, I made it up the stairs with my backpack. I had brought pyjamas, but I had no intention of sleeping. Tonight I'd be sleuthing.

Chapter 11

The room was spacious and clean. It had white and golden accents, and the bed was large. Normally I would be thrilled to stay in a room this beautiful, but it reminded me too much of the room that Victor had been in—even if the layout of this room was reversed. I threw my backpack on the bed and started unpacking my torch and lock pick set. In addition to that I'd also brought small ziplock bags that could function as evidence bags, and though I probably wouldn't need them, it made me feel like a detective.

Detective Black chuckled on the opposite side of the king-sized bed.

"What? I like to be prepared."

"Did you also bring a magnifying glass and handcuffs?" He raised his dark eyebrows as he grinned.

I scoffed. *Yes.* "Don't be silly."

"What exactly is your plan?"

"Have a drink downstairs, see what Mr Field is up to. Find Mrs Field and ask some questions. I'd really like to go into Mr Field's office, so I'll wait until everyone is asleep and snoop around."

"What if you get caught? What if he has cameras? What if you can't get into his office?"

"He doesn't have cameras outside of his office. I doubt he has them on the inside. If I get caught then I can just say I'm sleepwalking. I'll be in my pyjamas. Besides, I doubt he will be awake at three AM. And if I can't get into his office, well, at least I'll have tried."

"This would be so much easier if you were actually a detective."

"Would it? I couldn't snoop around if I was. I'd be restricted to interviewing people only. And people have their guard up around the police. They'll be at ease around me."

There was a knock on the door, and I froze. Eddie had gaming plans with Brian so that left Mr Field. What would he want?

"To murder you?" Detective Black said. "Maybe you should take a leaf out of your aunt's book and grab a kettle."

"Ha-ha," I muttered as I sauntered over to the door. "Who is it?"

"A certain detective," Alistair said.

I glanced back at Detective Black, but he was already gone. Before opening the door, I checked myself in the mirror.

"Hi." I smiled innocently.

He narrowed his eyes at me and stepped into the room. His gaze immediately travelled to the torch and lock pick set. "Planning on a relaxing stay?"

"Yes, I wanted to try out their poison and see what the fuss was about."

His jaw clenched. "Don't joke about that. What do you think you'll gain by staying here?"

"I just want to relax here. That's all. No biggie. How did you know I was here?"

"I overheard Eddie at the pub. And if you're planning to relax, why did you bring a lock pick set?"

"I always bring that. You never know when you might need it in a cosy English village with a maniacal chicken."

He folded his arms.

Perhaps I could use my feminine wiles. I started walking towards him, smiling, but my heel caught on the carpet, and I stumbled forwards. Right into his arms.

"Enjoy your trip?"

I chuckled. "Sorry, I guess I need to work on my walking skills."

"You should also work on your listening skills, but I doubt I can say anything that will make you go home." He was still holding me.

"No, sorry." I smiled. "You smell nice."

His pupils dilated.

Someone knocked on the door. "Did you bring DC Daniels?" I asked.

He laughed. "No, he's got his knitting club tonight."

"Really? Hmm. Good for him." I answered the door.

Several women spilled into the room. I stepped back in surprise. It took me a moment to realise it was the Castlefield Book Club. They all wore hats and sunglasses. Nancy wore a fake moustache.

Alistair groaned.

"Hi, Alistair. Here to help our Maggie?" Poppy asked.

If looks could kill.

"Alistair," Lily purred and sidled up to him. "What a lovely surprise. You know my daughter has recently split up with her husband—" she started.

"What are you doing here?" I asked Nancy.

Eleanor answered. "Eddie told Nancy you were coming here and we want to help with the investigation."

"Yes, we can be your eyes and ears," Olivia said. "Besides, there's nothing on TV, and Stanley is at the pub. We're bored."

"Until I get a new order of miniature furniture, I can't work on my new dollhouse, and it's driving me crazy. Let us do something," Phoebe said.

"I just came because I wanted to wear my new hat." Jessica struck a pose.

Ava lowered her sunglasses. "If we help solve this murder with you, we can make the local newspaper. That will be good for my new business."

"You're starting a new business?" I asked.

"Yes, I'm planning on selling mugs with mugshots on it. People can upload their photo and it will generate a mugshot. Then you simply choose a colour, and you have a mug."

"I'd like one. How much are they?" Poppy asked, and she already took out her coin purse as she counted pennies.

"Twenty pounds."

She put her purse away. "Never mind."

"So can we help?" Nancy asked. "It's me, Nancy. I'm wearing a disguise."

I kept from laughing. How could I tell them nicely that they were about as useful as a bag of porcupines at a balloon party? They were lovely people, but not exactly subtle. "Why are you wearing disguises?"

"Sherlock Holmes used them all the time," Lily said as if I'd just asked the most ridiculous question ever. And here I thought we'd bonded during the last book club meeting.

The door was still open and just then Mr Field passed with a trolley of whisky glasses and a cheese platter. "Oh, hello ladies. Are you having a book club meeting here? Enjoy." He disappeared out of sight again.

I raised my eyebrows at Lily who cleared her throat and slowly removed her sunglasses.

Still, if I truly wanted them out of the way, I had to give them something to do. Even if it led nowhere. I shut the door. "If I remember correctly, there's a library on this floor. I want half of you guys to scour it for any books on this property itself. If you find anything, let me know. The other half should stay in the lounge, grab a drink and talk to people who were here Friday. They'll probably be eager to gossip, so try to get as much info as you can." It was possible those people had already left, but the point here was to keep them busy.

The women chatted excitedly and started making groups. After several moments of quibbling, everybody was happy, and they left the room, their disguises still on.

Nancy was the last to leave and turned around. "Remember," she said to Alistair, "she's very single." Then she shut the door.

I laughed. "I think I need a drink."

"Yeah, me too," Alistair said.

The mini fridge was half-empty about an hour later as we sat against the bed. The women hadn't returned yet, but I figured they'd be having fun. They weren't the kind of women who'd do anything against their will. I liked that about them. Growing up around them meant that I had learned something from each and every one of them.

"So you're telling me," I said, "that instead of reading or watching TV, or even playing video games, your hobby is to perform magic tricks? Do you wear a cape for this? Do you have a bunch of bunnies because you can't put them back into the hat?"

"No, they're just fun tricks that I sometimes use to baffle people."

"Like what?"

He sat up straighter and put down the small bottle of vodka. From his breast pocket he grabbed one playing card.

I started laughing.

"Hey, keep an open mind, will you?" He handed me the card. "Rip it up."

"Really? Are you sure?"

He looked particularly sexy when he grinned. "Yes, I'm sure."

I ripped the card in half and then again.

He took the pieces into his hands and folded them over each other. Then he blew into his hands and opened them again. The pieces were gone.

I looked around on the floor and on my lap, but they weren't to be seen. "How did you do that?" My head felt fuzzy from the alcohol, as if it was filled with cotton balls.

"Look in your pocket," he said with a twinkle in his eyes.

I checked the pockets of my trousers and in my left pocket found the card, completely whole. "Wow, you are amazing. You should go on TV and become famous. Hey, do you require an assistant?"

"If the assistant is you, then yeah, totally."

A pause.

I grabbed his tie and pulled him a little closer. "You know what we should do?"

"What?"

WE STARED AT THE PULL-out ladder that led to the attic. "And why do we need to go up there?"

"Duh, my magician friend. We need to look for clues."

"Okay. And they'll be there?"

"They might be. How do we know unless we look?" I said.

"Good point. Can't argue with that," he said.

I wasn't sure if he was being sarcastic, but suspected he was serious. Sober Alistair would have probably shot down this idea and then set fire to it.

"I'll go up while you are the look-out." I took the first step.

"But by the time someone sees us, it will already be too late," he said.

"Shh, don't think about that. Too much logic will ruin it."

"Okay." He took a sip of the small vodka bottle.

"You took that with you?"

"Yeah." He held it out to me, and I finished the rest of it.

"You're both idiots," Detective Black said.

I jumped.

Alistair laughed. "What was that about?"

"I see imaginary people," I whispered, wide-eyed.

"I thought I could do that once, but it turned out I had a very sporadic roommate nobody had told me about."

"Yep, idiots," Detective Black said again.

I turned on the torch and climbed the ladder to the musty attic. There was a small window at the end. The light of my torch trembled as I shone it over the wooden floor and stacks of boxes. The space was clean and organised. This stuff was probably put here around the time of the renovation.

I opened one of the boxes and peered inside. There were candlesticks and pieces of cloth for decoration. They looked antique and images of people in old-fashioned, wide dresses flashed through my mind. The next box held kitchen utensils. They were mostly still in good condition. I picked up a rolling pin, looked at it, then put it back.

"A rolling pin, huh?" Alistair was right beside me.

I gasped. "I thought you were the look-out."

"Was I?" he asked. "Do you think the rolling pin could be the murder weapon?"

I frowned. "He was poisoned, remember?"

He chuckled. "I know. It was a joke." Then he turned serious. "Actually, that wasn't funny. Am I drunk?"

"Yes. Anyway, I don't think there's anything useful here." I stood up with difficulty, so did Alistair. I nearly lost my balance. "What should we do now?"

"Let's dance." He grabbed my waist, making me drop my torch, and started spinning me through the attic. It made me even more lightheaded, but I didn't mind. I liked the feel of his arms around me, the woody scent that clung to him, and the way he was looking into my eyes right now. A floorboard creaked as we stepped on it, and we continued towards the other corner. The fallen torch provided enough light for us to avoid the boxes.

"You—blast, what is wrong with you? Did you not hear that floorboard? It could mean something." Detective Black's tone was high, and he sounded exasperated. I'd never managed to get him to do that.

"My detective says we should inspect the creaking floorboard."

Alistair stopped dancing—or really just whirling me around. "I'm not your detective?"

"Aw, of course you are." I kissed his nose. "You're my real detective, he's my fake detective."

"Hey, watch who you are calling a phony," Detective Black said. "Now go." He pointed to the area of the floorboard, which was hard to spot without the torch.

I picked up the torch and went over to where it had creaked. It took me a few stomps to find it again, but it was definitely loose.

"Hang on," Alistair said and pried it open.

"Wow."

There were a few old papers in there that resembled blueprints. "I think those are of this building," I said as I grabbed them. The cotton balls were slowly disappearing one by one as I studied the pages. "We should take these to the room and spread them out on the bed."

Alistair put back the floorboard and grabbed my hand, directing me back to the stairs. "I'll go first," he said.

He carefully made his way down the steps, then waited for me to come down. I moved slowly, considering my propensity for tripping. Then he took my hand again as we ran down the corridor to make our way back to the room on the first floor. It instantly triggered the memory of that day we spent together—the way he'd taken my hand as we ran for the bus stop, giggling like naughty school children, which technically we were. And now we were doing something naughty again. Perhaps I was a bad influence. But that day hadn't been about skipping school, it had been about escaping reality for a day.

Alistair had found me on the roof where I sometimes went during lunchtime on rough days. They were rare, but each time my mother came to visit or wanted custody from my aunt, it made things very stressful. I'd really just sought solitude, yet I didn't mind when he found me up there. And even though we'd never spoken to each other before, not really, he'd mentioned the fair that was in the next town over, and he'd whisked me away for a day.

A day of sweet memories, and to this day my favourite Valentine's Day.

We made it to the room unseen. "Do you think the ladies were trying to find us while we were gone?" I asked.

"I'm sure they'll come back if they were." The sharpness in his gaze had returned somewhat, and I had the feeling he was sobering up. "I'm just going to splash some cold water on my face, I'm still too—" he said, not bothering to finish the sentence. He disappeared into the bathroom while I unfolded the blueprints and laid them out on the bed. My heart was thumping.

"Why are there so many?" Detective Black said. "And they don't look complete."

I studied them. The blueprints showed secret entrances and passageways, if I read them correctly. There were also illegible scribbles at random spots, but they were useless to me.

When Alistair came back out, he grabbed a bottle of water and stood next to me. "The woman who had this built used it to kill people, right?"

"Yes, she was a serial killer, and she hired different contractors so that nobody really knew the layout of the place but her. These must be those plans, and they'll reveal the rooms that were deathtraps." I shivered. Though the building was beautiful, to know that it was built to be a murder weapon was very disturbing.

"The hotel was owned by a rich couple after that, and they claimed they had those trap rooms sealed off, but still people disappeared. Only this time they were married men who were known cheaters, which is how the curse came about."

"And how will this help us?"

"I don't know. It might not." I bit my lip. "But it's worth studying, I think."

He checked his watch. "Sorry, it's getting late. I should probably go. I have to go to work tomorrow."

"I understand. Thanks for hanging out with me. It was fun." I smiled.

"It was. Though you do have a strange influence on me. You bring out a side of me I didn't think I still had." There was a certain sadness in his eyes.

"Do you remember that day we spent?"

"How can I forget?" His eyes dipped to my lips.

"What were you doing on that roof?"

He blushed. "I'm not sure I should tell you."

"Why not?"

He muttered something incoherent and then made his way to the door. "I'll see you around. Don't get into trouble." Before I could protest, he was gone.

"You really are an idiot. He was obviously looking for you in order to declare his undying love for you." Detective Black sniggered.

It had been Valentine's Day, and he did remember what I looked like when I was doing that poetry reading years ago. Would he really have liked me back then? And what about now? Why did he run away when he could confess something that would have likely landed him a kiss?

"Murder isn't complicated," Detective Black said. "Love is."

Unfortunately I would soon find out how true that was.

Chapter 12

When I went to find the lovely women of the Castlefield Book Club, I found them in the lounge. They were singing "Hey Jude" with the handful of other people in the lounge. I knew them long enough to know that they weren't drunk, just not ashamed to be themselves. Mr Field stood in the corner with a bemused look on his face. This was the perfect time to find out where his wife was.

"They're a wild bunch, aren't they?" I said.

"They certainly are ... special."

"Do you guys like Castlefield?"

Some muscles in his face tensed. "Yeah, sure. We like it just fine."

"Despite the murder?"

"Yes, that was unfortunate. However, we are now fully booked for the next few months, so I suppose it isn't all bad," he said in a business-like tone.

If I had the same volatile tendencies as Nancy, I'd have kicked his shin or hit him with a lamp. Even if Victor didn't deserve a husband-of-the-year award, he also didn't deserve to be murdered. "How's your wife?" I asked through gritted teeth.

"She's a bit upset, I suppose. She's staying with her sister in Rockfield."

Seeing as how cold he was being, it didn't surprise me. There was something reserved about him, and he didn't seem like a man to easily connect with. He also didn't seem to be worried about his wife. And for her to be so upset that she couldn't stay here anymore was perhaps also a clue in itself. Although, I wasn't sure if I would want to stay in this place if I were her.

I spent the rest of the time with the women, singing more Beatles songs even if Poppy slept through most of them. After they left—without having found anything—I went up to my room to sleep. I set the alarm for three in the morning when I'd be breaking into Mr Field's office.

THE CORRIDOR WAS QUIET and the wall lights provided ample light. Despite the fact that it wasn't dark, I still had to fight the urge to run back to my room or call Alistair. The fact that we had discussed the hotel's history had given me a nightmare and the feeling of terror still clung to me like wet tissue paper.

I made my way downstairs and avoided the reception desk. Mr Field had to have hired someone for the graveyard shift, but I wasn't keen on anyone seeing me at this time of night. So I went through the reception area and exited through the archway in the back as I hurried over to Mr Field's office. I tried the door, but it was locked; not that I'd expected it to be open.

"Stop dilly-dallying and hurry up," Detective Black said.

"I'm trying." I took out the lock pick set from the pocket of my pyjamas and got to work. It could take a while, but I couldn't give up. I knew this could work and if it did, then I could find something valuable and catch the killer. That would impress everyone in this village, including Alistair.

"When you get in, go for the desk first. Also check underneath it and be on the lookout for hidden cameras. I don't trust this man."

"I know," I muttered as I focussed on the lock. It took me about as long as ten minutes before I finally turned the lock and opened the door. I glanced around to make sure I was still alone and then hurried inside, shutting the door behind me. I put on gloves. It was dark, and I decided against turning on the lights. There were no curtains, so the moonlight enabled me to see. I'd brought my torch, but didn't want to use it in case someone was looking in. It was highly unlikely, but I was a bit paranoid and even if it turned out that Mr Field had nothing to hide, he wouldn't take kindly to some random author/shop owner snooping around in his office.

"Creepy," Detective Black said as he observed the mounted animal heads, their glass eyes staring at us. I told myself they weren't real so that I'd feel better. It didn't work.

The mere fact that I was trespassing made me tingle all over. I peered into the bathroom to the right and then checked his desk, searching top to bottom. There was one drawer that was locked, but after rummaging around for twenty minutes, I found the key in a small box behind a stack of books in his bookcase. *Hopefully my efforts will be rewarded.* I opened the drawer.

For this I did need my torch, and I turned it on so that I could read the small notebook inside. It had eight different dates, times and locations, including room numbers, which indicated it was right here in this hotel. I wasn't sure what they meant, but there was also an envelope that was sealed. I picked it up and squeezed it. "I think they might be photographs."

"Of what?" Detective Black asked.

"I won't know until I open them, but I can't do that, can I? He'll know."

"You can if you use steam."

I bit my lip. That was true. "No, it's too risky. I don't want him to get spooked when he finds out it's missing."

"He doesn't have to, you can open it now." Detective Black pointed at the teakettle that was on a table in the corner along with a few mugs and teabags.

There was a reason Mr Field kept this locked up, and it was probably worth it. And so I tried. I boiled the water and held the envelope over it, but there wasn't enough steam and it didn't do enough. "Wait," I said and went back to the desk. In one of the other drawers was a stack of envelopes.

I looked up at Detective Black and ripped open the envelope.

"What are you doing?"

I put the pictures on the desk and studied them with open mouth. "That's Mrs Field. And Victor."

"Oh, boy. He really did get around, didn't he?"

"This one definitely took place in this hotel. It looks like they were taken through a peephole. I bet if I study the blueprints, I might find a secret passage along the rooms. Holy pickle, that's creepy. I hope he hasn't watched Alistair and me."

"If he has these pictures then he could have used them to blackmail Victor. Or his wife, for that matter. It could also mean that he's the killer."

"He could have delivered the tea, or made his wife bring it up, not knowing it was poisoned. And if he isn't the killer then it might mean he knows who is, if he happened to be spying at the exact moment of the murder." I sighed. "I'll have to talk to his wife as soon as possible and tell Alistair this. Also, I really want to get out of here." I put the pictures in a new envelope and sealed it with glue because I didn't want to use my DNA. I kept the original envelope just in case and put it in my pocket. I didn't want to leave anything behind.

After putting everything back where it belonged, I turned off the torch and tiptoed to the door, which rattled as I reached it. My heart nearly shot out of my chest, and I ran into the bathroom, softly closing the door just as the other door opened.

There was a bath with a shower curtain in here and I thought about hiding behind it, but just then the bathroom door opened. I sucked in my breath and pressed myself against the wall as the door swung open wide. My whole body tensed with panic. I expected Mr Field to peer around the door and spot me, but instead footsteps moved away towards the bath. There was a pause and then the curtain was ripped open.

I closed my eyes as my blood turned to ice. Pure fear settled in the pit of my stomach, and I was too afraid to even breathe. Several scenarios played out in my head, all of which involved me fighting for my life and ended with me being buried in a shallow grave. My lungs were starting to burn.

It was so quiet, yet I knew he was there. Was he drawing it out? Did he enjoy playing with me?

Just then the door closed, and I opened my eyes to see I was alone. I let out a shaky breath and felt tears of relief sting my eyes. I blinked them away and listened at the door but couldn't make out much.

"He hasn't left yet," Detective Black said. "I didn't hear the other door."

My eye went to the window above the bath. It was large enough for me to fit through, and we were on the ground floor. Terrified that the bathroom door would swing open again, it took me a moment to compose myself and sweep up what little courage I had left. I thought about that cartoon I used to watch with that purple dog who was terrified of everything and still always saved the day.

"If you don't make a noise and move quickly, you'll be fine." Detective Black stood by the window already.

I joined him and pushed the window open slowly. It made some noise, but nothing that Mr Field could hear from the other side of the bathroom door. Especially if he was at his desk. This bathroom must have been part of the renovation. The window itself was clean and opened up wide enough for me to fit through it. It also wasn't placed too high and with a bit of wiggling and breath-holding, I managed to stick halfway through. Still terrified that my ankles would be grabbed at any moment, I let myself fall in the bushes below, even if it meant a moment of pain and several branches in my hair. I struggled to roll away as thorns grabbed hold of my clothes, but I managed. Without thinking about it, I ran.

The entire time I wrestled through the window, it had occurred to me that if I left without checking out and went straight to Alistair, that Mr Field would know what I'd been up to. I didn't want that yet, because it meant he could accuse me of trespassing, and then even Alistair wouldn't have much to go on unless he got a warrant. By that time Mr Field could get rid of the evidence, and all of this would be for nothing. If I went back to my room, stuck it out for the next few hours and checked out, it would buy me time to speak with his wife. I could even convince her to talk to Alistair and provide a statement. It would earn her husband a spot on the suspect list.

And so I ran. It was possible that Mr Field had left his office while I was climbing out of the window, but it was a chance I was willing to take. Without so much as a sign of him, I slipped through the front entrance and ran up the stairs two steps at a time. The carpet absorbed any sounds my footsteps made, though it couldn't silence the sound of my panting. I really had to start working out.

I encountered nobody on my way to my room. My hands were shaking, and I fumbled with the key. After seeing that my room was void of any murderers, I closed and locked the door behind me. Everything seemed the same, but just in case, I checked under the bed and in the bathroom. I took a shower, and the thought of spy holes made me get changed in the bathroom. Then I dried the bath, checked that the bathroom was still locked and got into the tub. The idea that someone could spy on me just made me too uneasy. If he did happen to look and not see me in my room, then so be it. He was probably already suspicious of me. I just hoped it wasn't enough to make him do something rash.

I MANAGED TO WAKE UP without having been murdered, which was a relief. My back was sore from sleeping in the tub, and in total I must have slept three hours, tops. Detectives had to make sacrifices for the good of the case, and I was just too thrilled that I had discovered actual useful information. It was funny how conveniently I forgot about the terrifying bathroom incident in Mr Field's office. But I suppose that if I dwelt on it too long, I would lock myself up in my own flat for the rest of my life. Or at the very least until the sun wiped out all life. At least I'd be safe from Mr Field then. If he was the killer.

It seemed like a good theory, except for one thing. If Victor had been blackmailed by Mr Field and he wanted help, why meet up in the hotel? Unless Mr Field did it anonymously, which was definitely possible. I still had some thinking to do.

Mr Field was at the reception desk that morning as I made my way down. I decided to have breakfast at home and didn't want to stay a second longer.

"I'd like to check out, please," I said in my most chipper voice.

"Did you enjoy your stay?" he asked, fixing me with a stare.

"I did. It's a lovely place." I handed him the key and managed a smile.

"How did you sleep?" He moved to the computer and typed on the keyboard.

"The bed was very soft. Was that all?"

"In a rush to leave?" he looked up and smiled. It didn't reach his eyes.

"Yes, I've got lots of inspiration and can't wait to start writing." I didn't like the way he was looking at me. How much did he know? Or suspect? Was he really the killer? Or was there something else going on here?

"That was all. Have a lovely day."

"And you." It took me great effort not to run out of there, but I picked up the pace once I was outside. It was seven in the morning and most people were on their way to work. I made it to the flat, had a hearty breakfast and then fell asleep on the sofa for a few hours. When I woke up, I changed into a new outfit, and after checking the hotel website, found Mrs Field's number. I had prepared a whole speech that would make her okay with me coming to visit, but she had immediately given me the green light when I told her it was about Victor Woodsbury. I left a note on the counter in my book shop so that Eddie would know where I was, just in case.

The sun was occasionally hidden by clouds, but it was still warm. I had taken off my blue cardigan and put it in my bag. From what Mrs Field told me, I needed to find the street behind the post office and then take a left turn, followed by a right turn. It would be the third house on my right.

This village was just as picturesque as our own. The streets were cobbled, and there were a few decorated lamp posts. Every front garden contained colourful flowers. They were big on gardening and held regular events related to it.

The house I was looking for was a semi-detached cottage. It had rose bushes in the garden along with sunflowers by the bay window. The white gate was already open, welcoming me to walk the paved path to the green front door. After I'd raised my hand to knock, the door flew open.

Mrs Field stood in the doorway. I still remembered her from the pub and the morning Nancy and I found Victor, though she looked more dishevelled now. She was wearing a green skirt and a white top, colours that didn't match her complexion. Her light-brown hair was peaky and had lost its shine. The woman at the pub had been beautiful, whereas this woman looked broken. She kind of reminded me of my mother, and I didn't like the way that made me feel. She also wore a heart-shaped necklace. The same one that Victor had the last time I saw him alive.

Chapter 13

We stared at each other for a moment.

"Mrs Field," I said as a way of greeting her.

"Barbara, please." She stepped aside to let me in.

The hallway was cluttered with women's shoes and Wellingtons. The coat rack wasn't even visible anymore, and even though there was a bin for the umbrellas, some were scattered across the carpet. I glanced at the narrow staircase that had a laundry basket and stacks of old newspapers on the steps.

"The kitchen is through there." She pointed ahead, past the stairs.

"Thank you." I made my way to the open kitchen door and peered inside. It was a typical country kitchen with wooden countertops and white cabinets. There was a dog's basket by the wall and a kitchen table with a fruit bowl and filled teacups.

"Go ahead," Mrs Field said as she stood behind me.

I walked over to the table and observed the cabinet filled with crockery while I switched on the recorder on my phone.

"I was just having tea, I made you some too." She sat down at the table and took a sip.

Considering the fact that Victor was poisoned, I couldn't bring myself to sip the tea.

"Just pretend," Detective Black said.

I put the cup to my lips and pretended to sip. The hot liquid touched my lips, and I wiped it off with my index finger.

"Is it good?" she asked.

"Lovely." I smiled.

"So you've come to discuss Victor Woodsbury." She sighed dramatically. "The thing is—"

"You were having an affair with him."

Her eyes widened. "How did you know?"

"It's kind of my job to know," I said with a little bit of smugness. This clue-gathering was getting to my head, but I figured this was the only time I could solve a real-life murder.

She looked at her hands. "Well, yes, you're right. I was his mistress," she said with a hint of pride. "We were very much in love, though. He was going to leave his wife, and I was going to leave my husband. We met up once a week, sometimes once every two weeks. It was bliss."

Victor sure was keeping himself busy. "Did his wife know?"

She wrinkled her nose as if she smelt something foul. "Patricia? No, I don't think so. She was a stuck-up cow, and there was nothing left between them. It wouldn't surprise me if she killed him, you know."

"Why do you say that?" I perked up.

"Because he always said that she'd kill him if she found out about us. He said that's why he wanted to divorce her first. She and her friends all had marriage troubles, but Patricia liked to pretend everything was fine. Appearances mattered to her."

That I could believe. "Did you notice anything unusual that morning? Did you bring the cup of tea up?"

"I did. He requested it especially so that he could see me." She blushed. "But he didn't feel well and I left quickly. He wanted to take a bath first."

"Do you know why? Why didn't he just shower at home?"

She shrugged. "He said he didn't feel well. I think he had been sick."

"He said that? Did you tell the police that?"

"It smelt a bit funny in there. And no, they didn't ask. Why? Does it matter?"

Of course it mattered. "It means he might have been poisoned already. Before he drank the tea."

She gasped. "Oh, my. I didn't think of that. I saw the police bag the tea cup."

"Yes, to check if there was poison in there. They wouldn't know just by looking at him how it was administered, or when. They need evidence to make sure. They also need to analyse it so they know what kind of poison it is. There are many different types of poison."

She eyed me warily. "Oh. Well, I wouldn't know about that."

"Luckily I do."

She shifted her weight.

"Did your husband know about the affair?"

She stared into her cup. "I don't know. I really don't know. He's been so distant. Ever since our daughter got admitted to Creedmoor. Do you know it? It's a mental institution."

"Yes, I know it," I said, unable to make eye contact as uncomfortable feelings rose to the surface. How long had Mum been there now? A year?

"All I know is that he's been so terribly obsessed with this hotel. If he was as interested in me as he was in the bloody place, we'd be fine." She shook her head. "Men."

Detective Black scoffed. "She's no peach either."

"Do you think that if your husband knew, he would have killed Victor?" I asked.

She looked up at me. "I really don't know," she said and her eyes filled with tears.

After I handed her a few tissues from my handbag, she calmed down. "Please find out who killed him. Victor was the love of my life."

"She sure as hell wasn't his," Detective Black said.

"I'll do my best to find the killer." I got up. "I just hope it's not your husband."

Barbara clasped my hand with both of hers. "If he's guilty, then I want him punished. If he's not guilty, I will still never go back to that place. Or him." Tears welled up in her eyes.

I nodded. "Okay." My brain searched for reassuring words, but they seemed to be in hiding.

"I heard you've solved mysteries before. Please, just find out who did this. Not knowing is just awful."

"Thanks for seeing me. I'll let myself out."

I was in the narrow hallway when I heard her shout: "You haven't finished your tea." The thought of drinking that tea made me scrunch up my face, and I ran the last few feet to the door.

As I reached the end of the street, I passed a woman with a small, white dog. She had a resemblance to Barbara. It had to be her sister. I wondered what Barbara would do now. Live with her sister for the rest of her life? Barbara didn't have a job, they probably put a lot of money in that hotel, and now ... That's why I was glad I had always followed my dreams and not a man.

BEFORE HEADING BACK to my bookshop, I stopped by Beth's cottage and shot a longing glance at the cottage where Alistair lived. He was no doubt at work now, but I couldn't help but daydream about what it would be like to live there with him and make him his morning tea. Humming a random tune, I picked up the key from under the flower pot by Beth's door and entered.

She was in the reception area and beamed when she spotted me. "Hi, Maggie. So lovely to see you." She had a book on her lap and a steaming cup of tea on the table next to her. Her eyes were also a lot sharper than usual. That was good.

"Hi, Beth. You look lovely." I headed over and kissed her cheek.

"I'll make you some tea," she said as she leaned forward.

"No, don't bother." I gently pushed her back. "I'll make it myself. You just relax."

The water in the kettle was still hot, and I used the teabag mix with chai and vanilla. I couldn't help but think about Victor as I poured the tea and still felt sorry for him, but I was also angry. Angry that he had played both Mrs Field and

Susan, perhaps even more women. I was even angry for Patricia, even though I still didn't like her. Victor had blinded me by being nice, and it had been foolish to not see him for what he was. If I had listened to my aunt earlier, I could have perhaps said something to him, make him see he was hurting people. Perhaps he'd be alive if I had.

Then again, it wasn't my responsibility even if I did feel like it was.

I joined Beth in the reception area. "I suppose you've heard about Victor, haven't you?" I asked. I wasn't sure how much she remembered from the moments she was foggy in her head. I also wasn't sure how good her memory was when she was more like herself.

"Terrible, isn't it?" she asked.

"It is. Do you remember when I stopped by a couple of days ago, and you were saying something about poison?"

She raised her eyebrows, and her glasses slipped forward. "I did? Oh, heavens. No, I don't remember that."

"Perhaps I heard you wrong, then," I said, so as not to alarm her any further.

"Did you hear that Molly Pearbottom made a nude calendar of herself for her husband? Only she'd made a mistake and instead having the printed calendar delivered to her home, it ended up at the vicarage."

My eyes widened. "What? Did Harold open it?"

"No, Eleanor. There was a sexy note with it as well. It nearly gave Eleanor a heart attack. After the initial shock, she realised it had to be a mistake."

"What a mistake," I said, imagining myself in Eleanor's shoes. "Did Dawn tell you this?"

"She did. She always has the best gossip. I suppose being a postwoman, you do see a few things."

I started telling her about Pandora and the night Alistair walked me home, but soon her eyes glossed over, and I could tell I'd lost her.

"Maggie," she said after I had grown silent. "When did you get here?"

"Just now," I said and squeezed her hand.

She eyed the cup of tea I was holding. "Be careful with that," she said.

"Why?"

"How are things with your husband?"

I smiled. "Fine." When she had these moments, it was best to go with it.

"It's not his fault, you know? Men are like that sometimes. There's no need for revenge."

My skin tingled. "Why? Did you hear Patricia say something when she visited?"

"Patricia? Oh, how is she doing?" she asked, a tender smile on her face. Just like that, her previous thoughts had vacated her mind.

After that it was difficult to strike up any kind of conversation. The topics were scattered and half of the time she made no sense, so instead I told her to read and then left after handing her a fresh cup of tea and some biscuits. I was sure that she was rereading the same page over and over again, but at least she couldn't hurt herself. Eleanor checked on her most nights, practically tucking her in, but I still felt uneasy each time I left Beth. Perhaps it was because she was so fragile, and it reminded me of those days with Mum.

I strolled back to the bookshop, thinking about Patricia and her gang of girlfriends, when the police car in front of the bookshop drew my attention. There was shouting and Nancy was being wrestled into the back of the car. Alistair's VW Beetle was parked behind the police car, and he was there as well. A small crowd had gathered and across the street Stanley and Olivia had come out of their bakery.

I pushed myself through the crowd and went straight up to the constable who was easily a head taller than me. "Excuse me, sir. What do you think you're doing to my aunt?"

"Let me," Alistair said to the police officer, who nodded and was about to get into his car.

"No, no. You're not going anywhere. Why did you put my aunt in your car, and where are you taking her?"

"To the police station, miss, and I'd appreciate it if you didn't raise your voice," the man said. I didn't recognise him, and I wasn't sure if he was from Castlefield. What I did know was that I had the desire to smack him in the face with a cactus.

"I'd appreciate it if you didn't hurl my aunt into the back of a police car, but here we are," I said, shouting even louder.

"Maggie," Eddie said, and he touched my arm. I wasn't sure where he had come from, but why was I the only one helping my aunt?

"Let her go," I said, and I moved around the police officer to get to the back door.

"Don't make me arrest you too," the officer said as I reached for the handle.

I glanced back at Nancy through the window. "Don't worry, love, I can take them all," she said in a muffled voice. "Go back inside and take care of Bailey."

"Why did you arrest her?" I asked.

"Because she hit me with a broom," the man now shouted, his face red. "She hit me in the head and on my bum."

People in the crowd behind him chuckled, and he turned around to glare at them.

"Constable Higgins, I'll handle this. Please go ahead to the police station." Alistair stepped forward and gently grabbed my arm, directing me to his car. I glanced back at Eddie who had a frown etched on his face.

"We were going to bring in your aunt for questioning, that is all, but then she started yelling and throwing things. DC Daniels called for backup without my knowledge since I was trying to calm your aunt down. When the police showed up, she started assaulting Higgins and he arrested her. There was very little I could do. We just have to wait for him to calm down and forgive her. The worst-case scenario is that he'll let her sleep it off a night in one of the cells."

"What? How could you let him do that?" I glanced back at the police car, which now took off as the people who were watching on started chatting excitedly before turning their attention over to us.

"Come on," he said. "Hop in. I'll fill you in on the way to the police station."

I shouted at Eddie to take care of Bailey and got in. Normally I'd be excited to sit in Alistair's car, but right now I was fuming. "Why do you need to question her?" I asked.

Alistair sighed. "We've completed the autopsy on Victor Woodsbury, and we found out he was poisoned with Amanita mushrooms. Your aunt sells them in her shop, which means that she has direct access to them. She also found the body and Victor invited her to his hotel room."

"And me. Besides, what motive do you think she has? They dated in secondary school, but that was ages ago. She's had nothing to do with him ever since then. Why would she want to kill him? And why put me through discovering his body?"

Alistair paused. "We'd like to find out. Hence the questioning. Look, if she hadn't hit Higgins, I could have asked my questions at her shop. But she did, and now we have to take her in. My boss will think it's suspicious that she was so defensive, so it's best to question her and rule her out as quickly as possible."

I stared at him. Then my eyes widened. "You're going to question me too. That's why you wanted me to get in."

Alistair's knuckles turned white as he gripped the steering wheel tighter. "I'm sorry. You and your aunt found him, and we just have a few questions. I'm only doing my job."

I gaped at him. "You just lured me into your car so you could drive me to the police station and question me about a murder. Yeah, no, great." I folded my arms. "Just doing your job, my ass," I muttered.

He looked at me. "I am. Do you think I enjoy this?"

"Maybe you do," I said without making eye contact.

"Well, I don't. I don't like this one bit, but we need answers, and I'm trying to get them."

"So am I."

He sighed. "But you're not a detective, I am. I have procedures to follow, and right now it helps if you answer a few questions. I'm sorry."

I said nothing. There was nothing to say. Even if I knew it wasn't personal, it felt personal. And it would be just my luck to get arrested by the guy I was in love with.

Chapter 14

The interrogation room wasn't very cosy. I suppose it wasn't meant to be, but I still didn't like it. The walls were painted a grey colour, and the table and chairs weren't very sturdy or aesthetically pleasing. There was also a large tape recorder on the table, which managed to intimidate me. This was all very serious.

"Remember that you can ask for a lawyer at any time," Detective Black said.

Just then Alistair and DC Daniels came in. They sat down in front of me, and Alistair slid a glass of water over to my side of the table. I figured that if things got really out of hand, I could throw it in someone's face, but now that they were here, I realised I couldn't do that.

"Too bad," Detective Black said.

They had kept me waiting for about twenty-five minutes, and I was getting worried about Nancy. I refused to show fear, though, and instead adopted a poker face. I just had to channel my inner Lady Gaga.

First Alistair stated the date and all of those present. Then he tapped the folder he'd brought and leaned forward.

"What was your relationship with Victor Woodsbury?" he asked in a professional tone. There was no indication at all that we so much as knew each other, not even in his eyes. He had flipped some sort of switch that eliminated our connection.

The question surprised me, but I did my best to hide it. "He lived in the same village as I did. I had once been invited into his home, and he had shown me photo albums and told me his life story. Well, the highlights."

"Why had he invited you into his home?" Alistair asked. Apparently he was the one asking the questions.

"He found me walking around, crying." I took the glass and sipped the freezing water. It hurt my teeth. "I had found out that my boyfriend at the time cheated on me." It was only because I was focussed on his reaction that I spotted the slight twitch of his eyebrows, as if he barely managed to refrain from frowning.

"I see. And all you did was have a friendly chat, nothing more?"

"Of course," I said with some indignation.

"A witness saw you two embrace in the street the day before his murder," Alistair stated.

"What? No, he didn't embrace me. He grabbed my arms. Look, I've seen him around, but that one time he comforted me was the only time we had a real conversation. After that I only saw him in passing. He stopped by a few times in the bookshop a few months ago, but apparently that was when he started ... dating Susan."

"Could she have gotten the poison?"

"The mushrooms are poisonous yes, but they are used by shamans in northern cultures. That's why Nancy sells them. She doesn't keep them in the shop, though. She keeps them in a special safe, and she only displays them on the site where they can be ordered. Susan wouldn't have been able to get to them. Not unless she ordered them, but then she'd have to fill in her address, and I doubt Nancy would have sent it to anyone she knows and who isn't a shaman."

"And your aunt? What was her relationship with Victor?" Alistair asked.

"They dated when she was fourteen or fifteen and after that, nothing. She had no reason to want to kill him."

"If I recall, she wasn't too fond of him. Didn't she bring a tea kettle with her to the hotel as a weapon?" Alistair was still leaning forward, his expression unchanged. He was good at this, but that also worried me. He had mentioned he was under pressure to close the case. What if he wanted a scapegoat?

I shifted in my seat and realised I had just admitted to being uncomfortable. "She did."

"Why?" His piercing gaze didn't waver.

"Because she thought it was weird that he asked to meet us at the Pembroke. She thought that maybe he wanted something sleazy. I told her he had seemed scared when he talked to me, but I agreed that it was weird."

"And why did he ask you?" DC Daniels asked.

"I don't know, do I? I still don't know what he could have been afraid of or what he needed advice for. What I do know is that Susan wasn't the only woman he was having an affair with."

At this, both men sat up straighter. "What do you mean?" Alistair asked.

I told them about Mrs Field and about the fact that he wasn't feeling well when she gave him his tea. "Those mushrooms take a few hours to actually affect someone, but by then it will be too late. Someone could have poisoned him much earlier, like six or seven hours earlier. Technically even twenty-four hours."

"You know a lot about these mushrooms," Alistair said.

I stiffened. "Yes, my aunt taught me a lot. I worked at her shop for years before I opened up the bookshop."

A pause.

"Is there anything else you'd like to share with us?" Alistair stared at me as if he could read me like a book, and I was tempted to tell him about Mr Field, but the tape was recording, and I didn't want to admit to breaking into his office. Instead I gave a shrug and swallowed a remark about them doing their job properly.

They left the room for about fifteen minutes before Alistair returned and informed me I could leave. He also told me that Nancy had to stay the night because she had assaulted that constable and then he walked me outside.

"I am really sorry," he said and touched my arm so that I would stop and face him.

"I'm sure you are."

His worried eyes scanned my face. "Are you upset with me?"

"I know you are just doing your job."

"That's not what I asked."

I sighed. "Yes, I'm upset with you. But I'm sure I'll get over it." Once I delivered him the actual killer in a neat little bow, and he would be so impressed he'd never doubt me again. "I think you should look into Patricia and her friends, as well as Mr Field. Patricia visited Beth regularly on Sundays and Beth, though struggling with her memory, mentioned something about poison and bad husbands." Before he could say anything else I strode away. Sure, he felt bad and he was just doing his job, but I still couldn't help but feel disappointed. Betrayed, even.

I took the bus that stopped near the post office and headed to my bookshop. It would undoubtedly be filled with curious villagers, but I figured I could handle them. It would also allow me to put a stop to a few rumours that had surely started circulating as soon as Nancy and I had been taken to the police station. Especially if someone had been telling people Victor had embraced me.

As soon as I entered the bookshop, it became quiet. It was busy, but that was because most of the Castlefield Book Club was there, as well as the vicar. Harold pushed his wheelchair over to me. "Maggie, are you alright?"

The women gathered around with worried expressions. "Please tell me Nancy hasn't been arrested?" Eleanor asked, her hand on her husband's shoulder.

Eddie rushed over from behind the counter and gave me a tight hug. "I'm glad you're okay. You are okay, right? Do I need to beat anyone up?"

I laughed. "No. I'm fine, I promise."

A couple of people whose faces I recognised were pretending not to listen. I didn't care. This was my opportunity to set things straight.

"Nancy was only arrested because she hit a constable with a broom, that's all. Then they asked some follow-up questions about Victor's death and that was it. There really is nothing to worry about. I promise."

The women sighed collectively.

"Good, because Nancy would not do well in prison. They don't have any scones there," Poppy said.

"Or kettles," Ava said and snorted. "She'd be so bored, not being able to hit someone with a household object."

The other women chuckled.

"Come, dear. Let's have some tea," Poppy said and dragged me to the corner with the armchairs. She plopped me down and pressed a few buttons on the coffee machine until hot water came out. The other women started chatting about their favourite Nancy moments that involved violence and household objects. They made me laugh, which is just what I needed.

AN HOUR MUST HAVE PASSED as the store became even busier. Eddie had the help of Brian since Susan still had time off, and both of them were sweating. Just as I was about to help them out and leave the book club ladies and Harold to themselves, Susan rushed in. Her cheeks were red, her fists clenched. Her eyes landed on me.

"You," she spat and dropped her handbag. "You were having an affair with him. How dare you lie to my face, pretending to care?"

I gaped at her. "I most certainly did not have an affair with Victor. I am very single, thank you very much. The other day I almost fell in love with an ad, that's how single I am."

"Liar!" She rushed over to me, and before I could react, she knocked me to the ground. I wasn't proud of my reaction, but I yanked her hair to get her off me, and we struggled for several seconds while the women shrieked in panic, except for Ava who kept yelling at me to stick it to her. I wasn't sure what it meant, but I was definitely trying to do that.

Just as Eddie came towards us, someone pulled Susan off me and I could breathe, even if it was a shaky breath. Eddie helped me to my feet while Susan started crying in Alistair's arms.

The whole thing hadn't taken long, but it felt like Susan and I had been on the ground for an hour. I adjusted my clothes while Eleanor came over to stroke my hair lovingly.

It took a while before Susan calmed down and the entire time nobody had said a word. Not even Ava.

"I'm sorry, I don't know what came over me," Susan mumbled as Alistair patted her shoulder in a wooden fashion. He clearly was not accustomed to comforting women he barely knew.

"Eddie, perhaps you can take her outside and let her calm down for a bit?" Alistair asked.

"I'm not sure I want to do that," Eddie said and glanced at me.

I was about to tell him it was okay when Harold moved forward. "I'll do it. Come along, love, let's enjoy that fresh air," he said in his pleasant voice, and she followed him like a meek lamb. It was hard to believe she had charged me like a bull a moment earlier.

Alistair took two steps closer. "Are you okay? Did she hurt you?"

"It's fine. She surprised me more than anything."

"Do you want to press charges?" he asked.

"No, of course not. She just lost the man she loved. Don't worry about it. I don't think she does this sort of thing on a regular basis."

"Are you sure?" Eddie asked. "Who knows? She might be a bit crazy."

"She's not. She's grieving. We can't judge her too harshly, we don't know all the things she's been through."

Eleanor squeezed my shoulder.

"Just please make it clear to her that I was not having an affair with Victor, because I wasn't," I said.

"She's right," Eleanor said. "Maggie would never do something like that, even if she had liked him. Which she hadn't."

The other women murmured in agreement, even Lily.

"Hiya," a chipper voice called out.

We all turned to Christina, who had just entered the bookshop.

Her smile disappeared. "Am I interrupting?"

Alistair moved away and towards her. "What are you doing here? I thought you were in London?" he asked with a familiarity that set off alarm bells.

"This is not good," Detective Black whispered in my ear.

The women were following this interaction as intensely as I was, though for different reasons. I felt Eddie tense up next to me. He glanced at me.

"Actually," Christina said loud enough for us to hear. "I've just officially moved in. I've sold the flat, and I called in a favour. The movers brought my stuff over just now. I wanted to come in and thank my new friend." She darted over to me and hugged me. "Thanks to you I've decided to give this whole thing a shot."

"Are you Alistair's girlfriend?" Lily asked with the kind of apprehension that I felt in my bones, though the answer was obvious. It was so obvious. It hit me like a tank.

She grabbed his hand. "Yeah. Didn't he tell you about me?"

Those words shot right through my heart.

"No," the book club ladies said in unison.

She raised her eyebrows. "I guess my Alistair's been a bit bad, then." She gave him a kiss on the cheek as he was staring at me.

My heartbeat sped up. Didn't we almost kiss after that chase by Pandora? I couldn't maintain my composure much longer. "I'm glad it worked out," I managed to squeeze out of my throat, but the words sounded a bit off. Like someone else was speaking them. "Excuse me for a moment. It's been a hectic morning. I just need to have a little lie down."

"Do you need me to come up with you?" Eleanor asked.

"No, no. I'll be fine." I kissed her on the cheek and said goodbye to the women, thanking them for their support.

Christina looked surprised at that, but I was sure Alistair would fill her in. During dinner. In their home. Where they lived. Together. In love. As soon as I was through the back door, I ran up the stairs and bit my lip to keep from crying. It was stupid to cry over this.

Even though my vision was blurry due to the tears, I made myself a cup of tea. As I opened the fridge for milk, I was confronted by all the shopping I'd done for the dinner we were supposed to have tonight. Clearly that wasn't happening. I had even bought extra candles to create an ambiance. I was an idiot.

I let out a sob as I poured my cup, and made it to the sofa without spilling anything other than tears. As soon as I sat down, I heard footfalls on the stairs. I froze, hoping Eddie hadn't let Alistair come up. I really didn't want him to see me like this.

But it was Eleanor. "Oh, dear," she muttered as she saw my poor attempt at a smile while tears still streamed down my cheeks.

I started crying again when she put her arm around me. After I calmed down, I told her the story of how Alistair and I spent that day at the fair and what had happened when he came back. That day at the fair had always been special because it felt like he had saved me from a particularly bad day, not to mention that he'd opened up about his own troubles. It had made me feel less alone. And now that he'd come back it was clear there was something between us, which was why the whole Christina thing had thrown me.

She shook her head. "He should have told you the truth."

"But he didn't. Why? Why did he do that to me? Or Christina for that matter?"

"It seems to me that this is his problem. I don't think it has anything to do with you or Christina. He is responsible for his own actions. Clearly, he should deal with his issues, but you've been hurt, and you should think about what you're going to do."

I made a face. "Why? What are my options?"

She rubbed my arm. "You can do whatever you want. You can ignore him, you can go and talk to him, you can make it clear you want nothing to do with him. Whatever will help you move on."

The thought of moving on made me even sadder, and I started crying again. It made it impossible to drink my tea, which was the only thing that could save me now.

Chapter 15

I spent the rest of the afternoon on my sofa, having wrapped myself in a snuggly blanket, with my remote in one hand, and a biscuit in the other. I had already eaten too many and felt my waistline expanding. The crying had made me feel a bit better, as had the tea, but now I had to brood. There was lots to brood about. There wasn't just Alistair's confusing behaviour, but there was also a murderer still on the loose. And even if I no longer felt the need to impress Alistair, I did feel the need to shove it into his face that I was a better investigator.

Also, the book club ladies had been so kind to me, I owed them some peace of mind.

The mushrooms that had killed Victor weren't hard to get. They could be ordered, but they could also be found in nature. The police were grasping at straws if they thought Nancy had anything to do with it just because she had them in her shop. But from what Mrs Field had said, the poison was probably administered earlier. Technically, it could have been when he asked me for help, but if he had suspected he was poisoned, he would have gone to a doctor, not me and Nancy. Still, he could have had a reason to think someone was out to get him. Threats? A fight? Was it related to the cheating?

There was no way to find out what it was about, but right now my suspect was Patricia. If I remembered correctly, she was part of the gardener's society, and they met on Mondays and Thursdays. Which meant it was likely she knew about the mushrooms, but also that she'd be out of the house tonight. My hands were itching to do something proactive after today. I needed results.

"If you're going to do what I think you're going to do, it's probably best not to go alone." Detective Black was right in front of me.

"I will be faster on my own. Besides, I don't have anyone."

He leaned forward to look me in the eyes. "That's not true at all. You have me."

That would have made me feel better if it weren't for the fact that he was a figment of my imagination.

"How dare you?" he said while I got up to take a shower.

I changed into a dark outfit and went downstairs to check on Eddie. The shop was closing soon, and I hadn't seen that much of him today. He had to be worried about me.

It was weird to think that Nancy's shop was closed on a Monday. She had always worked six days a week without fail. I felt teary-eyed just thinking about her in a cell, but I knew she wouldn't be too upset. She was a tough woman, and all a night in jail would do to her was make her cranky. Okay, crankier.

When I entered the store through the back door, Eddie was chatting with Nick by the counter. Brian was there as well. Nick was talking about something, and both men were hanging on his lips.

They turned to look at me as I approached them. "Hello," Nick said. "How are you doing?" He held up a flash drive. "I figured I'd come and play the recording of the ghost for you. Eddie rang me." He jerked his head towards Eddie, who smiled sheepishly.

"I figured it's about time you crack this case, Nancy Drew," Eddie said.

I smiled. "And you figured a so-called ghost recording could do that?"

"Aren't you curious?"

"Hey, just because a toothpick is enough to make you curious, doesn't mean it's the same for me."

Nick laughed. "Wow, just hearing this has made my trip to your bookshop worth it."

I tried to glare. "Anyway, I'll go get my laptop."

"You're not going to invite me upstairs?" Nick asked. The dimples in his cheek showed.

"O-okay," I said. "Follow me." When I glanced at Eddie, he held up a thumb. He probably hoped that Nick could make me forget about Alistair.

We went up the stairs to my flat in silence as I contemplated what to say to Nick, but somehow I had no inspiration at all. A writer who was at a loss for words. How blasphemous.

"Why don't you sit down," I said to him and gestured towards the sofa on which I had vegetated for most of the afternoon.

"You have a cute flat." He sat down as I rushed into my office and got my laptop. I also made sure I didn't have my browsers open on weird websites about poison and murder. Research as a mystery writer was quite dark and disturbing.

When I returned, I couldn't help but admire how natural Nick looked in my flat. He had his arm draped over the back of the sofa and appeared as if he always sat that way, waiting for me to come home. Man, I really had to start dating.

"So," he started tentatively, "you've been on the lips of a lot of people today. Should I be jealous?" One corner of his lips turned upwards, but his eyes remained serious.

"Ah, yes. I imagine you've heard lots of troublesome things about me by now."

"Nothing that has scared me off. In fact, I think we should have dinner together after this. But not in this village."

I chuckled. "Yeah, that will set even more tongues wagging."

"I don't care about that. I just don't want you to be mistreated or anything."

I raised my eyebrows. Did he really care about me that much? Nothing about his demeanor told me he was lying, but then again, I didn't trust my judgment after Alistair. "I have a cool group of women who support me, so don't worry. Sure, there will always be judgmental people, but that's their jam, not mine."

"Sometimes it's not that easy, but I admire your attitude." He smiled. "So, you didn't say no to dinner. Will you let me treat you?"

"I suppose so, but you should know I'm a hot mess right now."

Nick chuckled. "You look pretty good for a hot mess."

I felt my cheeks get warm. He sure was good at saying the right things, but I had fallen for that before. Still, he'd be a nice distraction from Alistair and Christina. "Okay, let's see what we have." I hit play on the recording.

After a few questions from Nick in a clear voice, there was some static and then a woman's voice. If I strained hard enough I could indeed make out the word 'justice,' but it sounded unusual. Was *hollow* the right word? When I had heard it in the hotel, it seemed to be more like a harsh gush of the wind. Still, something was familiar about it. Not because I had heard it at the hotel, but something else.

I closed my laptop and returned the flash drive, then tapped my fingers against my lips.

"What are you thinking?" Nick leaned closer.

"It sounds familiar."

"It does?"

I snapped my fingers. "I've got it." I went over to the TV cabinet and pulled open the drawer with DVDs. After a few moments, I found what I was looking for. I put the DVD in the DVD player and turned it on.

"What are you doing?" Nick asked.

"You'll see." I found the right scene and played the film. It was an old horror film called *Screams in the Night* that I'd once bought on a whim. It was actually a nice black-and-white film, not too spooky. But it also had a scene in it where a ghostly woman screams the word 'justice.' That moment was coming up. I glanced at Nick.

The apparition appeared in the corridors of a deserted manor. The main actor fell down the stairs, being shoved by the woman in white. She screamed the word, drawing it out.

"Wow," Nick said. He grabbed my laptop and played the recording again. It sounded the same, though less clear than the DVD, which made sense since whoever did this must have used a device not too close to us, nor too far away.

"Who would do this?" I said. "The killer obviously had a good reason for making everyone believe that ghosts were involved."

"At least we know for sure it wasn't a ghost. There's not much else to do. But if you're going to be thinking about this, perhaps a full stomach will help." Nick grinned.

"Sure. Let's go." I felt mild panic and excitement at the prospect of having dinner with Nick. He didn't seem like someone who played games, which I liked, but he was also from Wales and probably going home soon. What really was the point of this?

"To have fun," Detective Black said.

WE WENT TO A CUTE PUB in Lowfield, which was about a twenty-minute drive away. The village was even smaller than ours, and there were a lot of farms. On the side of the road, surrounded by fields of grazing sheep, was The Herder, which served food until 9.30, as it said on their blackboard outside. I had never been there before, but I liked the atmosphere. It reminded me of The Rose, and I expected Callum to pop up any moment to take our order. Instead it was a large woman with dark makeup.

We both ordered the fish and chips, and I had some rum and coke to go with it. I usually only drank alcohol on special occasions but felt the need for some booze.

"So, tell me your life story." Nick leaned forward.

"My life story? No, mine isn't interesting. I'd much rather hear yours."

"Come on, please tell me something about yourself. Anything. Tell me about what you write."

"I write mysteries about a detective who lives in this day and age, but is quite old-fashioned." I shrugged. "That's all."

"Enough to make a living?"

"Yes." I took a sip from my drink.

"But you still work at your bookshop?"

"Not always. I have two employees, Eddie and Susan."

"Right, Eddie. He's also your best friend, isn't he?"

"Yes, he's my little ghost-obsessed best friend."

"How long have you been friends?"

"Since secondary school. We met when we had to do our first project for school. We had such a blast, we never stopped hanging out. When my books started picking up and I had to go to London a lot, sometimes I took him with me. And otherwise we still texted and called like every hour."

"So you're close then?"

I nodded. "As close as butter on bread."

Nick smiled and played with a coaster. "But you never dated Eddie?"

"What? No. We're best friends. Men and women can be friends just fine, I hate that people don't seem to grasp that. Just because a woman likes men doesn't mean she likes every man and vice versa. Hence, they can be friends as long as they just happen to not be attracted to each other."

"But what if that attraction grows?"

"I'm sure that can happen, just like how you can stop liking someone."

He leaned back in his seat. "Has that happened before?"

"What? That a friend starts liking me or that I stop liking someone I once was attracted to?"

"Or that someone has stopped liking you. I find it hard to imagine, but I guess I'm asking if someone ever broke your heart."

I scratched my arms. "That's personal."

"I'm only asking because it would explain why you looked a little bit terrified when I asked you out," he said and leaned forward. He grabbed my hand and squeezed it.

"I did not look terrified." His hand felt warm and comfortable. I liked the intimacy of it.

He smiled. "That's okay. We've all been hurt before. I'm pretty sure it's a rite of passage."

"Doesn't make it more fun."

"No, it does not. But think about it as the process of weeding out the bad ones so that you're left with the good ones. At some point you'll end up with the person you're supposed to be with, and it will all be worth it."

I hope so.

Our food came, and we ate while Nick told me how he grew up in Wales with his five siblings and a sheepdog named Muffleton. He had always been interested in the paranormal, but his interest truly sparked after he believed to have seen the spirit of his deceased grandmother, with whom he had a special connection. He started out ghost hunting as a hobby, but eventually made a name for himself and started making some serious money.

"Actually, I have something I need to tell you about that." He dabbed his lips with his napkin.

"What?" I was too intent on my food to realise that he was nervous.

"Someone paid us to come to the Pembroke and do our recordings."

I looked up, mayonnaise on my chin.

He used his napkin to get rid of it for me. "That's not how it usually goes. We are hired to look into it, but never paid up front. There was something urgent about this message, and we decided to go and check it out anyway."

"And the only request was that you show up and do the recordings?"

"No. We also had to say it was haunted." He held up his hand. "We didn't touch that money, but it did pique our interest. That's all. With everything going on, I figured I should tell you. I didn't really know who else to tell, or what the point was. We never would have told anyone it was haunted if we didn't believe it. The recording is all we've got, so we told Mr Field that we needed to look into it further. I've done some readings with Eddie and Brian, actually, as the rest of my crew has already left. We didn't find anything, so I believe you're right, that there are no ghosts there."

"How did you get the request?" I asked.

"Email via our website."

"You should tell Alistair, he might be able to track an IP address."

"Consider it done. But, aren't you upset?"

"You didn't mean any harm. If I were you, I'd have been curious as well. Still, it would have been handier if I'd known earlier. It's likely it was the killer who hired you, to make it seem that the curse killed Victor. It might have been Patricia."

"Who? The wife?"

"Yes, Patricia Woodsbury. She's—well, I think she might have something to do with it."

"Then we should do something."

"What?" I asked.

"Everybody in the village is talking about how you'll solve this, but so far you've only gotten in trouble for discovering the body. Why don't you let me help you?"

"Well, I did actually have a plan that I was going to execute tonight."

He leaned forward with a glint in his eyes. "Tell me."

Chapter 16

We waited outside of Patricia's home until she left with one of her friends to go to the church where they held their meeting. It had a community garden where they would grow plants and flowers. I couldn't imagine what was fun about meetings like that, but Castlefield was big on clubs. There were obviously a book club and garden club, but also a knitting club, a model trains club, a stone skipping club, and even a tree shaping club. The last one was actually quite cool and consisted of training living trees and plants to grow into certain shapes. It could be used to create art or furniture. That club had four members, and they'd formed—get it?—the club a year ago and still had very little to show for it, but this was a time-consuming hobby.

"My heart is racing," Nick said. "Are we really doing this?"

"Yes. It's time we get some answers instead of more questions." I waited until Patricia and her friend were out of sight and then darted across the street, straight to the side of the house where there was a tall wooden gate that led to the garden.

"Okay, ready? No turning back now," I said to Nick who had followed on my heels and was grinning like the Cheshire cat.

"I'm ready." He bent forward.

"What are you doing?"

"You need to get over. Go ahead."

I glanced at the gate and pushed it open.

Nick looked at it, then back at me. "I was testing you." He slowly got back up. "You passed."

"Right." I walked ahead of him, smiling. I had to admit I was having more fun than I would have thought.

"Just remember to focus on the task," Detective Black said, walking next to me. "Don't let him distract you and don't lower your guard completely. You never know."

I had a small torch in my bag and got it out. Yellow roses were placed along the side of the house. It smelt sweet, much like Patricia's perfume usually did. The few times that I had encountered her, I could smell her ten minutes before she arrived.

The gate closed with a bang, and I whirled around, my heart in my throat.

Nick cringed. "Sorry."

"Let's go," I whispered. We made our way to the back of the house. There was a small patio with an iron table and four chairs. A plant with budding flowers was placed on the table. I shone the light in the window that looked out over the garden. It was the kitchen. The window itself was ajar.

"I'll try the back door," Nick whispered as he passed me. He walked soundlessly towards the door and tried it. "It's locked." Even partially hidden by darkness, he looked handsome.

"Do you see a security system or cameras?" I asked as I pulled on the kitchen window. It was big enough for me to get through, but I'd end up on the countertops. It wouldn't be a graceful endeavour.

"No, I don't see anything. Better try that window." He stood next to me, his hands in his pockets.

"Why do I have to do it?" I asked.

"I doubt I'll fit through there. Besides, this way I can keep watch for you."

"I know that, but it would have been chivalrous to at least pretend you were coming with me."

He smiled and stepped closer. "For good luck," he said and kissed me ever so briefly on the lips.

My cheeks got warm, and I handed him my torch. "Hold this, I'm going in." Before shyness made my whole body blush.

He pulled up one of the chairs and then held open the window as I got on the chair and leaned forward. I placed my hands on the clean counter and was relieved it wasn't cluttered with dirty dishes. Broken plates were as much a sign of a break-in as getting caught.

I placed one knee on the windowsill, which hurt, and then pulled up my other leg. One foot was on the shiny counter that smelt like lemons while I swung my other foot over a kitchen roll and next to my other foot. I was now crouched on Patricia Woodsbury's kitchen countertops and kind of felt like a badass.

I jumped off and landed on the tiled floor with a thud. In one swift motion I stood up straight and looked at Nick.

"Are you okay?" he asked.

I held up my thumb. "Torch," I said.

He threw it at me, and I caught it.

"Be careful."

"Don't worry." The words managed to leave my throat calmly, despite my rapid heartbeat and the tingling sensation that came with intruding someone else's personal space. I swallowed my fear and turned on the torch. The kitchen was tidy, almost sterile. She probably had a maid. I wiped the counter and checked all of the cupboards, making sure there were no murderous mushrooms. When I found nothing, I moved on to the corridor. The light was on, so I turned off my torch. Since I was most curious about their bedroom and bathroom, I headed straight upstairs where Detective Black was leaning against the wall. He nodded at me when I reached the landing.

I turned on my torch and went into the first room. It was an empty guest room. The second room was the bathroom. I opened the cupboards under the sink and put the small torch between my teeth as I opened my shoulder bag. From there I took the CSI gloves I had taken from my kitchen. They were actually just latex cleaning gloves.

"Bathrooms are always interesting rooms to check," Detective Black said as he was crouched beside me.

"Except that Eleanor already checked." And I indeed confirmed the pills for depression and the hemorrhoid cream. The sound of my footsteps was absorbed by the light yellow carpet. With hurried steps I reached the bedroom and closed the door behind me. The curtains were closed even though it was still light out. By the time Patricia would come back, it would be dark. My light scanned the big oak wardrobe and a black dress with a matching hat hung on the opened door. The tag was still on the dress. It was a funeral dress.

I wondered if she truly felt bad about Victor dying. She didn't seem remorseful, but she was good at hiding her feelings. If she had poisoned him, would she have done it in this house? In their home?

After looking around the bedroom, I moved to what turned out to be Victor's office. I imagined the police had already been here, but it wouldn't hurt to look around, especially since he had been worried about something before he died. I checked his desk and found nothing but useless papers that told me nothing about any potential secrets. But as I was rummaging through a few files on his desk, I found a DVD of *Screams in the Night.* I swallowed. Coincidences didn't exist in murder cases.

"This would imply that she hired Nick and wanted them to prove that the Pembroke was haunted," Detective Black said.

"It would. Perhaps she had hoped that they wouldn't find out about the poison, but she couldn't exactly be sure when he would die or show symptoms. Or who he would be with. It was always a huge risk. Perhaps that's why she wanted as many people as possible to think the Pembroke was haunted." I still wasn't sure about it. We needed more than just this. I took a picture of the DVD on the desk.

I looked around a bit longer, but found nothing and made my way down to the kitchen.

Nick looked relieved when he spotted me. "Are you okay?" he asked.

"Yes, I am." I climbed back onto the counter while Nick held out his hand. I grabbed it and pushed my way through the window. "You know what, this whole breaking in thing is way more fun when fictional people do it."

"Are you kidding? You're doing great," he said.

I shrieked and fell forward as Nick tried to catch me. One thud later, and we were both lying on the patio, me on top of Nick.

Nick chuckled. "This is an interesting development."

I felt my cheeks get warm again and smiled.

He looped his arms around me and rolled around so that I was now on the ground, and he was on top of me. He had his arm under my head as a sort of pillow, and grinned at me. "You look very beautiful," he whispered before he kissed me. His lips were soft and warm. I kissed him back, holding him tight as I enjoyed the fluttering feeling in the pit of my stomach.

When he broke away, I immediately missed the warmth and intimacy of the kiss.

"I've wanted to do that ever since I first saw you," he said.

"You did?"

"Oh, yeah." He kissed me again, briefly this time. Then he got to his feet and helped me up. "Did you find anything?"

I told him about the film.

"Damn, I can't believe it. So she's the killer?"

"I don't know that yet. It looks that way, though I still feel like I don't have all the pieces of the puzzle yet. Also, the DVD alone is suspicious, but circumstantial. Even if it might be enough to have Alistair ask some questions, we need more."

Nick took a step aside and pointed at a wooden shed in the corner of the garden. "We haven't checked there yet."

"Do you really think she'd keep anything important in there?" I asked.

"Why not? It's not the first place you'd think to look, is it?"

"True. Let's go." Nick was turning out to be a good partner, and not just because of his kissing skills.

The shed wasn't locked, so we could go right in. I used my torch to provide light in the organised shed. There were a few cabinets and a table with pots and garden tools. At the back of one of the cabinets, I found a basket with Amanita mushrooms.

"Wow," I said as I stared at the basket.

"What? Those are just mushrooms that grow in the woods," Nick said.

"No, these are what killed Victor, and she has a basket of it right in her shed. That's just—I mean—" my voice trailed off.

"So she is the killer then? Do we go to the police?"

"No," I said firmly. "I'm going to solve this case, and once I have a confession, I'll call Alistair."

"You really are hell-bent on solving this case, huh?"

"Yes, I am." And on showing up Alistair.

"So what's next then?" Nick asked.

I took a picture of the basket and returned it to where we'd found it. "I'm going to have to find a way to get her to confess. Perhaps get her to attack me."

"Whoa, what?"

"That's how it happens in books. The main character confronts the killer, and the killer who sees her as an annoying meddler decides to kill her and get her out of the way, and just then the police show up and have all the proof they need."

"Except you just said you didn't want the police involved and also, this isn't a story."

"How do you know?" I said.

"Okay, look, how about this: we invite this Patricia to a neutral, public place and discuss the mushrooms. See what she says?"

"I need to rattle her cage, make her angry. Also, if I make her feel like I'll be watching her, that I'll keep on looking for clues, then she'll feel cornered and snap. Hopefully."

"Do you hear yourself? We don't want her to snap, she might hurt you."

"Yeah, but we still don't have enough evidence to go to the police with and our only option right now is to get her to confess," I said.

"Okay, let's sleep on it, then. We don't want to make any rash decisions. Come, let's get out of here, I'll walk you home."

We still had very little to go on. I knew exactly what stupid Alistair would say. He'd babble about how it was all circumstantial, and that was after he'd bite my head off for snooping around. And then there was Mr Field, who had been spying on his cheating wife. Did he know who the killer was? Had he seen something? Should I talk to him about it?

"You're frowning," Nick said, bringing me back to reality. He grabbed my hand as we continued on our way to the bookshop.

It had been a while since I last held someone's hand and it was nice. Somehow this had turned into the weirdest date ever, but also a very cool one. I squeezed his hand and decided to enjoy the moment while it lasted. I could always worry about murder and mayhem later.

"I had fun tonight," Nick said as we were nearly at the bookshop.

"Me too."

"I've never been part of a break in before," he said.

"I hope it was all you've ever wanted and more."

He chuckled. "It was certainly thrilling, and I particularly enjoyed the kissing part."

"Yes, me too."

He stopped and pulled me in closer. He kissed my cheek and then my lips. I was apprehensive about doing this sort of thing in public, especially in a village that thrived on gossip, but as soon as his lips touched mine, those worries washed away. The kiss was over too soon.

"I'll see you around," he said.

"See you." I smiled.

It was getting dark now, and the sky had streaks of pink, as if someone had taken a brush to it. For a brief moment I felt happiness, but then Christina passed Nick and waved when we made eye contact. She had a big bag with her. "Listen," she said as she reached me. "I heard all about your troubles with the law today, and I've come to report for friend duty."

Inwardly, I groaned.

"I hope you don't hate Alistair too much, but if you do, don't take it out on me. You're about the only friend I've got here. Also, I brought snacks." She held out her bag to me, which contained a bag of Skittles, Snickers, marshmallows, and M&Ms.

I groaned even more on the inside. Why did she have to be so nice and cool? And why did Alistair have to be such a poopy face?

"Come on in," I said.

Chapter 17

Christina had kicked off her heels and pulled up her legs while observing my living room. The fact that Alistair's girlfriend was now on my sofa didn't unsettle me as much as it probably should. It helped that I had met her before I knew who she was dating. And I liked her. Which sucked, because if I had any sense of self-preservation, I would cut ties with both of them. That was difficult in a village like this.

My former English teacher Mrs Wilks got divorced from her husband, and he had a new girlfriend in two weeks. They moved in next door—it was the only affordable house for them at that time—and it started a lovely passive-aggressive war where Mrs Wilks placed trails of sugar cubes to her ex's house, put rubber snakes in the back garden, or borrowed the newspaper and then returned it with the coupons cut out. Once she even put wet cement in the boot of his car. Not sure how she did it, but she became a legend.

I made us both tea and then returned to the living room.

"Do you live alone?" Christina asked.

"I do, yes. Though I'm considering getting a bunny."

"Bunnies are cute," she said with enthusiasm. "You should do that. You can teach them tricks you know, just like with dogs."

"You can?" I asked.

"Yes, you should look it up. It's very cute." She shifted in her seat and took a gentle sip of the tea.

"So you officially moved in with Alistair, huh?" I tried to keep the pain out of my voice, not sure if I was succeeding.

"I figured I had to give it a real shot. You know, things weren't going that well with me and Alistair. I think we were on the brink of splitting up. He had a difficult time in London. He doesn't like talking about it, and he's been pushing me away. He had to fight a murder suspect that he was about to arrest. His partner got seriously injured and nearly died."

"What?"

"Yeah, Alistair ended up shoving the suspect, and he fell through a rotten banister and died." She made a face. "It was an awful ordeal, and it bothered him a lot."

"I can imagine," I said softly. "Is his partner okay?"

"He is now, yes, but it was touch and go. "He didn't want to stay after that. I think he was fed up with the city, and he wanted to go back to somewhere more innocent. Ironic that his first case is a murder case, but that just goes to show that nowhere is safe. Still, he seems happy here. Or at least, not unhappy. And at first I was upset with him for wanting to move back here. I felt like he was running away, but you made me realise I should give it—and him—a fair chance. He's worth fighting for, even if he has been pushing me away lately. I can't remember the last time we did anything fun." The corners of her mouth turned downwards.

"I'm sure you've done the right thing," I said, but my thoughts were with Alistair. I had no idea that this was the reason he'd come home. It was probably also the reason he had kept to himself ever since he got here. He hadn't even told anyone about Christina. He was also so serious all the time. Except when we were running for Pandora. He had a nice smile. His troubles still didn't give him an excuse to treat me the way he did, but I was beginning to understand it more.

I also realised that I was that connection to a simpler time, a safer time. Perhaps his attraction to me had been because of his desire to return to something safe and innocent. After all, we'd both changed, and there was so little we knew about each other. If we did get to know each other, maybe we'd find out that we made good friends and nothing more. Maybe he'd realise how important Christina is.

"He probably associated you with his time in London, and if it ended that traumatically for him, then that could be the reason he's pushing you away. By being here you show that you care about him and that you are willing to adapt your lifestyle with him. It's actually really romantic. Give him some time to make peace with the past and see you for who you are," I said.

She blinked at me. "Wow, you're wise."

"I have my moments."

"You know, the people in this village regard you with a lot of respect, not just because you write," she said.

I sat up straighter. "Really?"

She smiled. "Yeah, it's very sweet. It's like you are all a family."

"That doesn't mean that you can't be a part of that, or Alistair. In fact, it sounds like he needs that family now more than ever."

"I think so too." She squeezed my arm. "You're very sweet."

"So are you."

She laughed. "Well, enough about my love life. Are you seeing anyone?"

"No. Well, I did have a date tonight."

"Tell me all about it."

And I did, but I did leave out the part about breaking into Patricia's home. She would tell Alistair, and he would not take it well. The parts about the kissing I definitely did not skip, and Christina was as excited about it as I was.

"But what are you going to do when he goes back home?"

"I don't know. That's the one thing we haven't discussed yet. I doubt he'll stay here, and I can't go with him because my home is here. Just the thought of leaving this village is—just no."

She shrugged. "Long distance can work if you both want it to, but yeah, at some point you'll have to live somewhere together. Anyway, try not to worry about that. He's still here, and you should focus on having fun with him."

"Good advice." Hard to follow. My mind liked to worry, especially at three AM.

"The only thing that I need to do now is find a job. I quit working as a beautician in London."

"You were a beautician? Cool."

Christina blushed. "I liked it, but I wonder what I could find here."

I bit my lip. *Don't do it. Don't do it.* "You can work at my bookshop."

You did it.

"Really? You're looking for people?"

"Susan and Eddie work for me, Brian sometimes steps in as well. But now Susan is mourning Victor, and I could use the help. You don't have to, of course."

"No," she said quickly. "I'd love that. I promise I won't let you down, boss." She giggled and then hugged me, nearly spilling my tea. "I'm so glad I met you."

I patted her on the back. "Me too."

THAT NEXT MORNING I woke up with a pain in my neck. I had fallen asleep at my desk, looking at the blueprints of the hotel and going over all the things I had uncovered in the last day. I had written all the clues on Post-its and tried to see the big picture, but at some point I'd fallen asleep. The pain in my neck was enough to make me grumpy, but in addition to that, I also felt like I was letting my friends down. I had promised to solve the murder, but so far I had only managed to commit crimes myself.

After a warm shower and a quick breakfast, I went downstairs so I could sulk in public. Hopefully Eddie and Bailey could provide distractions. Today would also be the first day that Christina started work. I still wasn't sure if I was happy with that, especially if it meant that Alistair might frequent the shop. But I needed help, and she needed a job.

I got downstairs just in time for Eddie to open up the doors. Christina had already arrived and was waiting patiently outside. Brian was at the counter and Bailey had pranced my way to greet me. I scratched him behind his ears and then approached the counter.

"Hi," Christina said warmly, and she hugged Eddie, who immediately froze.

"What's happening?"

"I'm so excited to get started. Hi, Maggie." She hugged me as well.

"Good, welcome aboard. You can put your handbag and jacket behind that curtain. That's Eddie and this is Brian. Guys, this is Christina. She really needs a job and without Susan I figured we could use her help."

She had taken off her jacket and approached Brian. "Hi, Brian. I'm so glad to be here. This is going to be fun." She hugged him as well and then disappeared behind the curtain to dump her stuff.

Brian took out his inhaler.

"What are you thinking?" Eddie hissed. "That's Alistair's girlfriend."

"I know that, but she's very nice, and she needs a job."

"What about what you need?" he asked.

"I'm fine. You're fine. Brian, are you fine?"

Brian was about to open his mouth.

"See, he's fine too."

Christina emerged from behind the curtain. "What's on the other side of that other curtain?"

"My aunt's shop. She's indisposed right now," I said. The police still hadn't called me to pick her up, and if they didn't phone soon, I'd go over there and demand that she be released. I would bring Bailey and get him to bark until they all went mad and had no choice but to let her go.

"Oh, right. Alistair told me about that." She made a face. "Sorry about that. I'm sure it will sort itself out. Alistair felt really bad about it, I could tell."

Eddie narrowed his eyes at me as he observed my reaction carefully.

"Well, then we're even," I said and tried to chuckle, but it came out as a cough.

"Hi," a familiar voice said.

"Susan." Okay, this was awkward. Just when I'd hired a replacement for Susan, she showed up.

"I'm just here to say hi. I'm definitely not ready to go back to work." She smiled weakly.

I grabbed her arm and moved over to the armchairs in the back. "Are you okay?"

"I guess. A little better than before. How are you getting on with the case? Have you found out who hurt Victor yet?"

I bit my lip. "I'm sorry, it's going a lot slower than I thought."

"Don't feel bad. It was unfair to ask you to investigate. The police are doing their best. I just want you to know that it's okay." She touched my arm. "I appreciate your efforts. You're a good friend."

"No, I promise I'm not giving—"

At that moment my phone buzzed in my pocket. I nearly jumped. It was Alistair. "Excuse me. I'll see you once you feel better. If you need anything, let me know."

"I will. Bye," she said.

I went back through the back door at the bottom of the stairs. I didn't want anyone to eavesdrop. "Hello, Maggie speaking."

"This is Alistair." His voice sounded delectable, even over the phone.

"Hello, Detective Sergeant." My tone was cold. "May I pick up my aunt yet?"

A pause. "Yes, that's why I called."

"Good, I'll be right over."

"Maggie, listen—" he started.

I hung up. It should have felt good, but it didn't. Nothing about this felt good.

THE POLICE STATION was quiet on this Tuesday morning, and I was both excited because I would see Nancy and terrified because I'd see Alistair. Terrified might be an exaggeration, but I was certainly dreading it. I had been unlucky in love so far, and I had thought that Alistair was different, probably because he was technically the first guy I was ever in love with. When I thought he might feel the same, I had hope. And then that hope got crushed like a can of coke under a steamroller.

The waiting area had posters with tips on how to prevent car thefts and break-ins. It was too late for me. Had I been silly in trying to solve an actual murder? It had only gotten me in trouble, and in my eagerness to please people I had overlooked the fact that I was probably deluding myself.

Nancy showed up as if she hadn't just spent a night in a cell. Her hair was perfectly in place, her makeup flawless. How had she arranged that?

"Are you okay?" she asked me and kissed my temple.

"I should be asking you that."

"I'm fine. They were actually very nice to me, and the tea they have here is lovely."

"You're not still upset, then?" I asked.

"I was at first, but now I'm actually okay. Alistair told me he thought it unlikely that I was the killer, but considering the circumstances, he had to ask. His boss was friends with Victor and Patricia, so I guess that explains the eagerness to have this case closed." She rolled her eyes. "There is no justice in this world."

I had no idea that the DCI was friends with the Woodsbury's. That meant that even if Patricia had killed her husband, she might get away with it. Although I wasn't sure how far Alistair's boss would go to protect her. She could probably also afford good lawyers. I felt even more dejected now.

"Alright, let's go back. I can't leave my shop closed any longer. People need me, you know?"

I wondered if she knew I had been questioned too, but decided not to mention it as long as she didn't ask. She would probably find a way to assault someone in here with a mop or something.

Alistair was nowhere to be seen as I followed Nancy outside. It was a nice and warm day, but the rays of sunshine didn't reach me. I couldn't stand the thought of the killer getting away with Victor's murder. The police clearly weren't getting close if they had their sights on me and Nancy.

"Anything I missed?" Nancy asked. "Is Bailey still alive?"

"Eddie has been spoiling him, don't worry." I paused. "I've hired Christina, a new friend, to work in the bookshop."

"Oh, really? Have I heard that name before?"

"No. She's new. She's just moved in with her boyfriend. Alistair."

She looked at me sharply. "I didn't know he had a girlfriend. Did you know?"

"Only since yesterday. Anyway, she's really nice." I managed to keep my voice steady.

"Too bad. He's handsome, smart, and he likes mysteries. You two would have been a good fit. You sure you've never liked him?"

"Nope. Not even a little bit." If she detected any hint of the truth, she'd attack him with a rake. I could trust Eleanor to keep it a secret. The first time I had tried a cigarette was in front of her. She didn't want me to do it anywhere else and was very honest about the drawbacks, even if I still wanted to try it after that. It was disgusting, and I had never picked one up again, but I knew that Eleanor would always have my back.

When we neared the street to our shops, I turned the other way, dragging Nancy along with me.

"Why are we going here?" Nancy asked. "Please tell me you didn't make a fuss. It was only one night. I've spent more time teasing my hair than I did in that bloody cell."

"Regardless, just let us do this for you." I tugged her along to the vicarage and went around the back. Eleanor and Harold's garden was luscious and green with various colourful plants. They had a small pond with fish, and on the patio they had a lovely large table around which the Castlefield Book Club had gathered, apart from Olivia, who needed to help out Stanley at the bakery. She had clearly provided a cake, though, and it sat proudly on the table, being eyed by a water-mouthing Poppy.

"There she is," Phoebe exclaimed and all the women rushed over, showering Nancy in hugs and soothing comments.

"Alright, alright. You foolish girls," she muttered. "I'm perfectly fine. It was the police who had the most bother. One stare from me, and they waited on me hand and foot." She cackled.

"We hadn't expected anything else," said Ava with a laugh.

"Now, tell me, what gossip have I missed?"

The women all moved over to the table and sat down, chattering like energetic squirrels. The most exciting topic was, of course, Alistair's girlfriend. Eleanor eyed me and then tried to steer the conversation into a different direction, but to no avail. The women were too excited and once they got excited, not even a meteorite could stop them.

It wasn't long before I couldn't take it anymore. I had given them as much information as I could about Christina and still they found new things to discuss. Eleanor's sympathetic glances only made matters worse. I pretended to get a message from Eddie about needing me at the shop and then bolted. Though I didn't exactly relish the thought of returning, I also didn't really know what else to do. I wanted to solve the murder.

And the key to solving the case, I felt, was finding out what advice Victor had needed. He'd had a secret, he had been scared, and it was all linked to his murder.

I needed to know if Mr Field had seen or heard anything when he was spying on his wife, which meant that I had to set up a meeting with him.

"I don't fancy the idea of you meeting that spy-happy bastard," Detective Black said.

"Neither do I, which is why I'll ask Nick to go with me."

"Good thinking. And you'll have me, of course."

Pandora crossed the street with fluttering wings, heading straight for a middle-aged man who started swinging his grocery bag at the chicken. I shivered at the sight of her. The man climbed on top of the bonnet of a car.

I decided to ring Mr Field while I still felt motivated. My heart beat fast as his phone rang. There was a beep, and an automated voice told me to leave a message.

"Hi, Mr Field, this is Maggie. I need to talk to you, it's important. I'll stop by at seven tonight." Then I hung up and exhaled. I sent a message to Nick to meet me at closing time. It wouldn't hurt to have dinner with him first. In fact, I was looking forward to that. Not every man would have broken into a house on a first date.

"Unless he was a bad guy," Detective Black said.

My stomach felt heavy. "Don't say that."

"Just looking out for you."

I reached The Wicked Bookworm. Christina had attracted a bunch of younger women whose faces I vaguely recognised. They were asking her for beauty tips and where she bought her clothes. Granted, she looked good, but why had these women never asked me that kind of stuff?

I looked down at my boring jeans and shirt. *That's why.*

It was true that I had let myself go a bit. Most of my time was either spent in my office or in my bookshop. I had gone to London for some promotional stuff, but that was the biggest outing I'd had in a long time. It probably wouldn't kill me to put myself out there. Much.

I stomped towards the back door.

"Hey, Maggie. Back already?" Christina called.

"I've been busy, okay? I am still in the prime of my life," I shouted and then stormed off to my flat.

"Nice," Detective Black said dryly.

"Shut up."

I spent a short while reading and figured I'd prepare my talk with Mr Field over dinner with Nick. During lunchtime I decided to make it up to Christina and made sandwiches for us both, then invited her to eat them outside on the bench near my shop. It reminded me of how excited I had been when Alistair gave me his number, but I just had to get over that.

Christina told me stories about her previous work as well as the women she had worked with. She also told me the first time she had caused a wax-related injury, which made me wince in sympathy. "What about you? It must be cool to write."

I shrugged. "It's my passion. Books contain my favourite worlds. But I realised today that I also have the tendency to hide in them, and I should probably go out more."

Christina's eyes widened. "I could totally help you with that, if you want. I can give you a colourful make-over. You're very pretty, and you should wear clothes that highlight that."

Did she just insult and compliment me at the same time?

"Great, great. I'll think about it," I grumbled.

She laughed. "This will be so much fun, we could go shopping this weekend."

That was easy for her to say, she didn't have a murder to solve. Or to write.

Tuesdays usually weren't busy, so I spent the rest of the day writing and even got in half a chapter, much to Detective Black's relief. In that time I had also received two messages from Alistair wanting to talk, but I wasn't sure how to respond. Christina told me he was going through a difficult time, but that didn't excuse his behaviour. Still, if I was going to move on, I would need that closure. I messaged back saying I'd speak to him sometime later, not wanting to give him the impression that he was a priority.

Just around closing time I went downstairs to the bookshop to find Nick already waiting. He smiled when his eyes met mine, and I had done my best to put on some nice make-up and a black dress.

"You know you don't have to enter through the shop, right?" I said and gave him a kiss on the cheek.

"Yes, but then I would miss the chance to talk with Eddie about ghosts. My ghost-hunting buddies have left already, remember?" He smiled.

Which was probably so he could stay with me. Was he planning on staying much longer? I was afraid to ask.

We walked to the pub and sat in a quiet corner, though I knew people had started talking about us as soon as we walked in. Somewhere in this village someone had already started knitting baby clothes.

We both had the lasagna, and I told him about my aunt Nancy and the book club women. They were a great bunch and if he wanted to know more about me, I had to start there. I also talked a bit about my mum, not going into the details of her mental issues. Nick didn't seem too perturbed by it, so that was a plus.

"So what exactly is the plan for tonight?" Nick asked. "Am I to be your bodyguard?" He wiggled his eyebrows.

I giggled. "Sure, but I'd have to pay you in hugs."

"I'd love that," he said.

"Anyway, the plan is to confront him." I told Nick about the pictures of his wife and Victor, and that I suspected he knew more about the murder.

Nick made a face. "That is so creepy. And we have to go talk to that guy? I'm glad you asked me to go with you."

"Me too. I don't like the idea of talking to him either, but he might be able to get us answers. So we are going to be polite but clear. And if he doesn't spill any beans, we can always threaten to go to the police and see how he reacts."

"Do you really think that's wise?"

"If it was just me, no. But you're there. And I don't actually have to threaten him. I can allude to it."

Nick sighed. "There's no talking you out of this, is there?"

"No," I said and took a final bite of my food.

Chapter 18

The hotel was quiet, and there were only a handful of people in the lounge. Most would probably be out for dinner. Nobody was at the reception desk, and I gestured at Nick to follow me. Mr Field was probably in his office, awaiting our arrival. Hopefully he wouldn't do anything rash.

I narrowed my eyes as we headed through the corridor. Was I imagining this? Smoke drifted up from under the door. It was definitely real. I froze. Nick bumped into me.

"Look," I said.

"Crap," Nick said as we both ran to the office.

I took off my cardigan and wrapped it around my hand. I tried the door handle. It was locked. "What do we do?" I said, my voice high with panic.

"I'll call 999." Nick moved away as he dialed while I kicked the door. If only I had my lock pick set with me.

"Then what?" Detective Black asked. "What difference would that make? It's clearly already too late. And you don't know if he's in there. It's possible he wants you to think that."

I shushed him, trying to think. Nick was still on the phone, so I moved back and tried to kick in the door, but all I managed to do was hurt my leg. I tried again. And again.

"Stop, stop, stop." Nick grabbed me and pulled me back.

The smoke was getting thicker, and I started coughing.

"The police and fire department are on their way, come on." Nick pulled me away, and just then the fire alarm went off.

The fire department and police showed up quickly; even Alistair was there. We had been escorted outside and waited while they tried to put out the fire. Undoubtedly, Alistair would come and talk to us, knowing it was probably related to the murder of Victor, and my nosing around.

"Are you okay?" Nick rubbed my back. He had put his jacket over my shoulders at some point, I hadn't even noticed until now.

"Yeah, I just hope nobody got hurt," I said in a soft voice.

"Me too."

People had come to see what was going on, and Eddie found us in the crowd. "What happened?" he asked.

"There's a fire that started in Mr Field's office," I said, my eyes on the building.

"When will this nightmare stop?" Eddie muttered. "Come on, let's go to the pub."

"They'll probably want to talk to us," I said.

"So? They know where to find you. You could both use a drink."

"He's right," Nick said. "You're shivering."

Can you blame me? "Okay, one drink won't hurt."

The Rose was quiet since most people had gone over to the hill to speculate about what had happened at the Pembroke. They would probably blame the curse, and maybe they were right. Maybe the place was cursed to attract nothing but trouble. It was a shame since it was such a beautiful building.

Callum showed up at our table. "What is all the fuss about? Nobody can tell me anything."

Nick filled him in so that I didn't have to.

"Blimey," he said. "A fire? What is going on with people?"

"It could have been an accident," I said, not believing that for a second.

"That's too much of a coincidence," Callum said. "I'm surprised to hear you say that. Aren't you trying to solve this?"

"Okay, Callum. That's enough." Eddie glared at him.

"Fine, fine. I get the message," Callum said as he returned to the bar.

Nick ordered us drinks as Eddie distracted us by talking about a new shooter game he was playing with Brian. I was only half-listening and kept an eye on the door.

After what seemed like an eternity, it opened and Alistair walked in. He strode over, his professional attitude dripping off him.

Eddie yawned. It was almost nine o'clock.

Alistair sat down next to Nick and opposite Eddie. He didn't take out his notebook. "So," he started. "Any reason why you two were at the Pembroke tonight?"

"Is Mr Field okay?" I asked.

He stared at me. There was something like sympathy in his dark eyes. "No. He's dead."

My heart raced. "Was it an accident?"

"We don't know yet," Alistair said. "Now, what were you two doing there?" He was addressing us both, but only looked at me.

Nick looked at me. I knew that if I lied right now, he would cover for me. "We had an appointment with Mr Field. I rang him earlier, and told him I was coming over. He didn't pick up, so technically he didn't confirm the meeting."

"And why did you want to meet him?"

"Talk about books?" I said in a high voice.

"Maggie," Alistair said calmly, to my surprise. "I didn't bring DC Daniels, and I don't have my notebook out. Right now I'm just a friend. Tell me why you wanted to meet him."

"When I stayed the night at the hotel I uncovered a few things," I said.

"Like?" he asked.

All three of them were staring at me, and I shifted in my seat. I told them about the pictures and the fact that Mr Field had been spying on his wife and Victor.

"You climbed out of the window?" Eddie asked.

"Yeah, well, the point is, anyone else could have climbed out of that window as well. If the fire originated in his office, they could have left that way. Unseen," I said to Alistair.

"The fact that he was killed also implies that he did know something. Maybe someone overheard the message you left him, or he told someone," he said.

"Either way, the first person you need to talk to is Mrs Field. She needs to be notified, of course, but it's also a good opportunity to ask her some questions. She seemed a bit off."

"I'll keep that in mind," he said. "We have reason to believe that Mr Field blackmailed Victor."

"What? Really?" Eddie said. "It's always the quiet ones."

"He probably wanted him to stop seeing his wife. That could have been what Victor wanted advice for," I said.

"Exactly. And that could mean that Mr Field killed Victor when he realised he wasn't going to listen and instead asked for help. It could mean that the fire was an accident and the case is now closed, but honestly, I'm not sure. I am, however, glad you are both okay."

"Me too," Nick said.

"Does this mean I can go home now?" I asked.

"If you don't mind," Alistair asked Nick. "Can I walk her home? I'd like to discuss some things with her."

Nick and Alistair looked at each other for a moment, then Nick turned to me and raised his eyebrows.

"Sure," I said.

"Okay, then. I'll see you soon." Nick leaned over the table and gave me a kiss on the lips, warming my cheeks. I was too shy to look over at Alistair.

"Bye," Eddie said and gave me a hug.

Alistair got up to pull back my chair, and we left the pub just in time for the crowd that had been staring at the hotel to come in. They'd be gossiping all night.

It was darker now and Alistair put a hand on my lower back as he escorted me back to my flat. I didn't mind. In fact, I kind of liked the comfort it brought. There was no point in hanging on to any anger, even if I did have to decide what I wanted from him. Did I want to be friends? To be ignored? What was my plan?

The idea of not talking to him made me uneasy. I liked him too much, even after what he did.

"I'm sorry about my behaviour," Alistair said. "I hope one day you can forgive me, though if you can't, I don't blame you."

"I just need some time." We stopped at the back of my shop. "Why didn't you just tell me?"

He ran a hand through his hair. "I guess I was just surprised by what you made me feel, and I wanted to keep that feeling. It was selfish and cowardly. Obviously I have some figuring out to do."

I was too afraid to ask him if he really liked me or just the idea of me, so instead I smiled at him. "I also think you should talk to Patricia."

"What? Why?"

"I found the mushrooms in her shed. Also, Beth said something that made me think she'd overheard something, and I know Patricia visited her on Sundays for a while."

"Beth? Beth is still alive?"

"Yes," I said.

"How old is she?"

"Hundred-and-two and kicking."

"Wow, impressive. But let's circle back to the mushrooms in the shed. You broke in?"

"No, it was open. Before that I broke into her house, though."

Alistair's eyes widened.

"I found a DVD that was used to make it appear as if the hotel was haunted. I know it's circumstantial, but I figured I might as well mention everything now." *And let's hope he doesn't arrest me.*

"He won't," Detective Black said.

Alistair sighed. "That was dangerous."

"Nick was on the lookout."

"So Nick is your partner in crime now?" he asked.

"Problem with that?" I folded my arms and stared him down.

His shoulders tensed. "I appreciate you telling me, but you have to be careful with these things. If someone reported you, you could have been arrested. You do realise I have to do what my boss says, right?"

"Your boss who used to be buddies with Victor and who is still chummy with Patricia, you mean?"

Alistair bit his bottom lip. "I know, that bothers me too. But even if he wasn't friends with her, we still need evidence. We're the police, that's how it works. We can't just go around accusing people and hope for the best."

"I realise that, so perhaps we can work together. I just gave you a tip about Patricia's shed, maybe you can check it out?"

Alistair stared at me. "Perhaps. Just don't do things on your own. Or with Nick."

I smiled. "But he's such a good kisser."

He made a face as if he smelt something foul, then adapted a more neutral expression. "I'm going to go now." His heels clicked on the cobbled street as he moved farther away from me.

As much as I didn't want it to be true, he still did something to me.

"Perhaps the Pembroke isn't cursed," Detective Black said. "Maybe your love life is."

THAT NIGHT WAS THE first night I slept well. Knowing that Alistair was listening to me made me feel like I could breathe a bit. He was on it, and I could enjoy the feeling that I had helped. I didn't have to do everything alone, nor did I have to prove myself to anyone.

I spent the morning writing and doing some household chores. With my attention on the murder I had neglected my flat a bit, and the dust bunnies were almost becoming actual bunnies, with a similar reproduction rate.

Before lunchtime I went downstairs and chatted with Nancy briefly before returning to my shop. Christina was working hard and had been looking up information on a few new books, doing her best to pitch them to customers, so they'd buy them. I appreciated her proactive attitude and wondered what I would do when Susan returned. If she returned. It was entirely possible that she didn't want to stay here anymore. She had moved to this village only three years ago, and I could imagine that she would want a fresh start.

Christina clearly wanted to be my friend regardless, and I decided that would be good. It would help me get over Alistair, and I wanted to be friends with him.

"Good luck with that," Detective Black said.

"Hello, pretty lady," Nick said as he came in with a bouquet of wildflowers.

I beamed at him. "That's so sweet. Thank you."

"Do you want to have lunch?"

"I would love to. Why don't we go upstairs, and I'll make us a sandwich." I headed through the back and up the stairs to my flat while Nick followed.

"Are you feeling better? The fire was quite a shock, wasn't it?" he asked.

"Yeah, I just didn't see it coming. I also feel a bit guilty," I said as we went into the kitchen where I put the flowers in a vase.

"Why? You weren't responsible for this." He frowned.

"I can't help but think that our visit was the reason for the fire, even if it might as well just be an accident." I really hoped that was true. It would be so much simpler if it was.

Nick touched my cheek. "Don't think like that. You are not responsible for other people's actions."

I smiled. "What kind of sandwich would you like?"

"Anything you can make is fine."

"So a sandwich with soap and carrots?"

Nick chuckled.

"Or a sandwich with Post-its?"

Nick grabbed me and nuzzled my neck. "You think you're funny, huh?"

I laughed and started tickling him. I could get used to this, which is also why I was scared. In the past there had always been something that went wrong, and I didn't want that to be true now. The worst thing I could think of was that he was in cahoots with the killer, or that he had a family back home. My mind always assumed the other shoe would drop, and it took me considerable effort to keep those dark thoughts away.

"Okay, you win," Nick said and held up his hands in defeat. "You are an excellent tickler."

"And don't you forget it."

We had our lunch on the sofa instead of at the breakfast table, and the more time I spent with Nick, the more I realised I didn't want him to go back home. He made me laugh, and he was a good kisser. It also didn't hurt that he was handsome.

After our lunch I showed Nick the blueprints of the hotel and told him in more detail what had happened that night I broke into Mr Field's office. I left out the parts with Alistair in it. Even if the two deaths were in Alistair's hands for now, I still wanted to share this particular puzzle with him. It was fascinating, though creepy.

"See, this indicates that you have to twist the wooden markings on the side of the fireplace and it will open one of the rooms." I refused to call it a death trap, which is what it really was, but I didn't want to spoil the mood.

"You're discussing the layout of a murder house," Detective Black said, rolling his eyes. "Why can't you just make out with him like a normal person?"

I ignored him and showed Nick a few more examples of what I had uncovered.

"Wow, this is so interesting. Knowing the history of that place, I'm surprised there aren't any ghosts."

"Not that many people died there, actually, and my aunt is good at cleansing places. She probably scared the ghosts away," I said with a chuckle.

"Yes, I have heard that she can be quite intimidating."

"Definitely, but she's a softy on the inside. I think."

Nick laughed and pulled me close. "I'm glad you had someone like her looking after you."

This time I kissed him, and I didn't stop for a long time.

Chapter 19

I visited Beth the next morning with a spring in my step and a smile on my face. When I entered her living room, she was in a good mood herself and was even dusting the shelves with porcelain figurines of kittens.

"Hi, Mags," she said in a chipper voice.

How I loved those moments when she was herself. She had always been a lovely woman, and it was difficult to watch her confuse reality the way she did.

She kissed my cheek and then went into the kitchen to make me some tea. "How are you?"

"I'm fine," I said as I followed her. "I've been dating someone."

"You have? Who?"

"Nick. He's one of the ghost hunters that came to check out the hotel," I said.

"Ghost hunters, right. I've heard about that from Eleanor. It wouldn't be my kind of job, but it's good that nobody wants the same thing. That would be boring and pointless." She grabbed my arm. "And poor Mr Field."

"Yes," I said. "I know."

"Mrs Field must be terribly upset. She's probably not coming back to the village, and after she tried so hard to fit in."

"How so?"

"She came here a few Sundays along with Patricia and her friends. We played bridge."

My eyes widened. "You did?"

"Oh, yes. They were complaining about their husbands and making awful jokes."

"What kind of jokes?"

"Patricia made a joke about poisoning her husband. Terrible timing. She must regret those words more than anything." Beth continued making the tea and then handed me my mug.

"Now, tell me all about Nick, dear."

WHEN I ENTERED THROUGH the shop, Christina approached me. "There were two women here looking for your advice. They were very upset about something, and they nearly fought each other. I was very wrong about village life. It's not boring at all."

"Did you get their names?"

"Yeah, Phoebe and Jessica. They are apparently part of the book club."

"They're also neighbours, so I'm guessing they took this fight to their front garden. They love each other, but somehow they also end up fighting over things they both want. Thanks for letting me know. You're doing really well."

She lit up like a bonfire on a dark night. "Thanks, Mags."

We were at the nickname phase already.

"Before you know it you'll be besties, and Alistair and Christina will name their baby after you." Detective Black walked next to me.

I grunted.

Ten minutes later I was staring at the thatched cottages belonging to Phoebe and Jessica. They were both in their late forties and both single. Jessica had never married, and Phoebe had lost her husband a few years back. They were both opposites on the outside and quite alike on the inside. Jessica was short and wide and Phoebe long and thin. They were excitable, sweet women, but they were also stubborn and liked to get their own way. For example, they had both protested with self-made signs when the supermarket stopped selling their favourite brand of chocolate.

"I'm going on a date with him," Phoebe shouted over the neatly trimmed hedge. "Why would he want you?"

"Why would he go on a date with me if he didn't want me, you trollop?" Jessica shouted back.

Phoebe produced a toilet roll, seemingly out of nowhere, and threw it at Jessica.

"How dare you?" Jessica picked up a spade, and this was my cue.

"Ladies," I said, doing my best to imitate Eleanor when she was disappointed. A disappointed Eleanor was always worse than an angry Eleanor. "Why are you behaving like petulant children?"

The ladies stared at me and then erupted in a stream of verbal narration that ended up in a shouting match. I had caught enough to know that this was to do with a man they both met on an online dating website. "Wait, wait," I said, and they stopped. "This guy has a date with both of you?"

This again turned into a shouting match.

"Silence!" I held up my hand. "One person at a time. Phoebe."

Phoebe shot Jessica a smug look. "His name is Philippe, and we hit it off online. We've been texting back and forth and finally decided to go on a date. I told Jessica here, and she said she's also going on a date with a Philippe. When she showed me his picture, it turned out to be the same guy. It's not right, and I talked to him first." She stomped her foot for emphasis, crushing a daisy.

"Is this true, Jessica?"

She nodded. "But he likes me a lot. He asked me out very quickly, and I think that means we have a special connection. Phoebe should cancel her date."

"No, Jessica should."

"Do you both like him that much, even when he's agreed to dates with both of you?"

"Yes," they said simultaneously.

If he did end up with one of them, it would be bad. It would mean war. The moment he chose one of them over the other, there would be no recovery. Best would be if they both cancelled their dates, but they were stubborn, and it would mean admitting defeat. They were not likely to do that. Ever.

"Can I see a picture of this Philippe?" I said and held out my hand.

Phoebe was quicker, and she handed me her phone. I looked at the screen. The man was handsome and had a good set of hair and fake teeth. He seemed to love himself more than he ever would any woman. I gasped. "Hey, I know this guy."

"Really?" Phoebe asked and both women inched closer.

"Yeah. He used to date Nelly," I said, deciding that mentioning a name of someone who had moved away years ago was safer than someone they could actually confirm the story with. "He gave her and the other women he dated a nasty STD. I can't remember which one. Syphilis? Gonorrhea? Anyway, it didn't look pretty." I paused and stared at them. "He's got nice teeth, though."

They looked at each other and then back at me. Phoebe snatched her phone back.

"You know what? Being the generous woman that I am," Jessica said, "why don't you go on a date with him?"

"No. I'm the generous one, you go on a date with him."

"Ladies," I growled, before more toilet paper would be thrown, "you are both generous. Now go back inside and find someone else to date. Preferably not the same guy."

They nodded their heads at this.

"Phoebe. Clean up that toilet paper before you go. Jessica, go inside."

The women did as they were told.

Once Phoebe had gone back inside, I left. It was ridiculous to fight over the same man. This was also a good reminder that I should forget about Alistair. I stopped walking. Susan had reacted very angry when she thought I had an affair with Victor, even though he was already married. How would Mrs Fields have reacted? What if her husband was spying on him, and realised he was having an affair with Susan? What if he told her in order to win her back?

I took out my phone and texted this to Alistair. Instead of mulling things over obsessively, it was better to leave the info with Alistair so he could actually do something with it.

I was done trying to impress anyone. I just wanted the truth to come out.

I WAS SIPPING MY CUP of tea, forcing Detective Black to enter an abandoned church where the killer was waiting, when my phone rang. This afternoon had been productive, so I didn't like the intrusion and contemplated not answering. But it was possible that it was important. I finished typing my sentence and checked the screen. It was Mrs Field.

My throat felt dry. What could she possibly want? There was only one way to find out.

"Maggie here," I said.

"Do you know the street behind the vicarage with the red phone booth?" she whispered.

I paused. "Yes."

"Meet me there right now, and I'll tell you about the real killer."

"Oh, no. When that happens in a novel someone always dies. Tell me who it is now and then elaborate when I get there. Or better yet, go inside the vicarage and stay with Eleanor."

Pause.

"Hello?" She had hung up. "Damn it."

"People are so foolish," Detective Black said.

"I know." I kicked back my chair and rushed downstairs.

Christina was near the back door, restocking a few books. "Hey, Ma—"

"Street behind vicarage. Mrs Field. Alistair," I said to her and then ran out of the bookstore. People stared at me as I passed them, and I couldn't blame them. They hadn't seen me run since I was fourteen.

I was out of breath three times and had to stop before going on. At some point Pandora ran past me, and I swear she was chuckling. When I arrived at the street behind the vicarage, I was sweating and panting. A blue Fiat was parked in the street. With trepidation I approached the car. Instead of slowing down, my heartbeat only increased, and I prayed that all would be well. This wasn't a novel, so of course she would be fine. My imagination was just messing with me. She'd be in her car waiting, and within a few minutes I would know who the killer was.

I reached her car and tapped on her window. She was slumped forward. "Okay, not a good sign," I said with a quiver in my voice. "Maybe she's taking a nap."

"Sure, and guns are just elaborate firecrackers," Detective Black said.

Pandora screeched behind me, and I yelled out in surprise. "Evil," I said and made a cross at her with my fingers.

She screeched again, but remained where she was.

Just then Alistair turned the corner in a run. He didn't have a hair out of place. *Naturally.*

"What's going on?" he said.

"Mrs Field messaged me to meet her here and—" my voice trailed off, and I stepped aside. "She is slumped forward. I knocked, but she didn't respond."

"Okay, stand back." He peered through the window. "Her scarf looks very tight around her neck," he said.

I let out a whimper.

He opened the door and checked her pulse. "She's gone. I'll make the call."

"Are you sure we can't help her? Maybe it's not too late."

"It is, I'm sorry." He moved towards me and gave me a hug.

Eleanor showed up when the police rushed through the street with blaring sirens. She took me inside her home so I could calm down and Alistair could do his work. Harold had gone over to the crime scene to pray for Mrs Field.

I was mostly shaky and frustrated. She must have been killed right after she rang me. Had the killer been with her? Was it a set up for her, disguised as a set-up for me? Had she seen it coming? Had she suffered? I groaned and stared into my tea cup.

"I can't believe three people are dead within a week," Eleanor said. "This is supposed to be a quiet, peaceful village."

"Pandora is supposed to be the only homicidal maniac," I said, mustering a weak smile.

Eleanor squeezed my hand, then frowned. "But if she let the killer in her car, then it means she knew the killer."

"She was trying to be close to Patricia. She was there during one of the bridge nights. Patricia had joked about poisoning Victor."

Eleanor shook her head. "She's said distasteful things like that before, but do you really think she'd actually do something like that?"

"I know that you can't judge a book by its cover."

"Right."

A short while later Alistair showed up, followed by DC Daniels. Alistair sat down while his partner remained standing.

"How are you feeling?" he asked.

"Okay, I guess."

"Listen, I phoned my boss," Alistair said, the expression on his face pained, "and he wants me to take you in. He says he's not too happy with your name popping up every time, and he wants to scare you by taking you in. I'm telling you so that you know there's nothing to be worried about. We have nothing on you, because you did nothing. I've already called an old friend of mine who will be at the station shortly. He owes me a favour. You just have to do what he says, and you'll be out of there in no time."

Eleanor, usually composed and calm, slammed her cup on the table. "This is absurd. Maggie's been putting herself at risk trying to find the killer. I mean, that could have easily been her in that car, and you want to bring her in to scare her. She's already scared enough, I reckon." She had put on her stern voice.

Alistair looked at his hands. "I know it is absurd, but he's my boss, and if I don't do it, he'll just think it's suspicious. I don't want Maggie to have any more problems. This is the only way. Besides, my boss knows she's the local sleuth, he's heard the stories. Deep down I'm sure he knows she's not involved."

"But what if he thinks it's an easy solution? To arrest me, I mean," I said.

"I won't let that happen," Alistair said.

"Don't make promises you can't keep," Eleanor muttered. Then she turned to me. "Do you want me to come along to the police station?"

I shook my head. "No, if Alistair has arranged for someone to help me, then it will be fine."

"You better bring her back in one piece," Eleanor said to Alistair. "Or I'll send a certain chicken your way."

The corners of Alistair's mouth quivered, but he maintained his composure. "Understood."

The drive to the police station was a silent one. DC Daniels was in the front, and I was in the back. Occasionally I exchanged a look with Alistair through the rearview mirror. I wondered what Alistair was thinking. He really should be interviewing Patricia and scaring her. Perhaps he had already spoken to her. She didn't seem like the type to let the police snow her under. Once I was out again, I had to do something. I was done being careful.

Alistair got me a hot chocolate, and with his hand on my lower back, he escorted me into the same interrogation room I'd been in earlier. Soon it would become my second home. If they'd give me my laptop, maybe I'd get some work done.

Again I had to wait for a while before someone came in. This time it was a man I didn't recognise. He was dressed in a sharp suit with light-blond hair, and he had a dazzling smile. He looked like he could convince a vampire to sunbathe, if they existed.

"I'm Miles Mortimer, and I'll be representing you today." I held out my hand as he sat down next to me. "Alistair didn't tell me you'd be so lovely." He kissed the back of my hand.

I instinctively touched my hair, but realised how stupid that was and yanked my hand back. "If you could make sure that I don't get charged with murder today, that would be great." *I have a murderer to catch.*

Chapter 20

Even if the interview was supposed to scare me, I was nothing more than annoyed. They were supposed to be grilling Patricia, not me. Alistair kept asking questions that made me seem like some cheating, scheming murderer who liked to be the centre of attention. I figured his boss was watching through the two-way mirror. Miles Mortimer was not phased, though. Every time I opened my mouth to defend myself, he answered for me. And all of those answers weren't really answers at all. He kept telling them they had no evidence, and that I was not obligated to answer.

I loved it. Perhaps I could arrange to have a lawyer at my side every day.

"Any other questions?" Miles said in a syrupy voice.

"No, that was all." Alistair closed the file and pretended to be annoyed.

Finally the charade was over, so I could confront Patricia.

Miles held back my chair and then walked me out of the interrogation room. "That went swimmingly, don't you think?" he said with a self-satisfied smile on his face.

"Sure, you did great. Can you give me a ride?" I asked. The sooner I could be at Patricia's, the better.

"I'd be delighted. Follow me." He headed over to an expensive-looking BMW. Then again, don't they all look expensive?

"Hop in," he said. "It has seat warmers."

"How impressive," I said with the dryness of the Sahara desert.

Miles chuckled. "You're not like other women, are you?"

"I'm a writer. I'm weird. Now step to it." I got in.

"What's the rush?" he asked as he took place behind the steering wheel and started the engine.

"The rush is that someone who contacted me was murdered, and I think I know who the killer is. So if you could drop me off at her house that would be great."

Miles paused. "And then what are you planning to do, dear girl?" he asked, even though he was just a few years older than me.

"I don't know. Hit her with a plant. Hoover her hair until her wig comes off."

"Miss Matthews," he started.

"Okay, she probably doesn't have a wig, but still. And call me Maggie; we're about the same age."

"Maggie," he said and his eyes twinkled as he leaned in. "Please don't assault people you suspect of murder. If everybody did that, the ER would be busier than it already is. Now, I'm going to drop you off at your bookshop. Alistair said that The Wicked Bookworm belongs to you."

"How do you know Alistair? Are you from here?"

"We used to be childhood friends. When I turned ten, we moved away, but we always kept in touch. I am now contemplating moving here, actually. But we will see how it goes."

"He said you owed him a favour."

"Not anymore." He grinned, and I sensed that was all I was going to find out about it. For now.

When we arrived at the bookshop, Miles gave me one last warning. "There is no point. It will just get you into trouble. Let the police do their work." With a fluid gesture he produced a business card from his breast pocket and handed it to me. "In case you ever need anything. Or *want* anything."

I pretended to gag, and he laughed.

"I'll see you around, Maggie."

"See you." I got out of the car and bent down. "And thank you."

He nodded, and after I slammed the door shut, he drove off in his shiny car.

Christina showed up next to me. "Who was that?"

"Some lawyer Alistair knows."

"How did it go? Eleanor showed up and told us what happened. Someone died again?"

I sighed. "Mrs Field this time, yeah."

Christina patted my back. "Nick's inside. I'm sure he can cheer you up."

I smiled. "I hope so."

After I had filled in Eddie with the highlights, Nick and I went upstairs. I didn't want to repeat the story to anybody who stopped by for details.

Nick hugged me on the sofa, and he kept rubbing my arms even though I wasn't shivering. Anymore. I really didn't want to make finding bodies a new thing.

"I'm just so frustrated. I really think Patricia did it, and she's getting away with it. I want to do something and confront her, but I'm not sure if that will work, and it would be just my luck if it backfired and I got arrested." I grunted. "This killer is crazy and needs to be put behind bars."

"And you really think Patricia did it?"

"She had the poison in her shed, she cares about what things look like on the outside, she made a joke about killing him in front of Mrs Field. She couldn't bear to be a divorcee, and so she killed him. Mr Field probably knew because he was spying on Victor and his wife, and then Mrs Field was going to tell me about it and so she killed her too."

Nick inhaled. "When you put it like that—" his voice trailed off.

"But there's not enough evidence, that's the problem."

"Maybe I should talk to Alistair. There must be something we can do."

I shook my head. "I honestly doubt it. This is the real world, and things don't work like they do in stories. If it did, someone would come up right now and give us a new clue."

The door slammed downstairs and by the footsteps I could tell that it was Nancy. She reached the landing and stared at us.

We stared back, not breathing.

"Let's go to the pub," she said.

"See?" I said to Nick.

Nick sighed. "You read our minds. We could definitely use a drink."

"This entire village can use a drink. It's times like these that I wish I'd opened up a pub," Nancy said.

THE ROSE WAS PACKED and it could have been my imagination, but everyone looked up and got quiet when I walked in, even if it was just for a split second. They were probably hoping that I'd caught the killer by now, instead someone else died. They had relied on me, and I had failed them. Nancy and Eddie nudged me in the direction of the corner where there was still a table free. We sat down as chatter filled the pub, even if it wasn't as lively as always. Mrs Field hadn't been a local, people barely knew her, but it was the combination of the earlier events that had their impact. To know that someone in our village was doing these heinous things was awful.

The rest of the book club ladies started trickling in and joined us. People actually gave up their seats so we could sit near each other and communicate. This time there was no gossip, this time I told them about the case and everything I'd found, heard, and seen. I left out few details and told them I believed Patricia to be responsible. Normally they wouldn't have believed it, because Patricia is so popular, but after everything they'd heard, their postures changed. They had frowns on their faces and clenched their jaws.

"Well, that is just utterly unfair and ridiculous," Poppy said.

"Yes, you've done all this hard work and practically solved the case, and the police won't do anything to actually close it," Ava said, her Scottish accent becoming heavier as she got angry.

"We should do something." Phoebe stood up. "We should all go to her house right now and tell her we know what she's done and bring her to the police. That way she can't deny it. Not with all of us there."

"I'm not sure—" I started.

"I've always wanted to put that stuck-up cow in her place," Nancy said and also got up.

That did it. All the women rose to their feet except for Eleanor and me.

"We better go and make sure they don't do anything they'll regret," Eleanor said.

"Or to make sure that they do." They looked pretty excited to put Patricia to justice. Even Nick did.

I wasn't sure if it was a good idea, but I was desperate to get somewhere. And so the local book club, a mystery author and a ghost hunter went on a warpath.

Just a regular Tuesday evening.

"We're going to catch a killer," Poppy said with great enthusiasm to every person we encountered in the street. Which probably meant that Alistair would find out about it soon, if not Patricia as well. She could potentially be waiting with a hatchet.

We reached her house and the lights were clearly on in the front room, even if the drapes were closed. Nancy rang her doorbell, and when nothing happened, she knocked loudly.

"Are you holding a broom?" I asked incredulously.

"Yes," Nancy said.

"Where did that come from? You didn't have that with you in the pub." I would have noticed.

"I have my ways."

"Let's go around the back," Poppy said with a glint in her eyes. The door to the gate was open, and we followed her through to the back of the house, which was darker than the front.

"Maybe she's stepped out," Jessica said, clutching her bright orange scarf that made her look paler.

"Or she's on the lam," Ava said. "Okay, lassies, let's fan out. We should check the nearest bus stop and the train station."

Before I could say anything, the women dashed off, chatting about what they would do when they found her. They left me and Nick behind, and we stared at each other, then giggled.

"I bet this isn't what you expected when you came here."

Nick smiled. "I wouldn't trade any of this for the world. Although if I could have spared you from seeing dead bodies, then obviously I would have."

"Thanks." I looked down at my shoes. "When will you go home?"

He sighed. "I guess I should go back soon. I just don't want to leave you with a killer on the loose. Actually, I don't like leaving you, full stop."

I wrapped my arms around him and hugged him tight. We stood like that for a while.

He planted a kiss on my temple. "Come with me," he whispered.

"Stay," I whispered back.

He held me tighter. "I'm sorry."

"Me too." I pulled back and smiled at him.

"If you could stop batting your eyelids," Detective Black said, "you'd notice that sound."

I tilted my head and listened.

"What?" Nick asked.

"Do you hear that?"

He closed his eyes and listened as well. "Is it a banging?"

We both looked at the shed where the sound was coming from.

"There better not be any more dead bodies," I said.

"I don't think they make noises." Nick squeezed my hand. "Unless they're ghosts."

"You're the expert."

We etched closer towards the shed, still holding hands. My heart rate was increasing.

Nick placed his hand on the door handle and after a pause, he yanked the door open. It took us both a moment to adjust to the darkness, but it was clear that someone was lying on the ground.

"Susan?" I said and rushed to her side while Nick took out his phone and used it as a torch. Susan's ankles were tied with rope, and there was also rope coiled around her wrists, as well as tape on her mouth.

I carefully helped her sit up and took the tape off first.

She winced. "Ouch."

"Who did this to you? Are you okay?" I asked and was about to untie her hands when she moved them away.

"I've almost got this one, start on my ankles, please." She gave me a weak smile and then struggled with her hands. "She's a psycho."

I untied her ankles with some difficulty while Susan got the rope around her wrists undone. "Patricia? She did this to you?"

"Yeah, she pushed me and when I fell, she tied me up and put me here. I think she was going to bury me."

Nick swore under his breath. "At least we can go to the police now and end this madness."

I helped Susan to her feet, and we stepped out into the fresh air.

"What are you doing on my property?" a familiar voice asked.

Susan shrieked as we turned to Patricia. If looks could kill, we'd all be dead now.

"You are done now," Nick said. "Stay where you are."

I already had my phone out and messaged Alistair.

"I have no idea what you are on about, but I want you all off my property. I've suffered enough harassment from you, young lady," she said to me.

"There she is," Poppy shouted. Poppy, Nancy and Olivia had come back. They all rushed to stand between us and Patricia as if to protect us. Not that we needed it. Patricia wasn't going to do anything that bold with all of us here.

"This is utterly insane," Patricia said. "I don't know why you think it's okay to trespass."

"Because you're a murderer," Poppy said. "You killed poor Victor."

"Please, why would I kill my own husband?"

"Because he was going to leave you for me, you already joked about killing him," Susan said.

"As if he'd ever be interested in you, child." Patricia smirked.

"He was!" Susan shouted, and I had to hold her back. That fire I had seen in her when she'd attacked me was back. I'd have never guessed that about her.

"This is ridiculous. I'm calling the police." Patricia started to move away, but just then Poppy shouted that she was making a run for it and darted after her with surprising speed.

Patricia yelped and started running as well.

We followed the pair into the street. Pandora was there as well, and spurred on by the excitement, joined the chase. Bradley Walsh would have been proud.

"I've never seen an 83-year-old woman run that fast, or Patricia that scared," Olivia said.

"Damn, Poppy is catching up with her," I said. "Let's go." We hurried after them.

Poppy closed in on Patricia and in an unflattering dive took down Patricia. As we approached them, Poppy sat on Patricia's back with a gleeful expression. We stared at the scene, unable to speak just as Alistair joined us with some ketchup still on his chin.

"What the bloody hell is going on?" he asked.

"This. Is. Spartaaa!" Poppy shouted.

Chapter 21

I purposely spent the next morning writing in my office. I had gone to bed late, as we'd returned to the pub after Poppy's heroic tackle. We told anyone who was there about it. Poppy deserved the attention; she had been very brave. Still, I couldn't shake the feeling that I had missed something, and so I distracted myself with Detective's Black murder case. I was making some serious headway now and perhaps this actual case had given me inspiration.

I had on earphones so that even Detective Black himself couldn't disturb me, but it appeared that I didn't need to worry about him. When I felt a hand on my shoulder, I nearly jumped up to the ceiling.

"Sorry," Christina said after I took the headphones off. "I didn't mean to scare you."

"No, it's okay," I said. "I like heart attacks. They're so refreshing."

She chuckled. "I was wondering, now that my morning shift is over and Susan's back, if you want to go shopping? I was thinking I could give you that makeover."

I truly wanted to look more like this adult version of myself, one that had it together and had style. "I would love that. Maybe afterwards you can help me decide which of my old clothes I should donate to charity."

Her eyes sparkled. "Yes, I'm in. I love doing stuff like that. Before moving in with Alistair I decluttered my flat, and it was amazing."

The mere mention of Alistair twisted something inside of my stomach, but I masked it with a smile. "Excellent. Let's go."

The first thing that Christina did was take me to a hair salon. After checking with me that I was okay with anything, she gave the hairdresser instructions, and she worked her magic. We had gone to a nearby town that had more clothing stores and beauty salons than Castlefield. I was pretty sure that Castlefield didn't even have a beauty salon.

The hairdresser coloured my hair brown with red highlights and cut the bob in a sharp line, instantly improving my look. After that we went to a beauty salon where we had facials and manicures. That alone already made me feel like a million pounds. But Christina wasn't done, and we went shopping for two hours after that. I was exhausted by the time we returned to The Wicked Bookworm with six shopping bags.

"Wow," Eddie said when he saw me.

Christina beamed with pride, as if I were some sort of work of art that she'd created.

"Just a little makeover," I said and put the bags behind the counter. The store was already empty, since it was almost closing time.

Susan came to the front of the store. "We're clo—oh, wow, I almost didn't recognise you," she said. She looked a lot better now than she did before, and it seemed she truly was ready to get back to work. Even though she had been locked up in a shed the day before.

"She had a makeover, apparently," Eddie said. "Not that you needed one." He addressed the latter to me.

"Thanks, but I did. I feel more like myself. Well, not yet, I need to be wearing my new colourful clothes for that. Much better than the simple shirt and jeans." I smiled.

"Anyway, I have to go," Christina said. "But I'd like to have a film night with you and Nick sometime. When is he leaving?"

"Oh, I'm not sure. I guess soon." We had been texting today, but we were good at avoiding the heavy topic of goodbye.

"What about tonight, then?"

"Okay," I said before I could think about it too much, which was probably a good thing.

"We'll stop by with snacks at eight." She waved and then left through the front door, after which Eddie locked up, leaving me and Susan at the counter.

"How are you?" I asked Susan.

She shrugged. "Relieved, I guess."

"You must miss Victor terribly, though."

"Yes, I do. He was my soulmate."

"And where did you guys usually meet up again?" I asked.

"It differed. Why?"

"Just curious."

Eddie returned. "Okay, now that this nasty murder business is over, we can focus on fun things again, like not getting murdered."

"Why don't you guys both go home now, I'll take care of closing up properly," I said.

"That sounds like perfection. Have fun on your double date." He squeezed my shoulder.

"Bye," Susan said.

They both left through the back, and I listened to the silence.

"Maybe," Detective Black said, "you don't want this case to be over."

"I hope it's just that." I really did want this to be over, because I had no idea how stressful it would be. Three people had already died, and I kept fearing that someone else was going to be next.

NICK CAME AROUND AT six thirty so we could have dinner at my flat first. He didn't seem to mind or care that we were having a double date in a few hours even though we weren't officially a couple. I was wearing one of my new outfits: a light blue dress with white flowers and a black, cropped cardigan with short sleeves. Nick seemed to like my make-over and kept touching my hair.

I'd also put on my new eyeshadow and lipstick. It meant I had to get up earlier in the morning, but I didn't mind. It felt like it was part of my self-care routine.

"This pasta was really good," Nick said as he finished his plate.

"Good, it's very easy to make. Just make sure you have room for dessert. It's cheesecake."

He groaned. "I love cheesecake."

"Me too." I chuckled. "Nancy doesn't like it too much, she's more a fan of cherry pies and that kind of thing. She taught me how to bake."

"I know how to bake muffins, but not much else."

"Maybe I can tea—" my voice trailed off.

He narrowed his eyes at me. "Right."

"Right."

"I've thought about this a lot," he said.

"Me too."

"But I can't see any way around this. I have to go home, and you have to stay here."

"Yep."

"Even in the future I can't see myself moving here."

"And I can't see myself moving to Wales," I said.

"Which means that we just have to enjoy the time we have left."

"And how long is that?"

"I'll probably leave tomorrow," he said.

I gasped. "That soon?"

"Sorry."

I shook my head. "It's okay. You have a life to get back to. Really, it's okay. I'm just happy we already have such nice memories."

He leaned forward over the table and kissed me. We came up for air long enough to have dessert, and then we moved to the sofa where we continued to make out until it was time to prepare for Alistair and Christina's visit. I cleaned the kitchen while Nick lit a few candles and set up Netflix. We would just find something on there. The point of this was to have fun; I wanted to be friends with Alistair and Christina.

But the closer it got to eight o'clock, the more nervous I became.

"Perhaps despite telling yourself otherwise, you do still have feelings for Alistair," Detective Black said, appearing in the kitchen.

I said nothing. Why did I even like him so much? Was it the idea of Alistair? Because I used to have a crush on him? Or because I felt like he had saved me from a bad day when I was a teenager?

The doorbell rang and my stomach twisted. It was too late to change my mind.

"I'll get it," I said to Nick and ran down the stairs to open the door.

Alistair was dressed more casually this time in a long-sleeved shirt and jeans. It looked odd on him, since it wasn't what I was used to, but I liked it. I could only hope that he'd be less serious now that he was among friends. He was holding a bottle of wine.

Christina immediately fawned over my outfit even though she herself looked gorgeous as ever in a blouse with roses and red trousers. She had a bag with what I guessed were the snacks.

Alistair stared at me for a moment.

"Do you like her new look?" Christina asked.

He glanced at her and directed his attention back to me. "Yes, but her previous look was good too."

"Isn't he a sweetheart?" she said to me and hugged me.

"Go on up," I said.

Alistair came in, and we stared at each other. "You do look nice," he said.

"Thanks." My cheeks got warm.

"I'm glad we're friends." Then he gave me a kiss on the cheek, but his eyes lingered on my lips.

I cleared my throat. "Yes, me too. Go on up, I'll follow you."

"Right." He smiled at me, instantly looking even more handsome.

I would have to get used to that smile of his.

I followed him up up the stairs to my flat where Nick and Christina were setting up the coffee table with popcorn, crisps, and M&Ms. I took the wine from Alistair. "I'll pour us some."

"I'll help," he said.

I could feel his eyes on me as I led the way to the kitchen. *What was I thinking? I'm clearly not ready to be friends with him.*

I put down the bottle and grabbed four glasses. The least I could do was try the wine. It wouldn't kill me. Probably.

"So you and Nick are an item?" Alistair asked as he leaned against the counter.

"He is going home tomorrow. We're just making the best of our last day together," I said.

"And you're spending it with us?" His posture gave off an air of insouciance, but his eyes twinkled with curiosity.

"It was Christina's idea. Besides, I like Christina."

"But not me?"

"I didn't say that. But yes, you're awful. Ugh." I made a face as if I tasted something disgusting.

Alistair laughed.

I poured us all some wine and handed him two glasses while I took the other two. "Has Patricia confessed yet?"

"No. She's got a lawyer, and she'll be out on bail right about now."

"What?" I nearly dropped the glasses.

"That's the way it works sometimes. Unfortunately. At least Poppy got an exciting story out of it, diving on top of Patricia like that." He shook his head. "I'm sorry I missed it."

"Do you think she really did it?"

"Poppy? I should think so, she was sitting right on top of Patricia."

"No, I mean Patricia."

"She dove on top of herself?"

I glared at him, and he laughed again.

"I'm sorry," he said. "But yes, of course she did. We're questioning her friends as well. It's possible she used their help. They all have marriage troubles. I'm sure we'll get some answers soon. Not all of them can afford a good lawyer. But why are you having doubts? I thought you were convinced it was her."

Her friends, huh? That hadn't occurred to me. Patricia did make that joke about killing Victor in front of them. But would they cover for her now that the police was onto Patricia?

"Are you two coming?" Christina shouted. "We're getting thirsty."

"Let's just have some fun and forget about murder and mayhem," I said.

"Good idea."

We returned to the living room and handed out the drinks. I sat in the middle of the sofa with Nick on my left side and Alistair on the right while Christina sat in the armchair. "Have we decided on a film?" I asked.

"Here's one about Keanu Reeves as a hitman. It's supposed to be good."

We all agreed that was a fine enough choice and settled in to watch the film. There were a few exciting moments in the film where Alistair touched my hand. I wasn't sure if it was to reassure me, or if he was even aware that he was doing it, but I didn't move away. It wasn't as if he was holding it.

"I'm judging you," Detective Black said.

I'm judging me.

By the end of the film we'd eaten most of the snacks, and afterwards I put on the radio as background noise. Nick told Christina and Alistair some more about ghost hunting, and I admired Alistair's restraint in showing any scepticism. Somewhere deep inside of him, he was probably rolling his eyes. He was someone who liked to be in control, so I imagined anything inexplicable was something he didn't much care for. Christina, however, was riveted.

Alistair leaned towards me. "Can you show me where the magic happens?"

I blinked at him. "You're the one who does magic tricks."

He smiled. "I mean your office. I want to see where you write your novels."

"Okay, but it's not really special." I got up and went into the first door in the corridor. There was a desk with scattered notebooks on top, pens and Post-its, and my laptop. I had four bookcases and an armchair in the corner with the covers of all my books in poster size above it. On the other wall I had a white board with some notes about the actual murders here in Castlefield. I'd also stuck the blueprints of the hotel on the wall with tape.

"Wow. This is more like an investigation room," Alistair said as he studied it.

"Yeah. I may have gotten a little carried away." I rubbed my arm.

"Not at all. I mean, it shows that you care." He paused. "I think that Victor knew that he was being spied on, even if he didn't know it was Mr Field. It's possible he thought his wife hired someone. I believe that's what he wanted advice for. Nancy is respected and people turn to her for help, and you are also respected, people know you're smart. He wanted to find out who was watching him, but he was too late. Maybe Patricia realised he was going to ask for help, or it was just bad luck and she was planning on it anyway." He turned around to me.

"Either way, you did well," he said.

I felt a little teary-eyed, even though I didn't know why. "Thanks."

"Just promise me you'll stick to fictional cases from now on. Just to be on the safe side. Literally."

"I think I'd prefer that, actually. Solving a real case is nothing like I would have thought. It's very difficult."

"Welcome to my world." He grinned.

I looked down at my hands. "Christina mentioned something about London. About your partner."

His whole body tensed. "She shouldn't have done that."

"She meant well."

"I'm sure she did, but it's—it's nothing. I'm fine." He refused to make eye contact.

"You don't have to talk about it if you don't want to, but there are people who are skilled at making you see things you can't see for yourself. Or who can put things in perspective. If you want, I can get you some names of those people and email them, and you can see which one appeals to you. When you're ready."

He looked at me. "You don't have to fix or solve everything."

"There's nothing to fix, you're not broken. We all need a little help sometimes, that's all."

Alistair touched my hair gently. "You look very beautiful. Then again, you always have."

"Don't turn to mush," Detective Black said.

I swallowed. Why was he telling me this?

Before he could say more, I moved to the door. "Come on, let's get back out there."

Alistair looked disappointed but followed me out.

"Hey, there you are. Do you guys wanna play a game?" Christina asked. "What about Twister?"

The possibility of having my limbs entangling with Alistair's, having to move over him or be pressed up aga—

"No," Alistair and I said simultaneously.

Chapter 22

After a few innocent rounds of Texas Hold 'Em, we called it a night. Nick and I both walked Alistair and Christina downstairs and exchanged hugs, though the men shook hands.

"That was fun," Christina said. "We should do that again sometime." Then her face fell. "I mean, sorry."

Nick smiled. "No worries, but it was fun meeting you."

"And you. Bye." After another apologetic look, she waved and left with Alistair.

I wasn't sure what I was feeling as we watched them go.

Nick touched my back. "That was fun."

"Yeah," I said and yawned.

He chuckled. "I'll help you tidy."

"No, that's okay. I want to go to bed soon. If you want, you could come over for breakfast tomorrow. Would you like that?"

"Of course." He kissed me.

"Good. Here," I said and took an extra key out of the flowerpot outside my door. I wiped off the rest of the dirt.

"Wow. I've never seen anyone hide their key *inside* a flower pot."

"What can I say? I think outside the pot. Wait..."

He laughed and kissed me again. "I had fun. I'll see you tomorrow then."

"Bye." I also wasn't sure what I was feeling as I watched him go. Why did I have to have such bad luck? I finally found someone nice, and he wouldn't stay. Then again, I did have the whole Alistair thing going on inside my heart.

I went upstairs, cleaned up all the glasses and bowls and then took a shower. I was about to go to bed and message Nick when there was a text from a number I didn't recognise.

Meet me at the pembroke. It's about the murders

Who had sent me this? Was it a burner phone? Patricia was out on bail, but was it her? Would it be her? I ignored the small errors in punctuation and put down the phone so I could get changed into black trousers and a red blouse. I brought a voice recorder, a pocket knife and some deodorant that could double as pepper spray. Just as I left my flat, I phoned Alistair.

"Maggie, everything okay?" he said. His voice sounded hollow, like he was in a bathroom or something.

"I just got a text from a number I don't recognise. Someone wants me to meet them at the Pembroke. Apparently it's about the murder."

"What? Don't go. It's probably a trap. I'll go."

"I'm already on my way."

"Maggie," he warned.

"What? I've come prepared, and I'm calling you, aren't I? Just hurry up, and meet me there."

"Don't do anyth—" he started, but I hung up on him and started running. On my way I encountered Pandora, and she followed me for a bit but then lost interest when she spotted a black cat under a car.

The Pembroke looked dark and deserted. The street was quiet, and the stars were hiding behind a veil of clouds. I glanced back to see if Alistair was coming, but when I looked back at the Pembroke there was a flash of light. I dashed up the steps to the entrance.

"You should wait for Alistair," Detective Black said.

"I know, but—" There was a crash from inside. The front door was ajar. I couldn't resist and slipped inside. It was quiet. Too quiet. I took a few steps forward and used my torch to provide light. In the reception area was a broken vase and just as I walked towards it, I spotted a hidden room behind a bookcase that had been pulled open. I remembered it from the blueprints.

My heart started beating faster. What if there was another body?

"That's unlikely," Detective Black said. "But you should go outside and wait for Alistair. Now."

I was about to turn around and go back to the entrance when one of the floorboards creaked and a sharp pain spread through my head. I fell to the floor, and everything turned dark.

WHEN I CAME TO, I WAS leaning against something soft. There was a woody scent that filled my nose. I smiled, because I recognised it.

"Maggie?" Alistair asked. His voice sounded far away as if it was carried on clouds.

A dull pain spread throughout my skull, and I frowned.

"Maggie, are you okay?" Alistair's soft hand touched my cheek, but it was the pain in my head that brought me back to reality.

I blinked, staring up at his worried face, even though he tried to smile at me. He had me in his arms while I was on the cold and hard floor. It was dark, but there was a light aiming away from us. A torch?

"What—where—?" I started.

"It's okay, take your time." He still had his hand on my cheek, and he didn't budge.

I groaned. "My head hurts."

"I'm sorry," he said. "I really wish you would have waited for me."

Waited? "I can't wait. You have a girlfriend," I said, closing my eyes again as the pain came in waves.

A moment of silence. "I didn't mean that. What's the last thing you remember?"

"Film and poker," I muttered, then closed my again. I wasn't sure how much later it was when I opened them again. Where were we?

This time Alistair was stroking my hair. "Are you awake?" he asked.

"Yeah." I tried to sit up.

"Be careful."

I got up and clutched my head. "Where are we?" My torch was on the ground and shone on the opposite wall. We were surrounded by large bricks, not an opening in sight. My stomach flipped. "Oh, no."

"Yeah, I'm afraid so," Alistair said in a more casual tone than I had expected. He helped me sit up with my back against what appeared to be a door but without a handle. He made sure I could lean against him as well.

"What happened?"

"You were on the ground, and this bookcase was opened. I really thought—I mean, I thought you were dead," he said, not looking at me. "So I rushed in and someone closed the hidden door behind me. I didn't reach it in time. I'm sorry."

I grabbed his hand. "It's okay. We'll get out of here."

"I tried to make a phone call, but I don't have reception. What about your phone?"

I checked my pockets. "I don't have it. Weird."

"It must have been taken. Did you tell anyone you were coming? Oh, right. You don't remember."

"Sorry."

"Don't apologise. You were attacked. Do you think it was Patricia?" He shook his head. "She'll be sorry."

"I don't know." My head still felt foggy, and it hurt to think. "Just give me a minute to get my bearings."

"Right. Sorry for all the questions. I just—I don't want to stay here longer than necessary."

Now I could hear the panic between those words. "It will be okay. We're not going to die in here."

"How do you know?"

"I just know." I squeezed his hand. There was a pause. "My head really hurts."

"You're not bleeding, I checked. You might have a concussion, though. We'll have to go to the hospital after—I mean, if we—"

"We will get out."

"Yes."

"I suppose you already tried the door."

Alistair sighed. "Yeah, it won't budge."

I shivered. "Figured."

He leaned forward and shrugged off his jacket.

"Won't you be cold?"

"Don't worry about me." He placed his jacket over my shoulders.

"Thanks. You know, I'm sure your message will find a way to get through, and we'll be rescued."

"And even if that's true, how will they open the door?"

I swallowed. "Don't try to use your logic. It will just ruin things. Now, tell me something fun. It can be about anything."

His eyes scanned my face. "Fine. I'll share with you the reason why I was on that roof the day we went to the fair."

I looked at him. "Was it because you were going to practise your magic tricks?"

He smiled. "No. It was because I was going to ask you to be my Valentine."

"Really? Me? I didn't even know you—I mean, girls were always falling over themselves to get to you. Why would you be interested in me?"

"Are you joking? You're gorgeous, funny, smart, and you have the most beautiful smile."

I chuckled, too hurt to be shy. "Are you telling me we could have been together all those years ago?"

He shrugged. "No. You would have never left for London. Not that I should have gone. It was a mistake."

"I'm sure it wasn't. It made you who you are today."

"Exactly. I'm a mess. I haven't been treating you or Christina right. This is not who I am, I'm just—I don't know what I'm doing."

I said nothing. I could hardly argue with that. Whatever he was going through, he had to figure it out himself. "If you liked me, then why didn't you ever say or do anything during the fair? Or even after the fair?"

"Because that day was so perfect that I think I wanted to hold on to that idea of perfection. I was too afraid you would turn me down, I guess."

"Yeah, rejection hurts. I guess being hurt is part of being alive."

He inhaled. "My mother said you had a boyfriend last year, but that it didn't end well."

I put my head on his shoulder. "Yes. He wanted to get married and have babies and everything, but then he got a job opportunity that meant we had to move away, and I didn't want to leave. He chose his job over me and shattered my heart. It took some time, but I'm over it now. Still, he said all the right things, and I'm sure felt all the right things, yet he left me. It makes me a bit wary."

"Trust me, he didn't feel all the right things if he chose his job over you."

"I'd like to think so, but sometimes love isn't enough. I don't want it to be, but I think in real life that is true. Don't you?"

He narrowed his eyes at me as if he was thinking. "Maybe you're right. Maybe it's not just love, but also dedication."

"Dedication. I like that word. All the guys I've met have shown zero dedication. It would be nice to find someone who fights for me." I closed my eyes again. "What about you? What do you want?"

He said nothing for a while. "I guess I want someone I can be myself with."

"That's important. Wait, are you saying you don't feel that way with Christina?"

"I think I like the version of me that I am with her, but it's not—I'm not really that guy. Not fully. I guess I just forgot who I was when I was in London. Does that make sense?"

I touched his cheek. "It does. You're not weird. I mean, not weirder than any of us."

He leaned forward and kissed my nose. "You're pretty amazing, and you deserve someone who is equally amazing."

"Ugh. Deserve is a stupid word when it comes to love. Love is never about what you deserve. There are no rules or conditions when it comes to love. Love just is."

"And there is the writer in you." He chuckled.

"Yes, I can be pretty deep. The Grand Canyon has nothing on me."

Alistair laughed. "I'll remember that for when I need advice."

"Please do, I like giving advice."

"Don't say that, before you know it I'll be at your door all the time."

I smiled. Didn't he know I actually liked that idea?

"That's what friends are for," I said and resisted the urge to kiss him.

He put his arm around me, and I snuggled closer to him as it began to get colder. He held me tightly. "Rest for a bit," he whispered. "I'll wake you every now and then, in case you have a concussion."

"I'll be very grumpy," I said.

"That's okay. I'll just have to snuggle you to cheer you up again."

It warmed my heart to hear him talk to me like that. Like we were a couple. Why did he feel like he could do that with me and not with Christina? My limbs felt heavy, and I started drifting off again.

WE WERE JOLTED AWAKE when something behind us turned and groaned. It was the door. Alistair was on his feet faster than I was, and he pulled me up.

"Is it help or ... not?" I asked.

"It has to be help," he said. "But just in case, get behind me."

I did as he said. The noises stopped for a moment, then started again. It was as if someone was trying to figure out how the door worked. Which meant that it had to be help. I was so relieved that I almost cried.

The door creaked and then with a sudden noise, it popped open, letting in a gust of fresh air. The light of a torch shone in our eyes.

"Thank the goddess you're okay," Nancy cried out, and at the sound of her voice I moved past Alistair and rushed straight to her. I held out my arms and didn't stop until I felt the softness of her body and smelt the gentle scent of lavender.

"Are you okay?" Nick asked. I looked up and now that the torch wasn't shining in my face I saw that it was him, my aunt Nancy, and Eleanor. I hugged Nick and Eleanor next.

"Are you okay, son?" Nancy asked and pulled Alistair into a hug. "There, there. You're safe now."

He chuckled and hugged her back. "Thank you. You saved us."

"How did you save us?"

"I was walking back to my flat after the pub," she said, but in a tone that made me believe it wasn't just a visit to the pub. Was she lying?

"But why?" Detective Black asked.

"And I saw you running towards the hotel. I figured if Mags is running, something must be terribly wrong."

Alistair tried to hide a smile.

"So I followed, and then I saw Alistair go in, so I first thought, you know—" she wiggled her eyebrows, and I was glad it was too dark for anyone to see me blush, "but then I realised that Maggie is way too scared to go into that hotel if it wasn't important. So I decided to go in, and I swear there was someone here, but I didn't see or hear anything and your handbag was in front of that bookcase, as well as a broken vase, so I got a bad feeling. I called Alistair, but it went straight to voicemail and then I phoned Eleanor and Nick. Nick showed up with blueprints and we had a few tries to get it to open up. It worked." She beamed.

"Nick, you went and got the blueprints. How clever." I hugged him again.

"I'm just glad you explained them to me before this happened. I don't want to think about what would have happened otherwise."

"I would have charged through the wall, that's what would have happened," Nancy said. "Don't you worry. Nobody hurts my Maggie."

Again I was glad she didn't know how much Alistair had hurt me when I found out about Christina. But none of that seemed to matter now. Alistair had his path, I had mine. Maybe one day they would cross, or maybe they'd just run parallel to each other.

"So who did this to you? Patricia again?" Nick asked.

"You know it's not Patricia," Detective Black said.

"I'm going to kill her myself," Nancy said and was about to walk off.

"Actually," I said before she would go off on a murder rampage, "I think I know who did all of this." *And I hope I'm not wrong. Again.*

Chapter 23

I had never before been to Susan's house though I knew she lived on the outskirts of Castlefield. The cottage was small and appeared dilapidated, though that was mostly due to chipped paint and a garden that wasn't tended to at all. I rang the doorbell twice before the light was turned on, and I heard movement. It was four in the morning by now.

She opened the door in her pink pyjamas and her eyes widened, but then she composed herself. "Maggie? What are you doing here so late? Shouldn't you be sleeping?"

"Oh, she's good," Detective Black said.

"Quick, you have to come to the Pembroke," I said, proud that I managed to sound panicked. "Someone tried to kill me and Alistair."

"Really?"

"Yes, but Mr Field showed up and rescued us."

This time she took a step back. "What? How—I thought he was dead."

"Me too. Apparently the police lied because he knows who the real killer is. Alistair said that I should tell you to go to the Pembroke while I wait here."

Her eyes darted from left to right as she visibly contemplated her options. Alistair was on the lookout, and so were Nancy, Eleanor, DC Daniels, and Nick. Alistair and DC Daniels had eyes on us right now, whereas the others were either at the nearest bus stop or the train station, just in case. Since Susan was in her pyjamas, she would most likely get dressed, grab some stuff and try to run off.

But I wasn't so sure. She could have disappeared a long time ago, but instead she stayed and decided that murder was easier. She obviously had sociopathic tendencies, but there could have also been a part of her that believed she was doing the right thing. That she had been wronged and was simply protecting herself. I wanted to get to that part of her.

"You know what?" I said. "I'm kind of sick of this whole investigation. I'm not sure Victor deserves all this effort. Or Mrs Field."

She narrowed her eyes at me. Probably torn between keeping up the charade and vehemently agreeing with me.

"He was a selfish cheater who used people. I mean look at you, you're gorgeous, and yet he still couldn't commit to you. He stayed with that frumpy Patricia and then even dated Mrs Field. I mean, come on. I can't believe I respected him. He kind of had it coming, don't you think? I'm sorry, I'm not trying to be insensitive."

She bit her lip. "No, no, I understand. He could be very selfish. Sometimes he would—it would be like I didn't exist."

I shook my head. "Typical man. Doesn't even know what he wants."

"Exactly!" she said in a sudden outburst. "He didn't know that he wanted me. I kept telling him and telling him."

"But then he just started avoiding you because he was scared of his true feelings."

She grabbed my wrists. "Yes, that's right. He loved me. He loved me as much as I loved him, he just didn't see it."

She brushed her brown hair out of her face and looked up and down the street.

"Do you need help?" I asked in my most friendly tone. "Because of what you did? You're in trouble now, aren't you?"

She stared at me. "I didn't mean to kill him. I knew Mrs Field was trying to get close to Patricia, and so I got close to Mrs Field. Even though we were friends, she still made me call her 'Mrs Field', can you believe it? The tart. She was desperate to be like Patricia, and to have Victor to herself and be popular. I got into her head, it didn't take much of an effort at all. She barely hesitated when I told her we could get rid of Patricia. I ordered the mushrooms, and she was supposed to put them in Patricia's cup when she was playing bridge with that old woman and her friends. Except that she didn't get the chance to do it, the cow. So I simply walked into their house. They don't lock the gate to the back of the house and sleep with the windows open. It wasn't difficult at all."

"She's so stupid. She would have deserved to die," I said, hoping she couldn't see me tremble.

"Yes, she really should have died. There was a sweet tea that she had bought and mentioned in front of Mrs Field. I put it in there, not believing for one second that Victor would drink that stuff. Apparently he did." Her mouth turned downward.

Damn. We better warn Patricia as soon as possible.

"And Mr Field?"

"He was pretty much a stalker and found out about the plan. The greedy bastard. He was using it to blackmail his wife. He wanted her to come back to him, but I knew she didn't want that, so I got rid of him and the evidence by setting fire to his office with him in it. Crushed some sleeping tablets in the tea kettle in his office. His wife still knew all his habits, and he never changed his routine. He had insomnia, apparently. But when he was dead, she said she never meant for that to happen. What did she think I was going to do? Just destroy the evidence? Am I that stupid?"

"Of course not. That would be completely irresponsible. He had to go." I was beginning to feel nauseous.

"And I needed someone to blame. I was planning on blaming the curse first, but you started snooping around, so I decided to focus on Patricia. That's why I went back and put that DVD there and put myself in that shed. It was all a gamble, but it paid off. You thought she was the killer. But then you asked questions about Victor today, and I realised you had your suspicions. Why was that?"

"The way you got so upset when Patricia implied Victor wasn't interested in you and when you attacked me after you thought I was having an affair with him. You weren't sad or hurt, you were very angry. I also thought it was odd that you wanted to untie your own hands. I was aware that you knew I suspected Patricia, so it was possible that you pretended to be attacked and put in her shed. In addition to that, you also mentioned that Patricia made a joke about killing Victor. Technically, you could have heard that as a rumour, but all these things combined I just had a feeling."

"And now you're here."

"Now I'm here."

We stared at each other.

"You don't think Victor deserved it, do you? You just want me to confess?"

"You just did, so I guess it worked," I said, ready to bolt.

"I had a good run," she said. "I'm going back inside. Tell Alistair he can come arrest me." She moved back and shut the door.

I exhaled as I'd been holding my breath. There was a fluttering of wings behind me, and I jumped up. Pandora stared at me. From across the street, Daniels headed my way.

"If you were Susan, what would you do?" Detective Black said.

At that moment Daniels approached. "What happened?"

"She confessed. She said she was going to wait inside for you to arrest her. Where's Alistair?"

"I just saw him move around the back," he said.

"I think we should go in. She might try something stupid."

Pandora shrieked as if to agree.

Just then the front door opened again, and Susan lunged forward with a wooden cricket bat. She hit Daniels in the head since he was closer to the door, and he fell to the ground. He groaned, so he was still alive. She swung at me, and I ducked. She missed me by a hair's breadth.

I punched her in the stomach, but I didn't hit her hard since she moved back. This time she swung lower and forced me to move out of the way. She ran past me, but Pandora started her pursuit and pecked her in the heels.

Susan yelled and fell over. She had changed out of her pyjamas, but still wore her slippers. Her eyes were bulging, and she reached for her wounded heel.

I seized the opportunity and jumped on Susan. We fought for the bat, which she finally relinquished, after I bit her wrist. We struggled and she pushed me over, but just as she wanted to get on top of me, Pandora attacked her face.

Susan screamed again, and she flailed on the ground.

"Maggie," Alistair yelled as he came running. Within a few seconds he had his handcuffs around Susan, and Pandora calmly pecked at the ground, as if she wasn't the devil's spawn.

Although in this case she had saved me, so maybe she wasn't that bad.

Pandora shrieked.

THE SUN WAS SHINING and the temperature was nice enough that I didn't need a cardigan for my picnic the next day. After Susan's arrest, Nick had stayed the night and we slept until noon, but we set the alarm regularly in order to wake me. The doctor had confirmed that I had a mild concussion.

The weather was too nice not to go outside, and so we sat in a park near the vicarage with the woods in the short distance. The picnic basket was filled with fruits, sandwiches and nuts. His backpack was next to the picnic blanket; after this he would leave. Since this was the last thing Nick and I would do, he did his best to make me laugh, and I did my best to forget that I'd probably never see him again after this.

"How do you feel about having solved the murders?" Nick asked after we finished eating and lay down on the blanket, staring at the clear blue sky. There wasn't a puff of cloud in sight.

I hesitated. Several people had stopped us on the way to the park to check if the story was true and then congratulated me, but I didn't think I deserved their praise. After all, I had been wrong. Part of me wondered if I just didn't want it to be Susan, because I had hired her, and I felt responsible. I should have seen what she was. But then again, how could I?

"It took me too long," I said. "Because I made a mistake."

Nick turned on his side. "So what? You did better than the police. Without you they wouldn't have figured out it was Susan, and who knows who she would have become obsessed with afterwards? That shrine was creepy."

After Alistair had arrested her, we checked out her house and found what could only be described as a shrine to Victor. She had been following him for a while, probably ever since he'd stopped by at the bookshop a few months ago. They must have struck up a conversation. Maybe he put the moves on her, but changed his mind when she was a bit too eager. That had to be what he wanted to talk about. Perhaps he suspected the blackmailer was Susan, not knowing it was Mr Field. Or he suspected he was followed by two different people; that could explain why he was so scared when he spoke to me.

"Very creepy. I'm just glad Patricia hadn't drunk that tea. She could have been on her way to the grave as well."

"What will happen to Susan?"

"I don't know. Prison, most likely. She knew what she was doing," I said. "Anyway, it was pretty cool that you saved us. Without you we couldn't have apprehended her."

"What kind of knight in shining armour would I be if I didn't save my lady?" Nick said.

I laughed. "Well, I'm grateful."

He leaned forward and kissed me. "This has been fun, but I'm glad there are no more murders to solve."

"Only in my books."

"Which I am going to buy as soon as I get home," he said.

My smile disappeared. "I'll miss you."

"Come on, now. We won't say goodbye, okay? We have the internet and phones, we'll be fine."

But I knew that as soon as we both got into our routines, we would lose touch. That always happened, didn't it? Especially since we knew that neither of us wanted to move. My ex hadn't moved for me because he didn't love me enough, according to Alistair. Did this mean we didn't love each other enough? That wasn't odd; we had only known each other for a few days and most of that time we'd been running around trying to figure out a real-life mystery.

"Right," I said and snuggled closer to him.

When it was time to go, I walked him to the train station with my picnic basket in one hand and his hand in the other one. I held on tight until the train appeared. It felt like my stomach was being squeezed.

Nick leaned forward and kissed me. "I'm glad I met you."

"Same. I'll see you around." I tried to sound breezy.

"See you around."

He kissed me again, this time long and hard. This was more difficult than I would have thought, and I was tempted to follow him onto the train. Instead, I waved until the train started moving and I couldn't see him anymore.

Tears stung my eyes, and I tried not to cry, but when I turned around and saw the Castlefield Book Club standing there with sympathy in their eyes, I started sobbing. The women rallied around me and gave me a group hug.

"We figured you could use some support," Eleanor said into my ear.

"Thanks," I cried. How could I be lonely when I had these women in my life?

Chapter 24

A few days had passed and all had returned to normal in Castlefield, as well as my bookshop. Well, normal enough. Christina was now my new employee, and she was a welcome addition to our small club. She was cheerful and worked hard. We were starting to become good friends, and the sting I felt with each mention of Alistair had started to disappear.

My novel was coming along, and I was taking a well-earned break by taking down a display in the window. It was late in the afternoon, but not yet closing time, which was why it was odd that Christina ushered out the few customers that were in the shop. Eddie closed the door behind them.

"What are you doing?" I asked her. "What's going on? Why are you both grinning like that?"

"We're kidnapping you," Eddie said excitedly.

"Excuse me?"

"Not really," Christina said with a warning look to Eddie. "We're taking you to the pub, come on." She stepped out from behind the counter and ushered me out of the front door. Eddie followed and locked the door behind us.

"We still need to balanc—oh, sod it. I'll just go with the flow. It's been a long week." Whatever the reason for this sudden outing, I was certain I would like it. Especially since the pub contained alcohol.

After a few minutes we reached the double doors. Both Christina and Eddie practically pushed me through the doors. As soon as I entered the pub, a loud applause ruptured the air. I jumped and then looked at all the familiar faces of the people I cared about so much. Nancy was clapping loudly, as well as the Castlefield Book Club. Eleanor even whistled with her fingers, earning some surprised looks, including from her husband. Alistair and DC Daniels were also there.

I took a demure bow and then went up to Nancy to hug her, mainly because the whole thing was embarrassing me. I buried my face in her shoulder and held her tight. "Thanks," I said. The applause died down.

"You did so well," Poppy said. "We're so proud of you." She rubbed my shoulder, and I gave her a kiss on the cheek. The other women murmured in agreement.

Eleanor showed up next to me and put her arm around me. "We never doubted our local sleuth for a second, did we?" she said loudly and the others erupted in a few more claps and whistles.

"Okay, okay. Thank you. But I don't see any cake. If you're going to throw me a party, where's the cake?" I said and threw Olivia a look.

She grinned at me. "What kind of bakery would I run if I didn't provide cake at every opportunity?" A path was made as the others backed up. It led to one of the tables in the back. There was indeed a white cake on the right side of the table. On the left was a large rectangle covered in a sheet.

"What the heck is that?" I asked.

Nancy followed me closely. The others gathered around the table, some took out their phones to take pictures.

"If it's a collection of spiders, I'm out of here," I said.

Eleanor chuckled. "What kind of parties do you think we throw?" She was also filming.

Damn. I felt like a kid performing in a school play. I moved to the sheet and grabbed it tentatively. Then I glanced around at the expectant faces—even Alistair was smiling—and yanked off the sheet.

"A cage?" I tilted my head, and then I spotted it. A baby bunny. "Oh my goodness, a tiny bunny!"

People around me laughed and then started clapping again. I didn't even notice. With a swiftness that my PE teacher would be proud of, I opened the cage and got out the bunny. She was white with grey ears. Was it a she? I didn't even care. I planted little kisses on her head and kept stroking her. She was incredibly soft and didn't move. "Do you like it?" Nancy asked expectantly.

I turned to her. "It's—it's the best gift." My voice caught.

"Love, are you crying?"

"No, I'm not, and nobody better be filming my tears," I said defiantly.

There were some chuckles from the small crowd.

Nancy came over to hug me gently, since I was still holding the bunny. The women's club followed suit, and I heard Eddie shout: "Hey, I want to join too." They gossiped a lot, but they were good women, and even Eddie knew that.

The rest of the evening was perfect. The cake was delicious, and my friends and neighbours showered me with compliments. The bunny turned out to be a girl. I didn't have a name yet, but that would come.

Christina was cracking jokes with Eddie. She got our humour, she was smart and friendly, and I totally got what Alistair saw in her. It was time to move on. Instead of pining over someone I couldn't have, I would celebrate that I'd made two new friends. Alistair didn't make it easy, though, with his charming smiles or his long stares at me when nobody else was looking.

But for now, I was incredibly happy with the home I had, not just in this village, but with these people.

BAILEY TUGGED ON THE leash, ready to follow his nose again and enjoy the freedom that came with peeing on trees. I remained where I was, though, distracted by the moving van in front of the Pembroke hotel. It was a small van, and I imagined that not much would change about the hotel, except Mr Field's office, which was still damaged by the fire.

The thing I was most curious about was who would be brave enough to move in. After all that had happened, I had serious doubts that anyone would purchase the hotel, but it had been bought so quickly that nobody had had time to blink. In the past week there had been plenty of speculations, but the simple truth was that nobody knew. Patty the real estate agent was tight-lipped about the whole affair, despite several pub patrons buying her loads of drinks. I wondered what the secrecy was about. It had to be someone with a flair for the dramatic.

Someone cast a shadow over Bailey, and I looked up. I squinted at the familiar man. "Miles Fancypants, right?" I asked.

Miles smiled with his blindingly white teeth that even aliens across the universe could see. "That's right. I knew you wouldn't forget me."

"How could I forget? You made sure I wasn't arrested."

"And here I thought it was my dazzling good looks that you would have remembered me for. What are you looking at?"

"Some macabre idiot bought the Pembroke hotel," I said. "I didn't believe in curses at first, but now I'm not so sure. It's a gorgeous estate, but so much has happened there." I shivered.

"Ah, yes. Alistair told me about that. You were locked in a death room or something," he said.

"That's right. It was not pretty. I almost started eating Alistair's tie."

He laughed. It sounded melodious. "I'll be sure to keep my ties away from you."

"Does that mean you've decided to move here?" I gasped as it hit me, and he smiled.

"That's right. I'm the macabre idiot." He grabbed my hand and kissed it like he had the first time we met. "I look forward to seeing you around the village."

He was about to walk away when I pulled him closer. "Oh, I like where this is going," he said.

"Shut up, you fool. There's a monster behind you."

"A monster?" he turned around and looked back at me. He laughed.

"Don't laugh." I was experiencing a déjà vu.

"How can I not, dear? That's a chicken."

"It's an evil specimen sent from hell. Though she did save me, so maybe she's mellowed."

Pandora stared at us, but didn't show any signs of attacking.

"Alright, I'll see you. Good luck with your chicken," Miles said.

It wasn't until Miles had passed her that she made that loud screeching sound and started charging. Except that she didn't attack me, she went for Miles.

"Ouch," he said as she pecked his leg. He started running. "Get away from me, you winged beast!"

"Told you so," I shouted as he ran up the hill.

I FINISHED WALKING Bailey. It was Sunday and Nancy was having brunch with an old friend in a neighbouring village. Just as I opened the door so I could go up to my flat, someone called my name.

Christina gave me a deflated wave, and her mascara had run. She was carrying two suitcases and two handbags. She started crying when she reached me and dropped everything to give me a hug.

"Alistair broke up with me," she said after she had caught her breath.

I froze. *What?*

"Not this again," Detective Black said from behind me.

Bailey barked.

"I don't know where to go, I feel so—" she started crying again.

"I have an extra room, don't worry. You can stay with me."

Detective Black grunted.

What was I supposed to do? She needed my help and she was my friend.

"Come on," I said. "I'll make your bed and get you settled in. It will be fun, okay? You can play with Snowball. Bailey is afraid of her."

Christina managed a small smile. "Thanks. You're a good friend."

I wasn't sure if I had been, but I was going to be one from now on. Good friends were rare in this world, and you could never have too many.

DETECTIVE BLACK STARED into the killer's deflated eyes that were drowning in salty tears. As his partner cuffed him, he glanced at the smiling picture of Marlene Green. Somewhere in his heart he hoped that her smile was directed at him, that she was finally able to find the peace that she deserved.

He stepped out into the crisp autumn air and lit his pipe. He sauntered in the direction of the pub where he'd have a pint in honour of Ms Green and contemplate the beauty of life, as he did every Friday night. Luckily he got tipsy by the time he got to any answers. After all, what is life without a little mystery?

I LOOKED UP AT DETECTIVE Black, his dark eyes settled on mine. "Are you happy with that?" he asked.

"Of course. I'm the writer, and I know you." I leaned back in my chair and typed the final two words.

The end.

Excerpt The Chrono Unit

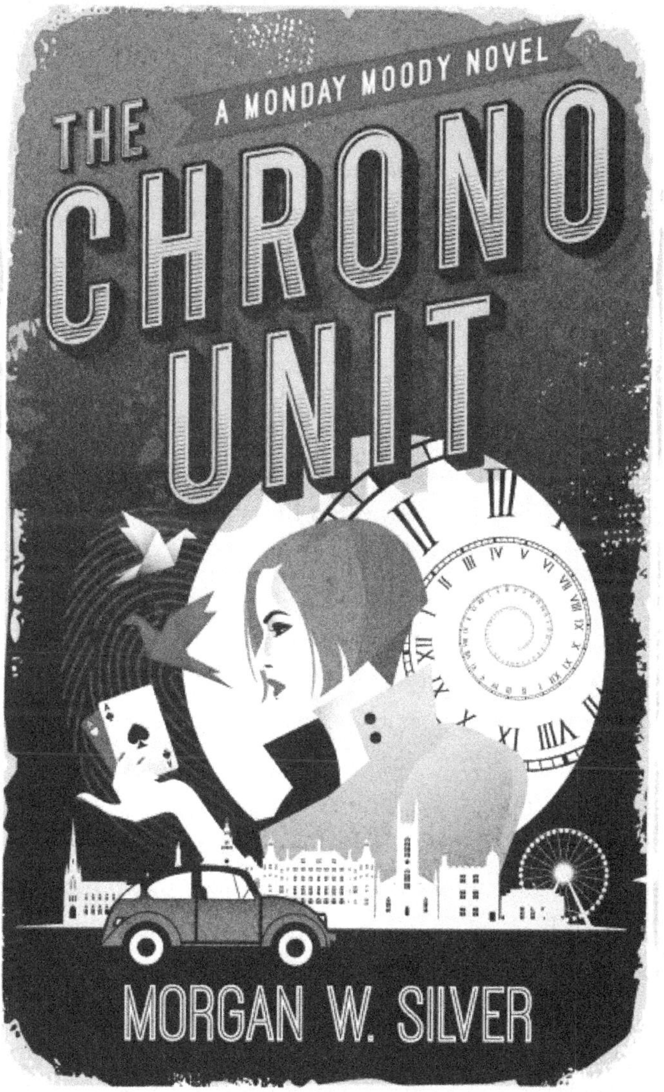

Chapter 1

"I am by no means an ordinary person, but considering the fact that the world is strange, I think it is a good thing I was prepared early." ~ Monday Moody

THE CALL COMES IN AT 2.36 minutes past ten in the morning. My watch, like any other CU officer's, is exact because time is of the essence and every second counts. The screen projects the necessary information. Code 103 at Fox Lane 15. That's Mr Woodacre's farm. The last time I went anywhere near his sheep, he chased me off his land with a pitchfork and such vigour that he lost his toupee. Unfortunately, his farm is close to where I'm enjoying my tea and scones, an unhealthy start of a disconsolate day in Yorkshire.

I could pretend to ignore the call, but who am I kidding? If I responded the time I had a fever, the most delectable scones of the county aren't going to make a difference either. That had been an interesting case since I had hallucinated yellow penguins and dancing daffodils.

"Chip," I call to the blonde waitress, a little person who always wears red clothes because she says it's the colour of seduction—something she maintains, even after having seen the horror that is my frizzy ginger hair after a drizzle. She hurries over, her blue eyes large and inquisitive, probably because she knows that even death can't separate me from my favourite food.

"I've just got a call. Can you bag this for me?" I say with an apologetic smile.

She raises her thin eyebrows and grabs my plate. "My scones not good enough?" Her voice is soft and low, as if her words are carried by an undercurrent.

"How dare you even suggest that? I sometimes dream about them. Even my dreams have dreams about them. No, I'm afraid duty calls."

"You work too hard," Chip says as I follow her to the counter. She disappears briefly and returns with a brown paper bag while I put on my bright yellow raincoat.

"I think I work the right amount." I clutch the bag to my chest.

"So you think you should take a call on your birthday?" she asks.

I smile at her. "Since I hate my birthday, yes. Thank you for the free scones." I bend down and kiss her on her soft cheek.

"Be careful," she calls after me, but the rain drowns out the last few letters. It is starting to let up a little, but I still have to run to my light blue Beetle. It takes me a while to straighten my sharp bob every morning, and I will not let a drizzle undo that hard work.

I gently place the bag on the passenger's seat and check that my red lipstick is still okay. I turn the ignition. It takes a few tries but then it purrs like a constipated, fat tabby. I tap the steering wheel lovingly before I reverse out of the parking space and drive towards the edge of town, to Mr Woodacre's farm. There is a fat chance he hasn't noticed the rip, but still I harbour hope that he will be absent.

DESPITE THE FACT THAT the morning started with gloomy feelings—I really don't like my birthday—and gloomier weather, luck appears to be on my side, because Mr Woodacre is nowhere to be seen. In fact, apart from a herd of sheep, the paddock is empty. In the distance is his cottage, his green truck gone. I exchange my red heels for red wellies and head over to the rip.

It is small, tiny, in fact, so it was probably someone's first time. Either that, or it is someone very skilled. The yellow and orange colours indicate that is not a rip in time, but only in space. Though messing with time travel is far more intricate and disastrous than messing with parallel universes, both are equally illegal. I hold out my scanner, but it comes up with nothing new. Parallel rips are easier to read, but in this case I can't tell if someone went to another world, or just came back from one. Filing reports on parallel rips makes root canals look like fun. This tiny rip will take me a few days, at least.

The hairs on the back of my neck stand on end and I turn around. By my car is a young girl, about seven years old, in a long woollen jumper that is too large for her and an open coat that has sagged off her right shoulder. Her two braids hang limply beside her pale face. Her brown eyes are large and even from here I can see that she's trembling. She must have been hiding in the woods at the edge of the field.

"Hi," I say in my most gentle tone. It is a tone that I have to use often, since most offenders are adolescents and scared at the realisation that they can manipulate space and time, and by having done so, committed a crime. This is the first time, though, that one is so young. And even if all of them remind me a little of me, this one does so even more. I inch towards her, but stop when her eyes dart towards the woods.

"I am Monday. Monday Moody," I say in a cheerful voice. "I suppose you made that happen?"

She says nothing. "I just need to do something, okay? Hold still." I hold out my watch to her face and after it scans her, it beeps. I check the screen. She appears to be from this world, since her name is immediately displayed.

"Hi, Lovelace. Did you make the rip happen?"

The girl looks at the rip and then at me. Her eyes tear up.

"Don't be sad," I say. "Listen, I need you to do me a favour." I check my watch. Six minutes have passed. "I need you to run home, okay? And don't mention what you did to anybody. Perhaps your mother, or someone you trust, but nobody else. You might be in trouble, you see? And I don't want you to be in trouble. I know what it's like and I wish I could teach you, but all I can say is: try not to be too upset. Your abilities are linked to your emotions." That sounds like lousy advice, even to me, but time really is of the essence. "Run, go." I nudge her arm gently and point at the woods. She runs off after a moment of hesitation, becoming smaller until she is swallowed up by the first line of trees.

The moment she is out of sight, another car comes up. A blue Hudson Hornet. Saoirse. She parks her car behind mine and at first her black curls come out above the car door. Then her pale face with sharp eyes and a lopsided grin. "Beat me to it," she says in an Irish accent.

"Can you believe I was eating Chip's scones when I got the call. Lousy timing."

"And on your birthday no less," she says and slams the door shut. She walks up to me and surveys the rip for a few moments.

"Ugh. I don't like to be reminded of the fact that my life is flashing me by with great speed," I say. That's not the only reason I hate this day. It may also have something to do with the fact that I nearly died on my 18th birthday.

"Oh, please. That's what happens when you have kids. You can at least do whatever you want." She squeezes my shoulder. "How I'd love to go back to a time of one-night stands and drunken make-out sessions, just for a day."

"Saoirse," I say, my mouth falling open.

"What? A mother of four can have desires." She chuckles and walks closer to the rip. "You haven't closed it yet, then?"

"I was conversing with Shaun over there about the reason for our existence." I point at the nearest sheep who is grazing languidly.

She chuckles. "Don't tell my kids. They'll get jealous." She takes out her Sonic gun and aims it at the rip. As soon as she pulls the trigger, the edges of the rip start weaving their way to each other until it disappears entirely. It is the only weapon we carry, and it's not even a weapon.

"The paperwork is going to be hell." She sighs. "I'll request some Ladybug Drones to survey the area for anything unusual, just in case." She swipes her watch a few times, then turns to me. "So, even if you don't celebrate your birthday, I still got you something months ago. I saw it and it's perfect for you." She grins.

I can't help but smile. Though I hadn't expected to make any friends as soon as I joined the Chrono Unit, she made it so damn easy. She is also the best partner I could have asked for. "Fine. Because it's you, I'll allow it."

She rushes back to the car and comes back with something hidden under her coat. "You're going to be so happy in a second."

"Stop stalling and give it to me." I hold out my hand.

In it she places a book and I nearly topple over. An actual book. "Oh, wow. *Alice in Wonderland*," I whisper. "Where—how—?"

"I have friends in high places. Well, only one. She was doing this cleanse—yes, that's what she called it—for her house and she got rid of loads of stuff she doesn't want. She's loaded and she's been hoarding crap for a while now. She was donating everything, but I fished out this copy when I spotted it."

"This must have cost her a fortune. Especially a book like this."

"Yeah, beats 3-D holograms, right? Well, you think that. I like holo-books."

I narrow my eyes at her. "They're not *books.*"

She chuckles. "Welcome to the 21st century. Now give me a hug already."

I smile and give her a bear hug. "You're amazing. Thank you." She smells like smoke, as if she's been burning wood in a fireplace. "I can't believe you have a friend in high places, you have to tell me the story sometime."

"It's a very boring one. I once helped her when someone Travelled back in time to Alter knowing her by crashing a party and inserting himself into her life. He didn't do a very good job and became frustrated that it hadn't worked out the way he wanted and became a stalker."

"I see. So you arrested him?"

"Yep, Collared and arrested. Though he's free now. Still Collared of course. Thank goodness."

"Thank goodness," I mutter, glancing at the woods, certain I'd done the right thing, but sad that I could never confide in Saoirse completely.

Both our watches beep as we get another call. The screen shows a 101 in progress, which causes Saoirse and I to frown. Two rips in one day? Usually we had two a month, at most a week. The address is a thirteen-minute drive. "Let's go," I say and hop into my car. I glance at the woods one more time before I turn around and follow Saoirse towards the town centre.

"MONDAY MOODY AND SAOIRSE Cavanaugh," I say as I point from me to Saoirse. We both tap our watches and a holograph of our badge with a serial number, name, and a photo appear above it. The constable barely glances at it, his face pale and his chin covered in a dab of ketchup. "I was—it's in there," he says and physically backs away as if he can get sucked in himself.

Inside the pub is a much larger rip that isn't a rip at all, but a portal. The size being the difference between the two.

The cause the same. The black and red colours swirl in a mesmerising fashion. A time portal.

The fact that it is still open means that someone is inside. We both take out our scanners. The rest of the pub is empty. Soft music is playing in the background. The person that steps through the portal has a certain feel to her or him, being from this time. The scanner shows it as the colour purple, a thread that leads into the black and red portal. All we have to do is follow the thread and forcibly remove the perp, though it only works if the person is still close to the portal.

Saoirse hates doing this and always calls it a hassle, but I know it's because she's afraid that something will go wrong and she'll be stuck in some past or future, lost to her loved ones. Which has happened to some of our colleagues. I have a similar concern, but I do not let myself get deterred. I don't like fear. I also don't have to worry about getting stuck in a different time or place, though I can't tell Saoirse that.

And so I step into the portal, surrounded by swirls of light and an immense pressure that soon subsides. A wave of nausea sweeps through me, and forces me to double over. I press my hand against my lips and wait for it to pass. Since the portal is still open, it means that the person stepped through, expecting to be but brief and in the vicinity of the portal itself. It has been open since the time it took for us to drive over, so something must have gone wrong.

"Hello," I say. The pub is empty and much seems unchanged except that I can sense it is not, and my scanner makes lots of gurgling noises, much like my old cat Sourpuss used to do when snoring. Something has disturbed this place and it feels heavy, as if weights have been put on my limbs.

"This is CU officer Monday Moody, please respond." My voice is firm and unshaken. One never knows what to expect on the other side of a portal, but to me, that is part of the challenge. Then, out of nowhere, I get tackled by a black blur. I scramble around on my back and realise it is not, in fact, a blur, but a woman dressed in black, trying very hard to incapacitate me.

"This is very rude," I manage to articulate with strain as her hands have found themselves around my neck. I poke her in the eyes with my fingers and knee her in the stomach before I push her away. She falls on the floor, giving me a brief moment to observe her. She has short, blonde hair and an athletic body. She's not afraid to attack a CU officer, so she might have had run-ins with the law before. Was she waiting for me?

By the time she gets up I crack a bar stool over her head. It breaks. "Please, don't get up."

I don't like that she managed to knock me off my feet, but at least she is unconscious now. Despite her athletic body, I've faced bigger and stronger enemies. I adjust my dress and glance around. I can sense that it is her that opened the portal, but I can't help but wonder what it is that took her so long. Did she want to hurt me? Or is there something else? Why Travel back to an empty bar?

I search for any signs that might tell me what she was doing and it takes me a few minutes before I find the reason for her outing.

A bomb. Strapped to the toilet on which there is an 'out of order' sign. I do not know much about bombs, but I know they are bad.

The timer says twenty minutes. I press my watch to check the time. It shows me the time here and the time where I came from. We have Travelled twenty minutes into the past which means it is set to go off as soon as we go back. Interesting. Was her plan to kill us? Members of the CU? If so, she didn't know who she was messing with. I can't disarm the bomb, but I can buy myself some time.

Now, this next trick requires a huge amount of concentration and an even bigger amount of guts. Luckily, a near-death situation is enough motivation to produce both. With sweat on my forehead and several knives from the kitchen, I manage to peel off the bomb from the tiles under the two sinks.

Then I close my eyes and focus. Going back a minute or so is enough. A tornado of feelings sweeps up inside of me until the momentum reaches a climax and I hold out my hand. A portal opens and I step through, nearly throwing up this time. I place the bomb in the toilet and peer out from the bathroom to check if the woman is indeed gone now. It means I have pulled her through in the near future. Then I step back through my portal which closes afterwards and this time I turn slightly green. I have no time to throw up though, and run towards the woman, dragging her through the portal.

I feel Saoirse's hands on my hips as she helps me pull the perpetrator through. As soon as we're through the portal she stops pulling, but I don't. "Quickly, we have to get her out of the building, there's a bomb. We have about a minute."

Saoirse turns a shade paler and after a split second of surprise, she grabs the other leg and we pull her out of the pub. The cold weather is welcoming after the sweat explosion caused by stress and nausea. Similar feelings I experienced on my first ever date.

"Did it go okay?" the constable asks, but I shout for him to get back. I shout for everyone to get back. And just as we push the majority of onlookers towards the opposite side of the street, the bomb goes off. It produces a deafening sound and its force shatters the windows and blows the door off its hinges. It also pushes the first line of people, me and Saoirse included, back into the nearest car.

A loud ringing in my ears is the least of my worries, as my nausea catches up with me. I throw up next to the car and nearly over the constable's hand, who has also fallen down. Unfortunately this also reminds me of my first ever date.

Not a bad start to my thirtieth birthday.

Chapter 2

"There is one kind of robber whom the law does not strike at, and who steals what is most precious to men: time." ~ Napoleon I

AS FAR AS BOSSES GO, mine is pretty okay. After all, she did once save my life. It also wasn't an easy task, because at the time I was pretty drunk, and the entire debacle involved a wedding cake knife and a clown. Fiona Steele calls me into her office at my earliest convenience, which means that I can freshen up first before giving an oral statement of what went down at the pub. Luckily, nobody was injured, but still, it was serious. Especially since no Traveller has ever tried something this destructive.

When I enter her office, she stops typing and presses twice on her typewriter, deactivating the holo-screen. Her desk is neat and minimalistic with only a mug of steaming coffee. She goes through about five cups a day, even though she claims she doesn't like it. The dark circles around her eyes indicate that she really does need them. I wonder if it's the job or if she and her wife are having troubles. They have an open marriage and have been together for a long time. As far as soulmates exist, they are soulmates, so I hope it's the job that's causing her stress.

Fiona smiles at me and it reaches her grey eyes. Her hair is dark, but has lightened over the years due to grey streaks. "Are you alright?" she asks. She has a quiet voice, but any temerity travels through her eyes, not her lips.

"I am still a bit shaky," I say, not one to lie. "I am relieved that nobody got seriously injured."

"Me too. What happened exactly? Can you walk me through it?" She folds her hands in front of her and nods at the chair in front of the desk. Her office smells like coffee and her sweet perfume lingers in the air.

Omission is key when handling sensitive information. "I entered the portal and something felt off. Before I could have a good look, I was attacked and we struggled. I knocked her out with a bar stool and then had a look around. I spotted the bomb in the bathroom and bolted. I mean, I ran and took the perp with me."

"How long did it take you to get there?" she asks. Her nail polish is a dark grey and matches her outfit.

"Seventeen minutes."

"And the perp had not left the portal then," she states.

I nod.

"Taking a bomb takes some time, but hardly seventeen minutes." She blinks at me, waiting for my input.

"I agree. Perhaps she had doubts."

"What time did she go to?"

"Not too long in the past. The moment I pulled her through, we had to hurry out of there." The large clock behind her desk makes no sound as it ticks on.

"It sounds like a trap. I don't like that."

"Neither do I, but we'll know more once we interview her."

Fiona drums her fingers on the glass desk. "Yes, but you won't be the one to do that. I need you elsewhere. Or specifically, someone else needs you."

"They do? Me? Are you sure?"

Fiona smiles. "No need to be diffident. You're a good officer. There's a case in Sheffield and the Head Officer asked for you specifically. It probably helped that you were in the news a few months ago."

"Hmm." I don't know what to say. I like working with Saoirse. I know I can rely on her and we have a good chemistry.

"It's just one case and we'll put you up in a nice hotel." Fiona activates the holo-screen, reverses it and types on the long keys to show images of a gorgeous Georgian estate where the rooms are spacious and old-fashioned. They also have a spa. She knows I love that.

"You know my weaknesses, don't you?"

She laughs. "Happy birthday."

MY DESK IS RIGHT ACROSS from Saoirse. As Level 1 Chrono Unit officers, there are six of us, each assigned to a partner. Most of the time we file paperwork on the people we Collar, arrest, or give a Warning to. Every registered Traveller only gets one Warning before being Collared.

Saoirse shoves a plate of biscuits in my face. "I brought extra since it's your birthday and was going to give them to take home with you, but I figured you can use them now." She smiles, the lines around her blue eyes visible.

"Thanks. I do need them. Badly. Did you know that hagfish eat their dead prey from the inside out? I wouldn't mind doing that with your biscuits. They are that good." I smile at her as I pick one up. It's a chocolate chip one with salt.

"You say the...sweetest things," she says as she makes a face. "You're lucky I'm used to your style of weird."

"It seems that someone else will have to get used to it. I'm going down to Sheffield. My help was requested for a case. Can't imagine why." I take a bite out of the biscuit and close my eyes. "Yeah, definitely want to burrow inside this biscuit and eat it," I say with my mouth full, yet skilfully comprehensible.

"Can't imagine it either." The corner of her mouth turns up. "Do you know what the case is about?"

"No, I'll find out when I get there."

"Don't your parents live in Sheffield?"

"Yeah, it will be nice to see them again." I call my mother every week, but with things being so busy in the past few weeks, I haven't stopped by.

"Then come over for dinner tonight. It's your birthday and I know you're not going to celebrate it otherwise."

"You got that right." I think about the four rug rats at her house and her husband who is always keen to discuss with me the dangers of air conditioning. Why he would think I find that interesting is beyond me and the rest of the universes. "No, thanks. I do actually have something planned that I would like to do instead." I take another bite of the biscuit and blink at her.

"It's sleep, isn't it?"

"How do you know me so well?"

"Time."

I RUB MY SHOULDERS and look up at the white ceiling. Saoirse left earlier to take care of her kids. Filing the report of the rip at the pub took up more time than I'd hoped. I press the button on the lift and contemplate if I should take a nap before dinner or after dinner when Gary appears next to me.

Tinkerers from the Parallel Division are interested in all sorts of things and are eager to spread that interest. Gary is no different and has a knack for running into me just when I am least excited to see him. His moustache trembles with excitement. I don't have to see it, I can feel it.

"Hi, Gary," I say without looking up.

"Monday. Have you seen this?" He holds up a small square with a screen and buttons below it. It also has a long wire attached to the front that leads up to two small buds.

"Yes, I see it, Gary."

"It's what they call an MP3-player in PU-39613. This is a mini device they use to listen to music. Instead of something like the chunky holo-radio, they have these. Aren't they adorable? I really like that parallel universe."

"They're a bit clumsy and big, don't you think?"

"Isn't that half the charm, Monday? Think about it. Twisting a few knobs and choosing any music from the HoloNet is so boring. This makes you put in an effort if you want to listen to music. They even have to download the songs." He chuckles. "Isn't that cute?"

"Yes. You're so lucky you can actually take things from the parallel universes." I mean those words. Despite his poor timing, I do actually find the objects he shows interesting. It reminds me of the stories my mother used to tell me about the places she's visited. And of the places I've visited, though most of that was for training, not leisure.

"Do you want it?"

The lift announces its presence with a ding and the door slides down into the floor. I narrow my eyes at him. "Is this some test? I know I'm not allowed to take things like that."

"It's frowned upon, but not forbidden. I requested this especially for you. Happy birthday." He winks at me conspiratorially and hands me the device.

I stare at it and then at him. "Thank you," I say and lean forward to kiss him on the cheek.

He turns a shade of red, mumbles something, and dashes off.

I chuckle and step into the lift. It brings me down to the garage and I tuck the new device into the pocket of my yellow raincoat. It takes me a few tries to start the familiar rattle of my car and I drive home, to my semi-detached house with three bedrooms. Being in the Chrono Unit earns a lot of money, mainly due to the fact that one of the occupational hazards is death. And we have notoriously bad coffee.

It is still light out and the sky is dotted with clouds, but it's not cold. I lock my car and run up the steps to my front door. The front garden is surrounded by hedges; I like my privacy and my neighbours are fox breeders. Despite the fact that many people don't know what noises they make, they do in fact make a lot of noise. As do their breeders. They keep wanting to chat about them, or about their collection of antique teacups. I may love foxes, but I don't need to know about their mating habits.

I reach my door when I realise I'm not alone. I turn around, preferring a serial killer over my neighbours. My eyes widen. It's neither. "Hi, Lovelace," I say after a moment of hesitation. How did she find me? Also, why? Does she not have a home?

The little girl from earlier today says nothing. She is dressed in the same outfit as before and looks just as upset as before. She says nothing and stares at me.

I walk up to her and ask her if she needs my help. She still doesn't reply. "Okay," I say. "Why don't you come inside." I let her past me and look down the street. Why do I have the feeling we're being watched? I wrinkle my nose and let the girl in. She looks around my hallway as if she's never seen one before. Mr Woodacre's farm is close to a lot of residential park homes, so that might be possible.

I help her take off her coat and hang it up. She follows me into the kitchen where I put the kettle on. "So, Lovelace, why are you here?"

The girl says nothing and looks at her shoes.

"Yeah, I get it," I say. "I like silence too. That's why I have a very relaxed pet. Do you want to see him?" I don't wait for her reply and head into the dining room and from there into the conservatory.

On a wooden sideboard is a case that houses my turtle. "This is Mr Turtleneck." I glance behind me. The girl has followed me. "You can pet him, if you want." The noise from the kettle grows louder. "I'll get us tea."

I pour us both a cup of herbal tea that is calming and relaxing. It will help her sleep. I sigh. What am I going to do with her? I can't keep her here. But I also can't have her running around. At least she's safe with me. I have to figure out what her story is.

I put some biscuits from Saoirse on a plate and turn around to put them on the breakfast table. The girl has quietly taken place at the table with her back to me. I startle and drop the plate. It shatters and the biscuits are lost to the floor. I curse under my breath and look up at the girl, ready to reassure her that it's okay. But she hasn't moved. She hasn't so much as twitched a muscle. That seems familiar. I step over the broken plate and my delicious victims and clap my hands behind her head. Nothing.

Then I tap her on her shoulder. She shrugs her shoulders, as if she's worried I might hurt her and then slowly turns around. She has question marks in her eyes.

"Are you deaf?" I sign.

Her eyes widen. "Yes," she signs back.

I smile. "Don't worry. I know how to talk to you."

"Only my aunt knew sign language." Her hands are hurried, as if she's been waiting to communicate to someone, anyone.

"Did she? What happened to her?"

The girl's face scrunches up like an accordion.

"Something bad?" I sign.

"Yes. I lived with her."

"There was a portal when we met. Did your aunt go through it?"

She nods.

"And you created that portal?"

The girl says nothing.

There is more going on here. "What's your name?" She doesn't know that I already know her name and I feel like an introduction is in order. I want to make her feel comfortable and strike up a conversation. The more I know about her, the better.

She spells her name slowly. "Lovelace Thomson."

"What a nice name. Very memorable."

The girl manages a feeble smile.

"My name is Monday Moody."

At this her smile grows wider. "No, that's a memorable name." She clasps her hand in front of her mouth as if she wants to stop herself from giggling.

I laugh. "You're quite right. What was I thinking?"

Lovelace turns serious. "Will you help me? I don't have anywhere to go."

"Why did you come to me? And how did you find me?"

"You are like me. Your energy tastes like strawberries." She smiles.

Travellers, Illusionists, and even vampires have more core energy than normal people. Some are talented enough to sense that energy in others, and it always evokes one of the senses. A taste, a smell, an image. For everyone that taste or image is different. Apparently to Lovelace, my life energy is sweet. With her I can see snowflakes.

"You just sit here for a bit," I sign. "I'll be right back." In the corner of the living room I have a desk with a typewriter. I sit down, activate the holo-screen, and type in her name. I need to decide what to do with her. She won't tell me much, but she's clearly in trouble.

I check her address and next of kin—her aunt—as well as the list of times that the police had to stop by because of noise disturbances or because her aunt hadn't come home. Her aunt was also arrested a few times for public indecency and the destruction of property while being drunk. What a stellar role-model.

Did she treat Lovelace poorly because she was a Traveller? Or is she simply a very bad caretaker? Either way, it is impressive that Lovelace managed to create that rip. She could have found someone to train with or perhaps she just happens to be that talented. It is possible.

It is likely that Level 3 officers will bring back her aunt and she'll be pissed and eager to point the finger at Lovelace. She will be in serious trouble, if the aunt even reports it. She sounds like someone who might just enjoy making Lovelace's life even worse. Regardless of what will happen, nobody is going to protect Lovelace. She doesn't have anybody on her side. Except maybe me.

Things could have been far worse for me without my mother. Things can easily become worse for Lovelace. She doesn't deserve that, she's just a girl.

The air cracks and a static tingles my skin. A portal? Here? I turn around. There is a bomb on the coffee table, much like the one I came across this morning. However, there is no rip to be seen. That would mean it's a very skilled Traveller. I get up and walk over to the coffee table. My breathing quickens as I glance at the timer. Less than a minute. Shit. I turn to run to Lovelace, but when I glance back at the bomb, it's gone. And still no rip. Did someone teleport here to remove it? Why? How? What? And why use a portal first?

I know time is the most elusive thief in the world, but this is a bit of a stretch. At least I know one thing for sure. Someone really is trying to kill me.

Chapter 3

"People told me that giving birth would be most painful. They were wrong. It was giving up coffee."
~ Mrs Eleanor Moody

THE FOLLOWING DAY I ring my parents' doorbell bright and early in the morning. I couldn't sleep last night anyway, and since they live in Sheffield, the choice was easily made. I glance at Lovelace, who is holding my hand, and think about the second, but poor attempt on my life. I'd rather stay with people I trust than in a hotel room. Though it is a good thing that anybody else might think that that's exactly where I'm staying.

I glance to my right where Beth, my parents' nosy neighbour, peers over her hedge. She's holding a pair of shears to make it appear as if she's doing garden work, but is in fact cutting air while gawking at Lovelace and me.

A shuffling sound. The door opens. My mother stands there in a purple dress and a black cardigan. She always looks fashionable. I doubt even a rainstorm could diminish her looks. Her black hair is done up and her eyes twinkle when she sees me, then widen as she spots the girl holding my turtle. "You weren't joking when you said you'd bring a visitor.

I thought you meant Mr Turtleneck." She hasn't blinked yet. "Come in, dear. Come in."

"Nice trimming, Beth. The air looks better already," she shouts before slamming the door.

I remember Beth was washing her windows when I went to prom. And when I had my first date and he picked me up, she was painting her front door. Even if it was dark by then. She also once washed her windows and fell off the slippery ladder as she was so focussed on the chat my mother was having with a handsome new neighbour. In fact, a similar accident occurred with a nail and a birdhouse. Clearly her trips to Homebase are sponsored by her curiosity.

After my mother sets us up in the kitchen, I share the highlights of my birthday while feeding Mr Turtleneck a piece of lettuce.

"I don't like this, Monday. Cheese-fisted attempt or not, it was still an attempt on your life. Nobody is allowed to kill you, only I can do that."

"It's 'ham-fisted' and why? Because you're my mother?"

"That's right. I gave birth to you. Even if it only lasted two hours." She smiles at Lovelace, who is playing with her tea spoon.

"I'm not letting anybody kill me, Mother. I am too stubborn to die prematurely."

She lets out a bark of laughter and places her manicured hand in front of her mouth, in an attempt to appear delicate. "You get that from me. That's why I'm not worried about you. We're strong. It runs in the family."

"Speaking of parental heritage, where is Dad?" The house is suspiciously plain.

"He's in his shed. I'm telling you, retirement actually makes me see less of the man." She shakes her head, then uses sign language to ask Lovelace if she wants more biscuits. She eagerly nods her response. I leave them to it.

The garden has a pool in the middle and a heap of begonias in the far right corner. On the opposite side is my dad's shed. He spends most of his time working on his Illusions since that has always been a passion of his. He's got several Illusions going on right now, mostly to protect our privacy from a certain nosy neighbour. The begonias are very real, though. My mother's pride.

The shed door swings open and I'm about to greet my father when a raptor comes out. The dinosaur stops in his tracks and cocks his head to assess me. Threat or snack? Unfortunately this is not the first time. Calling out for my dad won't help.

"Don't you dare," I say firmly. "I am not afraid of you." The quiver in my voice gives me away. The creature leaps forward and I shriek. With a few quick steps I jump into the pool. I stay under water for as long as I can hold out and then I resurface.

I curse under my breath, but at least the dinosaur is gone and I can climb out of the pool. My father stands in the doorway and his eyes widen as he spots me. He rushes over and helps me out. My dress is dripping wet and my shoes ruined. I push him away and sign angrily. "You knew I was coming over and you know how much they scare me."

"I'm sorry. I was trying a mixture of Illusions and this one sort of escaped. I am getting a bit forgetful sometimes and they take advantage. I'm so sorry. Are you okay?"

"Yeah, I am." I know they're not real, but fear doesn't work that way. That's why dangerous Illusions are forbidden. "You do know where I work, don't you?"

"I renew my license every year, and I know what I'm doing. Except for now. Really, I'm sorry." He adjusts his blazer nervously and eyes my drowned-cat look.

Apart from my red hair I am nothing like my dad. Which is probably why we get along so well. "It's okay." He still wears his blazer and neat trousers every day even though he's been retired for months now. "Hasn't Mother bought you new clothes?"

"I'm used to dressing like this." Then he smiles and hugs me, despite the fact that I'm soaking wet. "Are you cold?"

"No. I'll be fine. Show me what you were working on."

"First get a towel and dry yourself. Otherwise you can't enjoy it."

"So I am going to enjoy it, then? Sure you're not trying to kill me?" Too.

"Come on, I have a lovely birthday surprise. Just go and get a towel and I'll wait in the shed." He trots off excitedly.

"Wait," I sign, but he already has his back to me. I hurry inside trying my best not to leave a disastrous amount of water in my steps.

"The raptor again?" My mother asks as she eyes me over the rim of her tea mug.

I grumble incoherently as my high heels make squishy sounds with each step. In the guest room I dry myself off and change into a new outfit.

Instead of going back to Dad's shed alone, I take Lovelace with me. Hopefully her stay here will make her lower her guard. Maybe even my dad can get some more information out of her. Either way, my dad is one of the best Illusionists I've ever seen and his surprise will no doubt be beautiful. I have the feeling Lovelace could use something like that. She follows me obediently, holding my hand again. Despite never having been particularly fond of children, I find this quite touching and I squeeze her hand reassuringly. My mother stays in the kitchen, flipping through a magazine and wishing Dad hadn't made her throw out the coffee maker.

We enter the shed. Lovelace frowns as she looks around the large space, then she looks at me.

"It's larger on the inside, yes. You're not mistaken," I sign.

Her mouth opens.

"You ain't seen nothing yet." My dad is turned away from us so I have to tap him on his shoulder. He turns around with a smile, then adjusts his glasses to peer down at Lovelace.

"You haven't had a child, have you?" he signs as he speaks along.

"No," I sign back. I introduce them to each other and let them spell their name to each other. Lovelace asks him how long he's been deaf.

"For a long time. You?"

"I got sick when I was three," she signs.

"I'm sorry. Don't worry. You're in good hands. Monday is the best. The only downside is that she's afraid of dinosaurs."

Lovelace sniggers.

"I'd like to see how you do in the face of a dangerous predator."

Lovelace just smiles shyly at me.

"Now, my surprise, please," I sign to Dad.

My father holds up his finger, then turns his two armchairs away from the fireplace and towards us. "Sit down."

As soon as I do, my ChronoWatch beeps. I jump up. "Sorry, Dad. I thought I had time, but it waits for no woman. Please take care of Lovelace for me and ask Mother about my day. You'll want to hear it. If you wish, you can show the surprise to Lovelace without me, but I'll leave that up to you," I say, knowing my dad can read my lips.

Then, to Lovelace, I sign goodbye and let her know I'll be back for dinner. She waves and looks at my father expectantly, much like I did when I was her age. They'll get along just fine.

THE UNPARALLELED AFFAIRS building in Sheffield looks exactly like the one in York. In fact, all buildings across the country do. They do it so that even from afar it is recognisable. It has occurred that a stranded agent ended up in the wrong place and time. Without any bother they can find their headquarters, no matter what division they are in.

I tug on my sleeve and adjust my fringe. The Chrono Unit is always on the twelfth floor, so I take the lift up. It is filled with four other people. Based on their demeanour, outfit, and watches, I can tell what division they are in. For instance, the man dressed entirely like a burglar is from the Narcotics Unit. He is wearing gloves and a ski mask that only shows his eyes. They are currently battling a drug that makes you instantly addicted just by touching it, hence the outfits. As if confiscating such a drug isn't challenging enough, it doesn't help that their officers stick out like a lighthouse on the shore. I smile at a man who is clearly from the K-9 Division. He winks at me as his irises transmogrify into a golden colour.

I am the only one to stop at the twelfth floor. The first desk I come across is of the receptionist. "Monday Moody. I've been called in."

The woman's—her name tag says Susan—eyes grow wide. "Monday Moody, as I live and breathe. You look even prettier in real life. You were in the newspaper for fighting off a werewolf during an arrest." She gets up from her chair and walks around her desk to face me. Her round body is complemented by a dark blue dress that flares out at the bottom. She clasps my hands. "How did you feel when that happened?"

"I was rather upset that he was trying to eat the perp I was about to arrest."

She chuckles. "Yes, I'd imagine so. Goodness, you're funny. Listen, Janine from Level 2 wants to meet you. I told her you were coming and she had to fan herself. I promised her you'd give her your autograph. You're kind of her hero. In fact, I think you inspired her to kick out her husband." She leans in, her breath minty. "He cheated on her. Nasty business."

I glance at the door marked LEVEL 1, hoping someone will pop out and rescue me. I'm eager to learn what this new case is about and why they need me, but if everybody from the CU thinks of me like Janine does, that might explain why they'd request my help. Somehow I doubt that, though. "Sure," I say with a warm smile.

We head through to the LEVEL 2 section, which is a long corridor filled with doors and their different tags. We pass Wars, Famous People, Deaths, Inventions, and then stop at Crimes and Criminals. Susan swings open the door and immediately the smell of smoke and lemons assault my nose. In the middle of the room sits a thin woman. She's typing on her typewriter, which means she's discovered an anomaly and therefore a reason for Level 3 officers to investigate a possible Alteration.

The room holds nothing but the table, chair, and one filing cabinet. Janine doesn't look up. Instead she finishes her final sentence with her cigarette bouncing up and down between her thin lips. "And done," she says in a soft-spoken voice before she looks up. She lets out a yell when she spots me, dropping her cigarette on her lap, and immediately rushes over to hug me. She smells just like the room itself. It is an unpleasant combination, at least for me. But I've never particularly liked cigarettes or lemons.

"Monday Moody, as I live and breathe." She looks at me as if I'm the prodigal daughter who has finally come home. She's also clearly thick as thieves with Susan. I smile at them both as Susan looks on proudly.

"It is indeed me," I say. "Here." What else can I say? Good for you on leaving your husband? That werewolf wasn't that big? I've faced bigger and hungrier creatures? Do you have biscuits?

"How was it? Killing that rogue werewolf? It must have been terrifying."

I gasp for air so I can give some vague, general answer, just like I did when I was interviewed after the incident.

Paige Pageant, a reporter who now has her own talk show, eagerly shoved her microphone in my face and made the whole ordeal seem ten times more exciting than it was for me. In hindsight, after watching it myself, I realised I could have acted a tiny bit shaken. However, it made me a hero for a few weeks. Now, two months later, I hope most people have forgotten.

"I bet you were shaking in your boots, but you saved that person's life, even if they were a criminal. I mean, that just shows the world that us pencil pushers can be dangerous as well. We may not see a lot of the action, but we are also heroes." Janine smiles.

I nod, understanding now why she cares so much. Why anyone cared. I just wanted to move on as quickly as possible, uncomfortable with the sudden attention, but everyone wants to be a hero, right? And I reminded them that even normal people can be heroes. Except that I'm not normal. But they can't know that.

As I sign a piece of paper for her, the file cabinet shoots open and Janine jumps up. "Oh. Again?" She walks over to the cabinet and pulls out the file. "Bonnie and Clyde again. They are so popular."

"Altering it so they survive?" I ask.

"Yep. This is the third time." She types on her typewriter, immediately logging the new information and any possible suspect, though they rarely make the file. Not because there aren't any, but it's difficult to track Travellers near a Time Scene. Each Warning puts Travellers into the system, but there is no device made that can actually track their location. Not unless they leave a rip, and even then we may know who did it, but not where they are at that moment. She swipes on the holo-screen and sends the info along to Level 3, who then dispatch their people as quickly as possible to undo the Alteration. Some events are meant to be, and cannot be Altered.

"For all we know it could be the same person, but so far they haven't caught anyone. Level 3 is too distracted to fix the damage rather than arrest the Traveller responsible. I don't like it."

Susan nods her head. "They should make a Retrieval Unit for rogue Travellers as well. I mean, it wasn't bad before, but there are more and more Alterations, not to mention any insignificant changes."

"You've noticed that as well," I say, thinking back to the amount of Warnings I've had to give in the last month alone.

"Anyway, dear. Thank you for your autograph," Susan says. "We'd best leave Janine to it."

By now she's furiously typing, a drop of sweat on her forehead. "I'm so sorry, Monday," she says as her fingers fly across the keys. "I wish I could spend more time with you, but time waits for no woman."

With that we return to Susan's desk. She resumes her duties behind the typewriter, her fingers flying over the keys with the speed of a peregrine falcon. "P. Hosokawa. Monday Moody here for you," she murmurs into the chunky office speaker phone. "Wait here, dear. And thank you for obliging me." She winks and resumes typing.

"You're welcome." Not befriending the receptionist would be a bad move on my part, even if I'm only here to stay for a short while.

In a few seconds a man pushes open the doors to Level 1. He strides purposefully and keeps his warm eyes on me. When he reaches me he breaks out in a smile and holds out his hand. I shake it. "Perrin Hosokawa," he says. "My father was Japanese and my mother English, hence the unusual clash of names. You are Monday Moody," he says before I can introduce myself. "Daughter of Eleanor Moody-Parker, who has worked as a Level 3 officer for the UA, and Pip Moody, a well-known Illusionist."

"Indeed I am." Damn, he's done his homework. It shouldn't be a surprise since he requested me. I would have done exactly the same. Still, I better be extra careful.

"Excellent. I knew you were coming, and not a moment too soon. We have quite the situation on our hands."

"I see." I pause. "You're still holding my hand."

He looks down. "Ah, yes. That does seem to be the case." He slowly lets go, as if with reluctance. Then he sticks his hands in his pockets and smiles again. It is a charming smile.

"What's the problem?" I ask.

"There is a problem with the original Chrono Unit here."

Hmm. That indicates he isn't part of the usual six people who work here. "A problem? Are they in trouble?"

"Quite."

I raise an eyebrow. "Is it serious?"

"I'd say so. They're rather dead."

"Yes, I do hear that is a serious affliction."

Did you love *Prelude to Poison*? Then you should read *The Missing Maid*[1] by Morgan W. Silver!

[2]

When Clara arrives in the picturesque village of Greystone to work as a maid, things are about to get nasty. And not just because she's decided to open the door to her past and pull off one more con.

This con is different, though. It's personal. She just doesn't realise how personal, yet.

Because she's about to make friends, she's about to care, and worst of all, she can't stop thinking about that suspicious but charming detective. That's a mess she might not be able

1. https://books2read.com/u/bzdZqZ

2. https://books2read.com/u/bzdZqZ

to clean up, but things get messier when someone ends up dead. Her street smarts come in handy, and she's about to find out she's maid for murder.

Read more at www.authormw.com.

Also by Morgan W. Silver

Maggie's Murder Mysteries
Prelude to Poison
Poised to Quill
Booked For Murder

Maid for Murder
The Missing Maid

Monday Moody
The Chrono Unit
Unparalleled Affairs

Standalone
The Exciting Life of a Minor Character

Watch for more at www.authormw.com.

About the Author

I considered writing this bio in the third person, but my other voices wouldn't let me. My name is Morgan W. Silver. I have a BA in English Language and Culture and a Master's degree in Creative Writing. Which means I have a licence to write, and it will be extra awkward if I make spelling eroiers. Oops.

All my novels contain mysteries, but the subgenres may differ. There are, however, always shenanigans and quirky characters, as well as a dash of romance.

Read more at www.authormw.com.

Made in the USA
Monee, IL
10 February 2026

43688926R00173